BEST MAN

A CLOSE PROXIMITY NOVEL

LILY MORTON

Warning

This book contains material that is intended for a mature, adult audience. It contains graphic language, explicit sexual content and adult situations.

BLURB

Zeb Evans doesn't do messy.

The product of a disorganised and chaotic childhood, Zeb likes order and control, and as the boss of his own employment agency he can give that to himself. Life runs along strict lines and he never mixes business with pleasure. Everything in his life lives in neat, alphabetized boxes. Until Jesse.

Jesse Reed is Zeb's complete opposite. He's chaos personified. A whirling cyclone of disorder. He's also charming and funny and a very unwanted distraction.

Which is why it comes as a complete surprise to Zeb to find himself asking Jesse to pose as his boyfriend for a few days in the country at a wedding.

Zeb doesn't do impulsive, but as the time away progresses, he finds himself increasingly drawn to the merry and irreverent Jesse. But can he bring himself to break the hard-won lessons he's learnt in life? And even if he can, how could Jesse be attracted to him anyway? He's so much older than Jesse, not to mention being his boss.

From the bestselling author of the Mixed Messages and Finding Home series comes a warm and funny romance about one man's fight for control and another man's determination to circumvent it.

This is the first book in the Close Proximity series, but it can be read as a standalone.

For Hailey
A wonderful friend

"To live is the rarest thing in the world. Most people exist, that is all."
Oscar Wilde

PROLOGUE

Three Years Ago

Jesse

I settle back into my chair and try to find a comfortable resting spot. However, the hard plastic makes that as unlikely a possibility as Keanu Reeves descending to Covent Garden and declaring his undying love for me.

I've just drifted off to a lovely dream of licking his beard when the office's inner door slams open and a young man comes marching out with high spots of colour glowing over his cheekbones. I look at him with interest. It's a marked change from when he went in all high head and confident dazzling smile.

Not that it's a surprise. All six previous interviewees have gone in the same way and left just as quickly. I settle back and watch as he exits the office in a cloud of angst and Hugo Boss aftershave, letting in the faint twang of petrol fumes from outside and a whiff of bread from the bakery next door.

Several of the other people dotted around the room stir and look at each other while the man at the desk, obviously well used to this, carries on scratching away with his pen on a piece of paper.

He shows no sign of calling anyone else for an interview and the inner door remains shut, so I stand up and edge over to him. He looks up. He's not pretty, but he has a very striking appearance with big hazel eyes and a tumble of black hair around a thin face. But my purpose isn't to flirt today.

I perch on the edge of the desk, and he eyes my bum. His mouth quirks. "Can I help you? Did I not give you a chair? How very remiss of me."

I look down at the nameplate on his desk and smile. "Yes, Felix, maybe you can help me. Is there any chance of me being interviewed today, or should I just settle down and wait for death to find me?"

He smirks. "Mr Evans has a long queue of people waiting."

That's not surprising. The Evans Agency is well known in London for catering to the needs of its customers who are largely from the LGBTQ community. Its employees can help a person with their business, do their gardening and their shopping, walk their dogs, or even pose as a fake boyfriend or girlfriend to help in awkward social situations. No job is too small for them, and the agency has become a byword for discretion and capability.

I'd heard about the job vacancy from my friend. His boyfriend had cheated on him just before his office Christmas party, and within a couple of hours an extremely gorgeous bloke turned up and escorted him to the party, much to the displeasure of the cheating ex.

"Mr Evans is very busy," Felix says happily.

I look at the outer door which is still swaying gently in the breeze from the previous applicant. "He's busy pissing people off from the looks of it," I mutter. There's a stack of post on the desk, and I lean closer and whistle. "Zebadiah Evans. Fucking hell, that's a mouthful. Sounds like someone who'd be at home on *The Tudors*. Wearing a wimple and chucking brimstone at a peasant."

Felix's eyes widening are the only sign that I've just stepped in shit. That and the low, posh voice from behind me.

"I know *The Tudors* took a lot of liberties with facts, but I don't think that even they went that far."

I stiffen and then spin round. A tall, wide-shouldered man is leaning against the open doorway of the inner room, and fucking hell, he's gorgeous. Thick, black, wavy hair frames a craggy face. There are faint lines around his eyes telling me that he's quite a bit older than me, but his eyes are the deepest blue I've ever seen. As blue as a corn-flower. He's wearing a very expensive pinstriped suit with a white shirt and red tie. I pause. And a very sardonic smile. *Shit, this is the boss man.*

I straighten up slowly, prepared to apologise. But one look at his expression and I change my mind. My student loans need this money, and I'm just going to have to brazen this out. So I look him up and down slowly instead. "No wimple, then?"

"Not in office hours," he says primly, making me smile. His voice is deep with a slight husky catch to it. For a second we stare at each other, and then he shrugs and gestures to his room with one large hand. "You'd better come in. Felix might need to do some actual work on his desk at some point today."

I swallow hard and, standing up, I edge past him, getting a waft of very expensive cologne that smells of orange and sandalwood. "Watch out for the brimstone," he mutters. "It's over by the window."

I snort and shake my head. "What exactly is brimstone, anyway?"

"Your extensive knowledge of *The Tudors* didn't give you that knowledge, then?" he says, gesturing me to a seat in front of an enor-mous desk piled high with very neat stacks of paperwork.

"I must have dozed off at that point. If Henry Cavill wasn't naked, I lost interest."

"What a discerning viewer you are," he murmurs. He looks at me as he settles back into his chair and slips on a pair of black-framed glasses. "Brimstone is an alternative name for sulphur. In the Bible it was called brimstone, which means burning stone."

"Ah, good job, you're educated. I must have missed that page of the Bible when I passed out due to boredom."

For a second he stares at me, and I think I catch a faint twitch around his mouth which might denote amusement, but more likely it just means he'd like to throttle me. That's the more common reaction I'm used to.

I gaze at him, the only sound in the room that of the chatter of people wandering in the courtyard outside which filters in through the open window. It brings with it a faint breeze, and I strain to catch it, feeling the sweat dampening my underarms and the faint track of grime on my skin. England is in the middle of a heatwave and there's nowhere more miserable than London when it's hot.

I sigh, and he looks up from the piece of paper he's holding. "Something wrong?"

"It's just that you look as cool as a cucumber, and I look like I've been thrown in an oven and then pushed down a hill." He blinks and I bite my lip. "What does that mean, anyway?"

"Are you asking me to decipher your entire sentence? Because I've a feeling that the Greek gods setting Hercules his labours wouldn't have tasked him with that one."

I shake my head. "What does 'cool as a cucumber' mean? Cucumbers aren't particularly chilled. I mean, they're not in the fridge at Tesco's. They're out in boxes. So, why cucumber? Why not as cool as the pre-cut carrots?"

He blinks. "This is not the way I thought this interview would go." He shakes his head as if to try and empty it. "Moving back to business, Mr Reed?"

"Jesse," I say helpfully. "Just call me Jesse. Mr Reed sounds like my dad."

"How lovely that we're circumventing the awkwardness of the interview format. What a joy," he says dryly, and I grin at him.

"I do my best."

"Okay." He peers down at the piece of paper. "So, looking at your resume, it appears that you don't stick at jobs, Mr Reed."

I clear my throat, and when he looks at me, I smile. "Jesse."

He stares at me over the top of his glasses. "Oh, of course. Well, it appears, *Jesse*, that you have all the sticking ability of a plaster on a cut after a few days."

I sit back in my chair. "That's probably a fair summary."

"Your old boss, who gave you a reference, has written something that's very ..." He seems to pause to look for words. "Nebulous. If the army ever need a code writer, they'd do well to contact this man. He manages to say so much while not actually saying anything at all."

"Not in person," I assure him. "In person he managed to say quite a lot." I shake my head. "All the way through my lunch hour and somebody else's too."

He slowly puts the piece of paper down and takes his glasses off. "Jesse," he says slowly. I sit forward, waiting to hear words of wisdom. "Your job history is spottier than Boris Johnson's."

He surprises a laugh out of me, and I grin at him. "Well, look what job he got," I say. He shudders and I laugh. "I just wasn't the right fit to be a taxi rank operator or a dog groomer."

"Or a bus driver," he says wryly, stabbing the paper with one long finger. "Apparently, you diverted the route you'd been given to pick your mate up."

"That's a long story," I say cagily. "It's best that you don't press me for it."

"Oh, okay," he says faintly.

"Look," I say, leaning forward. "Let's chuck the CV away."

"Oh, please do," he says, waving a hand. "But unfortunately, the thing's engraved on my brain now."

"Try and wipe it clean," I advise him. I look around the office. "The truth is that you need me."

"I do?"

I nod, and then do it again more emphatically in case he missed the point. "This is an agency that deals a lot with LGBTQ customers, isn't it?" He nods and I sit back. "Perfect, I'm gay."

He blinks. "It's a *teeny* bit more involved than that."

I wave my hand airily. "Not much."

"Okay, then please enlighten me as to how with your atrocious job history you'll be a boon to me."

"Well, I'm charming." He opens his mouth and I wag my finger at him. "I am. You might not recognise it, which probably makes you a bit odd, but few are immune to my charm." He looks like he wants to argue, so I carry on quickly. "I just have a bit of a problem with my attention span in that I get bored easily. I can't abide to be backed into a corner and stuck doing the same thing all the time. Which makes me perfect for your jobs. I can do most things I turn my hand to, mainly because I've had a job doing nearly everything." I pause. "Hopefully you won't need the funeral company experience, but you never know." His mouth quirks, and I spread my hands. "Ta-da! Perfect match."

"So, the fact that you're a jack of all trades and master of none is an attractive quality. Oh, I see now," he says mockingly. "How can I have been so blind?"

"That's a potential problem for you," I say sympathetically.

I can see that the laugh he lets loose shocks him, which makes me smile.

He looks down at the paper again. Damn that CV. "You're very young," he says doubtfully.

"I'm twenty-one," I say indignantly. "I hope you're not going to be ageist."

He blinks. "I wouldn't dream of it," he says faintly. He leans back in his chair and considers me. "So, if I were to give you this job, how would you approach it?"

"What do you mean?"

"Well, every case is different. We help people with their needs. Sometimes it'll be someone who needs you to do their shopping, sometimes it's to act as a PA, and sometimes it's pretending to be a boyfriend for a family party so the person doesn't lose face. How would you approach all these people with their very different needs?"

I stare at him in surprise. "Well, like they're people." I hastily try to cover up the "duh" tone in my voice. "Every person is different, Zebadiah. Can I call you Zebadiah?"

"I really wish you wouldn't," he says testily.

"Okay then. Zeb." I nod. "I like that. Makes you sound less like a manager and more like a DJ in Ibiza."

"Oh joy, that's my life goal attained, then."

"I'm sure sarcasm isn't appropriate for a job interview."

"I do beg your pardon." His face is alight with amusement.

"What was I saying?"

"You were talking about how every person in this world is different. I'm halfway expecting you to launch into the chorus of 'We All Stand Together'."

This time it's me that laughs. I sober and smile at him. "People are really difficult. There's a reason why Basil Fawlty was so popular." I shrug. "But I like them better than a computer or a typewriter." I pause and shudder. "Or a funeral hearse and the cremation machine." His eyes go wide, and I shake my head regretfully. "I'm afraid I agreed never to discuss that matter." I think hard. "I'm respectful, diligent, obliging, and focused."

"And you've obviously swallowed a thesaurus at some point in your life." He sighs and looks at me, and his gaze is suddenly piercing. "There's to be no sex."

I blink. "Zeb, this so, *so* sudden." I put my hand to my chest. "I'm not that sort of boy."

He shakes his head and this time doesn't bother to contain the laugh. "You're impossible." He turns serious. "No sleeping with clients. It's the number-one rule. This is not the littlest whore house in Neal's Yard."

I look him up and down, and the heat from the summer day seems to run in my blood. "Does that apply to the boss?"

He stares at me, and the silence stretches for a second. "It especially applies to the boss," he says gruffly. "I don't shit where I eat."

"What a charming expression. I'm surprised your dance card isn't filled up for the millennium."

Another laugh. I'm beginning to like peeling them out of him. He sobers. "So, no fucking the clients."

"I won't even kiss them on the lips," I promise. "I feel like Julia Roberts," I say with a sigh. "I'll be lying on a grand piano in my dressing gown soon. But that would make you Richard Gere, which is a crime."

"You don't like Richard Gere?" he asks, and I shake my head.

"Face like a ferret and a personality to match. If he'd stopped that car for me, I'd have waved the fucker on."

His laughter bursts out loud and joyful, and the door to the office opens and Felix pokes his head around. "Everything okay, sir?" he asks cautiously, looking like he thinks zombie hordes are about to flood the room.

Zeb wipes his eyes. "I'm fine, thank you, Felix. Come and meet the newest member of staff."

Felix looks insultingly astonished. *"Really?"* he says in a doubtful voice.

Zeb nods. "May God help me?"

"You don't need him," I say earnestly. "You've got me now."

"I need a new religion." He sighs and I smile, getting up to shake his hand. I swallow at the tingle I get when our palms meet, and, looking at him, I know he feels it too.

"Shame," I say softly so his assistant doesn't hear.

His face twitches, and I watch the cool expression slide over his face. "Not where I eat," he reminds me, and I step back, walking towards the door.

"It's because the inside of cucumbers are twenty degrees cooler than the outside air," he says just as I get to the door.

I stop and turn back. "What?"

"You asked where the idiom 'cool as a cucumber' came from. That's what it means."

"I don't know how I lived this long without knowing that," I say solemnly, and his face creases into a smile.

"Welcome aboard, Mr Reed."

"Aye aye, captain," I say. "And it's Jesse."

"Welcome aboard, Mr Reed," is his reply. "Don't let the door hit your arse on the way out."

CHAPTER ONE

Three Years Later

Jesse

I walk through the narrow, whitewashed alley, coming out into the glory of Neal's Yard. Even after three years, this place still makes me happy. It's almost a shock to cross from the main road with its cars and noise into this small courtyard full of the scent from the window boxes hanging from the tall, narrow buildings that are painted intensely vivid colours from pink to lime green to sky blue. It's hidden in plain sight and I've always thought it was like a psychedelic Diagon Alley, full of small shops, restaurants and cafes, and tourists taking the perfect Instagram shot.

According to Zeb, the area was once the home of occultists and astrologers, and to me it seems that atmosphere lingers a little in the open and welcoming feel of the courtyard.

Zeb's building is one of the prettiest. It's four storeys in the original brick with windows painted bright orange. It has the original bay doors from when it was a warehouse, and pretty Juliet balconies. His front door is painted lime green with a discreet sign advertising the name of the agency, and when I open it and walk into the hallway, it's blessedly cool and filled with the scent of roses from the flower arrangement on a low table.

I saunter through the reception area, which contains the usual load of people waiting to see Felix or Zeb. Felix grins at me.

"Why the sunglasses inside, Brad Pitt? Hiding from the paparazzi?"

I shake my head. "They're needed today."

"Have you got a hangover?" he asks sympathetically.

"Why does everyone always leap to the conclusion that anything I do is alcohol related?"

"Because it is," comes a deep voice from behind me. I whirl round to see Zeb standing in his doorway. He's in his shirtsleeves, his tie at half-mast, clutching a handful of papers and wearing a sardonic smile.

"I feel judged," I say. They keep looking at me, and finally I sigh and lower my glasses.

Zeb drops his papers and strides towards me immediately. "What the fuck?" he says angrily. "Who did this?"

I gape at him as he lifts my face and examines my black eye intently.

"Well?" he says. His voice is sharp, but the fingers he touches to the side of my eye are gentle. I blink at him, smelling the scent of oranges. I'm sure he doesn't realise how close he's standing, but I'll take the time to enjoy it while I can.

Felix shifts position and realisation comes into Zeb's eyes as well as discomfort, and he drops his hands from my face.

I mourn the loss of his closeness before I realise that he just said something. "Huh? What?" I say.

He shakes his head. "Did you hit your head when this happened?"

"No?"

He sighs. "Okay, this is just normal behaviour, isn't it? I keep forgetting that."

Felix breaks into laughter, and I shake my head before putting my glasses back on. "It's a long story," I say slowly.

"Ah, would it have anything to do with the very long email I received from Mr Sampson this morning?"

"It depends on whether that email is praise or recrimination." He stares at me and I shake my head again. "Okay, a bit of both, then," I say sadly.

"Into my office, Mr Reed," he says, waving his hand towards the door as if I've forgotten where it is.

I square my shoulders. "Just so you know, this is totally like being called in to see the Head. And not in a good way."

"Is there a good way?" he asks, his mouth twitching at the corner as he shuts the door.

"In porn there is."

"Ah, I can't help feeling, Mr Reed, that watching porn has given you rather unrealistic expectations of life."

I slump into the chair opposite his desk. "Maybe. But I have realised by now that it's never that easy to get a plumber."

He can't help the smile this time, but he quashes it remorselessly and sits down in his chair before resting his elbows on the desk and steepling his fingers together. It's a thoughtful pose, but I can testify that it's a better interrogation technique than anything MI5 use. *And more threatening,* I think morosely.

"Well?" he murmurs.

"Oh, okay then," I say sulkily. "There might have been a tiny fight at the wake."

He blinks. "And did you cause it?"

"No, of course not," I say indignantly. He stares at me and I slump some more. "But I might have finished it. You should have seen Peter Sampson's family. All of them glaring at him like he was Voldemort arriving for the wake, rather than just a gay man with his partner."

"*Pretend* partner."

I stare at him. "Of course." I furrow my brow. Surely he can't think it's anything else? I know the rules and I abide by them. No fucking the clients. I open my mouth to break in, but he speaks and the moment is lost.

"So, what happened?"

"The coffin was set up in the front room, and Peter tried to go in, but his elder brother was drunk and barred his way. Said no faggot was coming into his house." Zeb grimaces but motions for me to carry on. "Anyway, he laid his hands on Peter and pushed him, but Peter shoved him back." I grin. "Quite surprised me. Made me feel almost proud." I shrug. "But then it was open season, and in the fight that happened next, there was a lot of pushing and shoving and a great deal of family members who appeared to have very strong feelings about homosexuality. And not the good, strong feelings you get at Vibe at midnight."

He frowns. "So, what happened? How did you finish it?"

I shift in my chair. "I punched the eldest brother. He deserved it," I say quickly. "The homophobic git slapped Peter round the face."

"And then?" I look at him and he sighs. "There's more. I know there's more." He shakes his head. "There's always more," he says with weary resignation.

I try to summon up indignation, but I can't manage it because he's telling the truth. "I punched him, and I must be a great deal stronger than I ever imagined because he flew through the air and landed on the coffin."

"Jesus Christ," Zeb mutters and rubs his eyes.

"Do you know that in Spanish that's *Jesu Christo?*" I nod. "I know that because it was shouted a lot after that."

"Why?" It's the voice of doom.

I bite my lips. "Because the old lady sort of fell out of the coffin."

"Sort of? How does a body *sort of* fall out of a coffin?"

"Your voice goes alarmingly high when you're angry," I observe.

He breathes in slowly. "Jesse Reed," he says ominously.

"Okay, okay. Since you actually used my first name, I'll tell you. But it wasn't used terribly nicely. You could really do better." He glares at me. "So, the old lady's body sort of fell out of the coffin, and the brother landed on her." I shrug helplessly. "It brought the party to a bit of an abrupt stop."

"I should imagine it did," he drawls. "Is that how you got your black eye?"

"I'd like to say yes, but the undignified truth is that one of the old lady's shoes flew off and hit me in the eye."

There's a very long silence as he steadily goes red in the face. Alarmed, I wonder if I should ring for an ambulance, but at that moment he starts to laugh. And laugh. And laugh.

I stare at him, feeling my own lips twitch because his laugh is so contagious. You could actually catch his laughter like a little germ and feel it taking root in yourself.

After a few minutes, he stops laughing and looks contemplatively at me. I try a smile, but I think the true glory is a bit wasted today with my sunglasses on. I probably look like I'm still pissed.

Zeb shakes his head. "That explains Mr Sampson's email." His voice wobbles slightly and I frown at him. "He apologises for the fracas at the party and would like to tell you that the package was picked up and put back where it belonged." His voice falters again but he firms his expression. "He says how happy he was with the service and would definitely like to use you again."

I stare at him. "So, that's good, then. Brilliant." I clap my hands together. "Another satisfied customer."

"Let's not speak too rashly. That goes against the grain." I open my mouth, but he holds his hand up. "No, I'm not explaining that." I subside back into my chair. "Let's face it, these last few months have been rather eventful for your career at the agency."

"I wouldn't go that far," I say uneasily.

"Really?" he says silkily. "You wouldn't? Hmm, let's see. Last month you were asked to escort Mr French to an office party and what happened?" I mutter something and he smiles mockingly. "No need to whisper."

"I fell on the buffet table," I say clearly. "Because someone tripped me up."

He smiles. "Yes. Yes, you did, and then what about the next week when I asked you to sort out Miss Hendon's garden, and you decided that her prize collection of ferns were actually weeds and pulled them up?"

And he's off. It's almost admirable how he can speak without notes. He'd have a great career on the after-dinner speaking circuit. Although only if the title of the speech was The Misadventures of Jesse Reed, I think sulkily.

There's a big, expensive-looking, square envelope on his desk with Zeb's name on it in italics. It looks like an invitation of some sort, and I crane my neck to try and see more while he rants on. However, I can't, so I'm forced to grin and bear it.

Finally, after what seems like a week, he lets me go with the suggestion that I pull my socks up. I contemplate telling him that I'm not wearing any, but I abandon that when I see the glint in his eye. Instead I half salute and scarper.

Once the door shuts behind me, I look at Felix and fall to the ground, groaning dramatically.

He laughs. "Was it bad?"

"Define bad," I mutter into the carpet. I raise my head. "He's vile sometimes."

He shrugs. "But fair."

"He's even more bad tempered than usual," I mutter, getting up and slinging myself into the chair next to his desk. "Is Patrick giving him a hard time?"

Patrick is Zeb's partner of six years. He's a beautiful man and quite a bit younger than Zeb, but from the photos I've seen of them together they seem to be happy. I consider that. Maybe. Patrick looks like he'd be bloody hard work, but luckily that's Zeb's problem and not mine.

Felix stares at me. "Didn't you know?"

"Know what?"

"They split up."

"Get away. When?"

He smiles. "Last year sometime."

I sit up straight. "Why didn't I know this?"

"Didn't know the subject interested you," Felix says casually as he rifles through the paperwork. He shoots me a quick glance and I feel my cheeks flush.

"Well, obviously I like to know these things," I say robustly. "His mood directly impacts my job security situation."

"Oh, okay," he says, overdoing the nodding. "Of course."

"Does everyone know?"

He shrugs. "Probably. Zeb hasn't advertised it, but he hasn't exactly hidden it. Plus, Patrick came into the office shouting a few times which sort of gave the game away, as did the furniture removal."

Zeb lives in a three-storey flat over the agency offices. I've heard it's lovely. Heard, because I've never been invited up.

"I'm surprised I didn't cotton on," I say slowly.

He laughs. "Well, usually your meetings with Zeb don't run to the format of a cosy chat."

"No," I say morosely. "They're more hurricanes, earthquakes, and a fucking great tsunami."

"The earth moved though."

I laugh, but it's thoughtful, and the news about Zeb is still on my mind as I let myself into my flat later on.

"That you, Jesse?" comes the call.

"Is there anyone else who has a key?"

My flatmate Charlie appears in the door. "Eli's got a key."

I smile at the thought of my best friend who now lives in Cornwall in domestic bliss. "Eli is shacked up with a famous actor. Don't think he needs a key to this shithole anymore."

He smiles. He has the widest grin that seems to light his whole face up, and with that and his long blond hair, sometimes he fairly glows. That smile led to him being nicknamed Charlie Sunshine. It suits him because he's the prettiest and most angelic-looking man I've ever met, with a head full of blond waves and green eyes. He'd have made a fantastic model but instead chose to be a librarian. His beauty is almost startling.

"Aww, they're so happy together," he says.

I'm sorry. I forgot that. His smile *and* his outlook on life led to him being called Charlie Sunshine. He sees the good in everyone. When Eli and I set up interviews for a flatmate, we took one look at Charlie and crossed everyone else off the list. We've never regretted it. He's funny and calm and like my baby brother.

I look a bit closer at him and then frown. "You're very pale. Are you okay?"

He waves his hand airily. "I'm fine."

I narrow my eyes. "You don't look it. Did you have a turn?"

He turns and wanders back into the lounge. "A small one." He catches my eyes. "Only a little one. I was only out for a bit. I'm fine. Just feel like I've got a hangover now."

"Are you out with Vic tonight?" I frown at the thought. It's almost like a reflex now when I think of his arsehole boyfriend. Born with a golden spoon in his mouth, it's always seemed a shame that he didn't choke on it. He's been with Charlie for a year and while he's ecstatic to have such a good-looking man on his arm, he doesn't treat Charlie right at all. He talks to him like he's shit most of the time and Charlie waves it off, making excuses for him like "he's tired" and "he works so hard."

I sigh. Who am I to judge anyway? I haven't exactly done well in the boyfriend stakes. Three of them cheated and one stole my wallet. Not to mention the charmer who took out a credit card in my name.

Charlie sneaks a glance at me and shakes his head, lowering himself to the sofa with a weary sigh. I hover slightly because he looks fragile. "No, Misha is coming over tonight," he says, closing his eyes.

Unseen, I sag with relief. Misha is Charlie's best friend. They're closer than two peas in a pod but as different as broccoli and a nuclear bomb. But it seems to make their friendship stronger, and

Misha has always been very protective of Charlie. If he's here, nothing will happen.

"Good," I say. I settle down onto the sofa next to him, raising his legs so they rest on my lap. I massage the calves while he makes happy sounds. "I like Misha," I say slowly. "Good-looking bloke." I pinch his knee. "And your best friend."

He shakes his head disapprovingly. "Stop matchmaking, you're shit at it. Misha and I are friends. I love him and he loves me, but that's it. It'll never be anything else."

"Why?" I ask curiously. We've spoken about this before, but it's the first time we've done it sober. I'm sure he's answered it before, but either it didn't make sense, or I wasn't listening, or I'd passed out.

"Because Misha is a complete tart and I'm not," he says, smiling at me. I'm relieved to see the colour coming back into his face. "And we don't see each other like that. We were friends too long for that."

"Oh, okay." I was right. It doesn't make sense.

"Do you want to get Chinese?" he asks.

I shrug. "Sounds good. You need an early night then and so do I. My eye is killing me."

He smiles kindly at me. "Do you want me to get you an ice pack?"

I shake my head. "No." My phone starts to ring and I raise a finger and answer it, surprised to hear Felix.

"Jesse, are you settled in for the night?"

"Not really." I tug at my tie. "It's only seven o'clock. I'm not sixty and *Midsomer Murders* is a repeat."

He chuckles. "Can you come back in?" he says apologetically.

"Now? Why?"

"Zeb needs to see you."

"Oh, has he forgotten a misdemeanour he needs to bollock me about?" I say sourly. "What a tragedy."

He laughs. "Can you come in or not?"

"I notice you're not denying it." I look at Charlie and sigh. "Okay, I'll be there in a bit."

I click End and Charlie grins at me. "Going to pay a late-night visit to Mr Super Sexy?"

"I wish you wouldn't call him that."

He nudges me with his foot. "You wish I wouldn't, or that you didn't call him it in your head?" I groan and he laughs. "You're in denial, Vivian."

He likes to call me this, and no matter how much I tell him that I'm not a prostitute with thigh-high boots, he keeps at it.

"I didn't kiss him on the mouth, Daddy," I say in a high voice.

"You're my boy now," he growls, and I snort.

"Okay, enough. It's making me uneasy. I'm going to have a shower."

"Make sure you clean all your crevices," he says and chuckles to himself.

Half an hour later, showered and dressed in Levis and a black shirt, I push my hand through my still-wet hair. "Right, I'm off. I'll be back later. You sure you're okay?"

"I'm fine," he says firmly. The doorbell rings and his face brightens. "That'll be Misha."

"I'll get the door on my way out." Kissing him on the head, I walk into the hall and open the front door. I grin at Misha. He's dressed in a grey suit and with his black hair, olive skin, and bright blue eyes, he looks as good-looking as normal. And as irritable. Surly and handsome looks great on him.

"You scrub up nicely." I laugh, and he grins at me.

"Not half as nicely as you. Look at you with the whole matching-your-eye-to-your-shirt-thing you've got going on."

I snort. "Baby, I wrote the fashion bible."

"I'd be slightly more reassured if you'd written the actual Bible."

As I step back to let him through the door, I grab his arm. "He had a turn," I whisper.

Worry flares in his eyes. "Is he okay?"

"Bit fragile. But it wasn't a bad one."

"I hate them," he says slowly but fiercely. He gives me a half-hearted smile. "You on your way out?"

"Been called back in."

"What have you done now?"

I shake my head sadly. "So predictable. You staying with him?"

He instantly nods. "I'll kip on the sofa if you're not back." He eyes the lounge. "I might kip here anyway."

I nod and wave goodbye before clattering down the stairs.

An hour later I knock on the front door of the office. All the windows are dark, and I frown and knock again. Then a light switches on and I see the fuzzy form of Zeb appear.

When he opens the door, I nearly swallow my tongue. In the three years I've known him I've never seen him in anything other than his very expensive suits. Tonight he's barefoot and wearing a grey T-shirt and an ancient pair of jeans. Worn white in places, they hang on him, perfectly cupping his package like an overeager man at kicking-out time in a night club. His hair is slightly dishevelled, as if he's being running his hand through it, and he has thick stubble on his chin.

"Hello," he says and then pauses. "You okay? You look a bit shell-shocked."

I recover myself. "Just getting my expression perfectly right for the bollocking you're surely going to give me."

He shakes his head. "You have such a pessimistic outlook for someone so young."

"I'd say realistic," I mutter, following him in as he gestures. I look around the dark office. "Is this going to be one of those events where they torture people so that the office bonds as a group? Or like that SAS programme where they blindfold people and bang wooden spoons?"

He blinks. "Why on earth would I want to bang wooden spoons around you? And since when is torture associated with office bonding?"

"That's a question you'll have to take up with all those companies that offer team-building exercises. All I'll say is that if you want your workplace to bond, take them to the pub and pay the bar bill."

He shakes his head and moves forward, gesturing for me to follow him. "I'd be bankrupt within twenty minutes."

I laugh and then stop as he opens the door next to his office. "Oh my God," I breathe. "Are we going up to your flat?"

He pauses, looking worried. "We were, but we can stay down here if you want. I was cooking dinner, so I thought we could talk while I do that."

"So, it's not some surprise appraisal."

"I'm not quite sure you understand the ways of the workplace. I don't spring appraisals on people at eight o'clock at night. What do you think happens? That I shin up a drainpipe and shout through their bedroom window?"

I follow him into a hallway decorated with whitewashed walls and a lovely parquet floor. An olive tree sits in a huge stone container next to a tall window. He moves up a flight of stairs and I follow, trying not to look too much at that very fine arse of his. Oh, okay, I totally seize the day and look to my heart's content. Carpe diem and everything, as Robin Williams said in *Dead Poet's Society*.

He opens a huge battered wooden door, gesturing me through, and I find myself in a long hallway. I trot behind him as he moves away, looking through a door and glimpsing his lounge. It's lit by three floor-to-ceiling windows and they've been thrown open, letting in the sounds from the courtyard below. The Juliet balconies are painted the same bright orange as the windows and complement the huge turquoise sofa that sits catty-corner to a battered leather sofa. Two of the walls are lined with floor-to-ceiling bookshelves and there is bright artwork on the walls.

I look ahead and pick up my pace to catch up with him. Signs of the building's previous history as a warehouse are everywhere, from the original loading doors to the sandblasted beams. Some of the walls have been stripped back to the bare brick while others are painted clear, warm colours. The floor is the original wood planks and they've been refurbished to a soft sheen. Someone very skilled did this renovation, and looking at my boss's broad back, I somehow know it was him. I think what most surprises me is the feeling of warmth and comfort here. I'd imagined him in something pristine and modern, not this place with its bright walls and comfy furniture and books everywhere.

However, it's still extremely neat, which feels *very* familiar after three years of watching Zeb organise everyone around him to an inch of their lives. I try to imagine living here, but I'm pretty sure that after twenty-four hours of my mess he'd chuck me out of a window. We pass a laundry room with not even a sock on the worksurface, and I amend that to two hours.

"This is lovely," I say. "Bang smack in the middle of Seven Dials and all this space."

He glances back, looking suddenly almost shy. "Thank you. I like it. There are another two floors above us. This floor has the kitchen, dining room, and lounge. Next floor has the spare bedrooms and then at the top is the master suite."

"I bet this cost a fortune."

He shakes his head. "My father was a property developer. He left me this in his will. He bought it for a song years ago when Neal's Yard was derelict and just a place for bins and rats. But even though the other buildings got renovated, he never did anything with this. I think he actually forgot about it and when I inherited, it was very dilapidated, so I had to spend a long time doing it up."

So it was him. "Did Patrick help?" I say and hold my breath. That's way too personal, but I'm curious about his ex.

He smiles. "No, he didn't, and if you knew Patrick you'd be thankful for that. He hardly knows how to change a bulb, so the idea of him tackling wiring is rather scary." He shrugs, leading me into a huge kitchen. The cabinets are painted navy with a wooden worksurface and the floor is made of navy-and-white patterned floor tiles. It could look cold but it's warmed by the exposed brick wall, battered-looking sideboard, and the bright paintings giving it a slightly shabby chic look. "Anyway, this was mine before Patrick came along. And it's stayed mine," he says thoughtfully.

"Yes, I heard you'd split up."

A funny expression crosses his face. "Is it a topic of conversation now? It was a year ago."

I shrug. "I only found out recently. Sorry."

There's an awkward sort of pause as he stares at me without saying anything. Then a lid on one of the saucepans rattles, and it breaks the stasis. He gestures me to one of the barstools at the central island. "Sit down. Do you want a glass of wine?"

I stare at him as I sit down where instructed, looking at the very healthy-looking herbs in their ceramic pots. If this was my house, they'd be dead. "Okay," I say faintly. "That would be lovely." *Is this a dream?* I wonder. *If it is, hopefully we'll have sex soon.*

"What are you thinking? You've got a very funny expression on your face," he asks, pouring red wine into a large glass.

"Oh, nothing," I say quickly.

"Hmm." He sounds suspicious. He turns back to the oven. "Are you allergic to anything?"

"Erm, penicillin," I say slowly.

He laughs, and now I'm convinced he's an alien that's stolen the real Zeb. He's a hot alien, though, because when he smiles and laughs it takes over his whole face. He fairly glows.

"No, I mean food allergies."

"Oh no, nothing. I'll eat anything." I pause. "Are you feeding me?" The latter part of that sentence is a bit high, but this is Zeb. In his home. In those jeans. And he's cooking. I feel like I've wandered onto the set of a very high-class porn movie.

"Your face is very animated even when you're not speaking." He smiles, sliding the glass to me and turning to the cooker. Within a few minutes he's plated up two meals and is placing one in front of me.

I stare down at the rustic-looking white plate piled high with food.

"It's only chilli." He hesitates. "If you don't want it, you don't have to eat it. I'm sorry. It just seems that as I called you away at dinnertime, I ought to feed you."

I slap my hand on his as he goes to move the plate away. "No, leave it," I say quickly. "It smells bloody lovely."

He stares at me, and I realise that I'm still holding his hand and, as a latter thought, that it feels nice. I feel the flush on my face and drop his hand and shove a mouthful of food in.

"Shit, that's hot," I gasp.

He smiles. "It usually is when it's just come straight out of the pan."

He lowers himself into the seat next to me and unfurls his napkin, and the next few minutes are spent eating. It's absolutely delicious. Meaty-tasting and spicy. He's served it with rice and home-made guacamole.

I eat hungrily. When I've satisfied the food gremlin inside me temporarily, I lean back. "So, why did you need to see me?"

He fiddles with his fork, drawing the tines through the sauce on his plate, making patterns like a child with sand.

"I have a favour to ask," he finally says.

"Okay," I say slowly.

There's a short silence and then he sighs. "I need to hire you."

I blink. "To do what?"

He bites his lip. "It's a long story, but the short version is that Patrick is getting married."

"Patrick, your ex?"

He nods. "He's getting married in a month."

"*That's* what the invitation was on your desk," I say out loud, unfortunately, and hurriedly gesture. "Tell me more," I say quickly.

His mouth quirks. "That's about it. He's having a house party for a few days in a country hotel. They've rented out the whole hotel."

"For a *few days*? Is he Richard Branson?"

He laughs. "No, but his future bride is the daughter of someone worth the same money."

"Oh, okay." The record comes to a jerky screech. "What? A *bride?*"

Incredibly, he smiles. "Yes, a bride."

"But he was with you for five years."

"There is something called bisexuality," he says mildly.

"Are you bisexual?" I want to gasp because that was incredibly personal, but he just shrugs, an almost sad expression on his face.

"No, I'm gay." He pauses and then waves a hand as if dismissing the conversation. When he speaks next his voice is very brisk and businesslike. "The house party will be a few days full of activities for the wedding party at a hotel in the Cotswolds. Then they'll get married a month later. I'd like you to come with me to both events."

"Do you really want to do this?" I ask softly. "That's a hard thing to do. You were together for five years. Spending that amount of time with him and his new partner won't be particularly nice."

He shrugs, looking awkward. "I have to. I'm the best man." I make a choked sound but he ignores me, still speaking like a model of a businessman. "I meant to do something about it before, but the time passed quicker than I noticed, and now the week is on me and I need to take someone with me."

"And that's me?" He nods. "You do know you could find someone —" I snap my fingers. "—just like that?"

He shakes his head. "I don't want any romantic complications. I'm a private person, and this is a lot of time to spend with someone. If I take you, we both know it's just a business transaction. I'll pay your usual fee and double it. Would you be interested?"

"But you think I'm incompetent."

He looks startled. "I do not. Where on earth did you get that ridiculous idea?"

"The amount of times you've bollocked me in your office."

He shakes his head. "You just care about people," he says. "Too much," he finishes darkly. "You get involved and want to help and sometimes that goes wrong. I have to tell you off, but it doesn't mean I don't understand."

I stare at him. "This would have made the last three years much more understandable," I say faintly.

There's a flush on his cheeks, and he has the appearance of someone who's being tortured, but he looks at me determinedly. "So, would you be interested?" He smiles slightly. "I promise not to tell you off while we're away."

I stare at him, thinking hard. All that time to spend with him. To be in close confines with someone I have to admit I'm attracted to and who plainly doesn't fancy me back wouldn't be most people's idea of a good time. Then I shrug. I've always been contrary.

"I'll do it," I say softly and his shoulders slump slightly in relief. I hold up my hand. "But I don't want paying."

"Don't be ridiculous," he immediately and predictably starts, and I shush him.

I take a second to enjoy him obeying me, albeit with a dark look, and carry on talking. "I don't want paying. I'll do this for you on one condition."

"What?" He sounds wary.

I smile. "You have to call me Jesse."

He groans. "Okay," he finally says. "It goes against the grain, but I'll do it." I open my mouth but he holds up a hand. "A phrase made famous by Shakespeare, meaning if you planed the wood in the wrong direction, you'd rough it up," he says, well used to our conversational detours by now. He pauses. "Why would you not want to get paid?"

"Because I respect you and I quite like you. As a boss," I say quickly as alarm floods his face. "I will not accept payment," I say firmly. I don't know where this is coming from because I always need the money, especially with my student loan running thin now, but somehow it feels right, so I carry on. "If you try to pay me, I will leave you in the Cotswolds with the wedding party from hell."

He looks like he wants to argue, so I give him a cross look and he subsides.

"I'm not comfortable with this," he mutters.

"Is it because you're not in control suddenly?" I say sweetly. "Oh, how the mighty have fallen." He glares at me and I grin. "And a few days in the Cotswolds is never a hardship," I say lightly and smile. "Just think what fun we're going to have."

He looks faintly sick. "What have I done?" he mutters.

"I'm not sure," I say comfortingly. "But it's probably best just to relax and go with the flow." I laugh. "Last time I said that, I ended up with a night in the cells."

CHAPTER TWO

Zeb

I hear the door opening behind me as I stare down at the paperwork on my desk.

"Are you not supposed to be halfway to the Cotswolds on a dirty mini-break with the office hunk?"

I look up over my glasses at Felix. I think about trying a frown, but it would just be a waste of my facial muscles. He's been my assistant for seven years, and I know that nothing cows him. *Nothing.*

Instead, I grimace. "I'm going. I just..."

My words trail off and he shakes his head before sitting down on the chair in front of my desk.

"I was only joking about the dirty mini-break." He pauses. "Well, actually I wasn't."

"What?" My voice is a bark of astonishment.

He shrugs. "I've always wanted to see you and Jesse together."

I take off my glasses slowly and stare at him. "Have you been drinking this morning?"

He grins. "He'd be really good for you. So much better than bloody Patrick."

"Would it be any good for me to say for the five-millionth time that I wish you wouldn't talk about Patrick like that?"

He considers it. "No," he finally says, and I slump.

"I'm sure my company details list me as the boss. I'm almost positive. Can you get the paperwork for me so I can check?"

He sighs. "You're nominally in charge, but I've known you for far too long to take any notice. I've also known Patrick for far too long, but that's just something between my therapist and myself."

"He's not that bad," I say slowly, driven to stand up for him for some godforsaken reason.

"Zeb, he's a selfish twat. He's far too in love with himself to ever make a good partner for anyone. I'd send pitying thoughts over to his new bride if I didn't have a sneaking suspicion that she's exactly the same as him."

I think about arguing, but some of what he's saying does skirt perilously close to my own thoughts on the matter.

I sigh. "I know all that."

"So, why are you being his best man? You spent five years doing that, and he rewarded you by cheating on you."

A year ago I'd have flinched at that, but somehow, now it seems to have happened a decade ago. Like a distant memory. It's how I know that I'm healed. "I have to," I finally say. "I made a commitment to doing it, so I'll go through with it."

"Why did you promise?"

I shrug. "Because he was full of pretty apologies, and once upon a time I loved him." I hold my hands up. "I honestly don't know, but he caught me at a weak moment blathering on about wanting to be friends, and I gave in. There's no going back. I can't do that."

"Zeb." He hesitates, and I know he's got a zinger in store. "Zeb, you're not your dad. It's a statement of pure fact that I'm giving you now. You are not him. So bending over backwards to not let your wanker of an ex down won't mean you'll slide into bad habits."

I try to think of a clever answer but end up just shrugging awkwardly. "Let's not talk about this anymore," I suggest, sliding the paperwork towards him. "That's the Hawley file. Get Simon to do it. He's got a degree in horticulture, and he's got a good relationship with them, and they're comfortable with him. Also, make sure you pay Jesse and give him a bonus. He's doing me a huge favour at short notice."

He nods, accepting the paperwork. He's not just my assistant. He's the office manager and the company would fall into disarray if ever he left. He's got a mind like a steel trap. He demonstrates that immediately. "I thought he didn't want paying. That's what you said yesterday."

I shrug awkwardly. "I'd prefer to pay him and keep this–"

"Businesslike?" he offers sweetly.

I glare at him, trying silently to move him along. "Yes, of course, businesslike. What else would it be?"

"You should think about taking on a partner."

I stare at him, reeling at the switchbacks of daily conversation with him. They leave me with mental whiplash. "Why?"

"How can I put this delicately?" I groan, but he carries on relentlessly. "Because we're getting busier every week, and I love you, Zeb, but you're better with the details than you are with the customers. You're pretty shit with them."

"*That's* your version of delicate?"

He shrugs. "We each have to make the best of our own pluses and minuses." He grimaces. "The problem is that you're too intimidating."

I draw back, stung. "I am not."

"I don't mean personally," he says, shaking his head in exasperation. "I mean you're very organised and thorough and somehow people feel a lot less when they're with you. Some of the customers are already feeling that when they come to us. Try explaining to a hot as fuck man who has his own business and wears bespoke suits made on Savile Row that you need to hire someone to be your boyfriend for an office do." He holds his hand up when I open my mouth to protest. "I know you're kind and so do they after a bit, but it's not easy to confide what you see as a failure to someone who looks like they've only had sunny days. Impressions are everything." I stare at him and he smiles. "Just think about it."

"I will." I grimace. "God help me, but you do sometimes give good advice and I usually end up taking it."

"Hope you do with this last bit, then," he says cheerfully.

"Oh no," I groan, covering my face. "I knew you hadn't dropped it."

"Oh yes. You're going away with a fucking gorgeous bloke. If you get the chance, I want you to do what comes naturally."

"You want me to organise my paperwork and colour code the filing cabinet?"

He shakes his head. "You're hopeless."

"I'm realistic. Have you actually seen Jesse?"

"Seen and salivated over. Yes."

"Well, you know how he is." He gazes at me and I shake my head in exasperation. "He's twenty years younger than me, as fickle as the weather, and a total walking disaster."

He looks at me for a long second and a mysterious smile crosses his face. "One day you're going to listen when I talk to you. And when you realise that, you're going to apologise for thinking I talk a load of crap every day and know far too much gossip."

"I have no idea what is happening at the moment," I mutter.

"Just at the moment?" he says tartly and then seems to relent. "Jesse is actually a lot of things besides gorgeous. He's also smart and, most importantly, he's very kind." I stare at him, and he nods. "You know he is. You said it yourself the other day. Half the messes he ends up in are because he cares about people and he goes two steps further than anyone else to help them. He's never met a stranger, he's sociable, and genuinely interested in people. He's like a throwback to olden times. He should be in *Miss Marple*."

"Hopefully not as a dead body," I grumble. "But he'd be in the midst of it if he was. He's flippant and like a fucking butterfly."

"He's funny and he has a conscience," he corrects me. "I'm sure you already know this, but it's easier for you to pretend in your head that he's stupid."

"Why is it easier?"

He settles back in his chair and eyes me like I'm appearing before him in court. "Because you fancy him," he says calmly.

"I fucking do not," I start to splutter, and he holds up his hand. To my chagrin I immediately stop talking.

"You do, Zeb. You always have. Right from the first moment you met him I saw the sparks, and you've always been so protective of him." He stands up. "I saw other things too."

"What?" I say reluctantly.

"He fancies you too." I close my mouth with an audible snap, and he smiles. "That's me done."

"I feel like getting on my knees and offering thanks."

"Try getting on your knees and offering the gorgeous Jesse a nice blowjob."

"Oh my God, I'm old enough to be his father."

"He's twenty-four, not a teenager, and what you don't know about him would fill a football stadium."

I stare at him. "And just what does that mean?"

"It means you should seriously consider doing him."

"*Doing him.* What a delightful turn of phrase you have. Have you gone through *any* workplace training? He's my employee, in case you've forgotten."

"Pah, that's a silly detail."

"Says everyone who's ever ended up in a tribunal."

He waves his hand cavalierly and leaves my room on a tide of misplaced righteousness and Miller Harris aftershave.

I stare down at my desk. I need to go and pick Jesse up. I think of his high-boned face, the neck-length shiny brown hair, and his warm brown eyes, and my mouth waters. I call up the image of his long, wide-shouldered body and swear at the tightening in my groin. Then I think of having him to myself for the next few days. All of those warm smiles and eager curiosity, the silly jokes and that easy manner of his. Despite all the shit going on in my private life, Jesse has always managed to cheer me up. Just seeing his face makes me smile.

I might speak about his butterfly tendencies, but he's so much more than that. There's something very steadfast about him. And something inherently very beautiful that has nothing to do with his looks. He has a way of commanding your attention, and I've always left his company feeling lighter in myself.

I'm well aware that I've always had a small crush on him, but I put that to the side one day when Patrick seized on the subject of Jesse. Apparently, I talked too much about him and Patrick objected. I can still recall the argument that followed, and how, after that, I pushed my enjoyment of Jesse down into a hole inside me and turned the key.

It was easier all round for me to concentrate on his youth and put everything else aside. However, he isn't a kid anymore. He's a very handsome twenty-four-year-old. I shake my head. And I'm still twenty years older than him.

I wander over to the mirror and make myself take a long look at myself. In my head I itemise the crow's feet at the corners of my eyes, the wrinkle appearing between my brows, and the flecks of grey that are starting to show in my hair. Then I make myself look down at my body and remember that I am practically middle-aged and things are not as tight as they were.

I remember Patrick sneering at me when we were arguing once, telling me how ridiculous I was with my crush on a boy. The words still manage to hurt me, and with all that in the forefront of my mind I let myself think of Jesse's looks and body again, confident that I've come to my senses at last. My cock stirs despite all my efforts. *I'm fucking screwed*, I think dolefully. *What have I done?*

I'm no nearer an answer when I pull up outside his flat and honk the horn. I look around curiously. At one point this must have been a well-off area because the houses are beautifully proportioned, but then it must have fallen victim to the steady encroach of bedsit land, and here we are. Windows are dirty with sheets hung up at them rather than curtains. Rubbish blows idly round in the faint breeze and two dogs are fighting nearby over an upturned rubbish bin.

Movement catches my eye, and I turn to see Jesse coming out of the door of the block of flats. He's dressed in faded jeans, a pale blue shirt, and blue and white seersucker striped Vans, and he's wheeling a suitcase. He grins at me, and I can't help the uptick of my lips. I've tried many times but it doesn't work. There's just something about him that makes me smile.

Then I notice the man following him carrying a suit bag and my smile falters slightly. He's stunningly beautiful, and the laughing conversation they're having and their body language displays a familiarity with each other. I'm so busy staring ahead and trying not to analyse why my spirits have sunk that it takes Jesse three gos at calling my name through the window.

I lower it. "Shit, sorry. I was daydreaming."

His brow quirks and he grins. It's glorious at such a close range. "No problem. I just wondered for a second whether I was expected to run behind the car all the way to the Cotswolds."

"I'm not discounting that option yet," I say wryly, just to hear him laugh. He has a wonderful laugh. Rich and full and almost dirty.

I open the door and climb out, going round to the boot and opening it. "Stick your case in here," I say briskly, watching as the other man ambles over. He's dressed in old jeans and a navy T-shirt and he's wearing flipflops, but he moves like he's on the catwalk. I blink and Jesse laughs and nudges me.

"I know," he whispers. "It happens everywhere."

I turn to him. "I'm not looking at him like that," I start to say, trying to explain that I'm not leering at his boyfriend. It would be impossible when all my senses still seem to be tuned to Jesse's wavelength despite the all-round hopelessness of that silly yearning. Luckily, he saves me the humiliation.

"Charlie has this effect on everyone. Good job he's oblivious."

"Don't you mind?"

He blinks. "Why would I mind?"

"Isn't this your boyfriend?"

To my astonishment, he laughs loudly. "*No*, he's my flatmate. He's far too happy for me." He looks sideways at me. "I like them older and surlier," he says slowly and no less brutally effectively. I feel my cock stir under that clear brown gaze and leap into evasive manoeuvres.

"Hello." I smile quickly at Charlie and ignore Jesse. "Do you want to give me that? I'll hang it in the back of the car."

He smiles and it's seriously like an angel has descended. God knows how he goes about his normal life without his way being littered with smitten bodies. "Thank you. Bloody coat hanger was hurting my fingers." He hands it over and reaches out to hug Jesse who's still smiling curiously at me. "Have a good time," he says happily to Jesse. "Don't do anything I wouldn't do."

"That actually doesn't leave me with a very wide field. While the saintly existence seems to suit you, I can't say I'm gagging to live it with you," Jesse says. "I'll deal with things my own way, thank you."

"Badly then," the blond man says sadly, surprising a laugh out of me. He smiles at me. "Have a good few days," he says cheerfully. "Try and keep this one in order."

"I don't think I have that level of power. I'm not exactly sure who does." We smile at each other and I turn to find Jesse staring at me. For once there isn't a trace of a smile on his face and it looks wrong somehow. He has a face that's built to display his warmth and charm. I wonder if he's having second thoughts.

"You still okay to go?" I ask hesitantly. His expression clears and I contain my sigh of relief when the smile appears again, poking at the corners of that wide mouth like the sun around a cloud.

"Of course," he says. He hugs his flatmate. "You going to be okay?" he asks somewhat anxiously, and I watch them curiously.

"Of course," Charlie says. "Don't worry."

"I'm not *worrying* exactly." I tilt my head slightly. Even I can hear the worry. "I'd just be happier if Misha was around. Not that you need him, but you've had quite a few episodes lately."

Charlie steps back, his face closing down slightly. "He'll be round tonight. He's got the week planned." Jesse's shoulders sag, and his friend smiles. "I'm an adult, Jess. I don't need to be treated like a–"

"Like a child," Jesse fills in, smiling wryly. "I know the tune, and I know the lyrics."

"Well, sing it properly, then," Charlie advises happily, and, smiling at both of us, he turns and heads back into his flat, oblivious to the woman who nearly walks into a postbox as she stares at him.

Jesses looks at me and laughs. "Happens every time," he says cheerfully. "You ready?"

"As I'll ever be," I say wryly as we climb into the car. I drive an Audi which, according to the salesman, is known for its spacious interior. He obviously hadn't travelled with Jesse before though, because sitting next to him it's like the space has suddenly shrunk. Like we're in a reverse Tardis where I'm preternaturally aware of the scent of green tea that seems to cling to his skin and that sun-warmed long body.

I should probably break into conversation, but instead I turn the radio up and drive off. We travel in silence for ten or fifteen minutes while I navigate the early morning rush hour. Or at least I travel in silence. Jesse talks, but it's an easy-going chatter that doesn't require much beyond an occasional yes or no or a grunt.

It isn't until we're heading out of London on the motorway and it's calmed down a bit that he steps up the chat. "So, tell me about the people who are going to be at this do," he says, stretching his long legs out and sighing happily.

I shoot him a quick look and go back to staring at the road ahead. "Well, there's Patrick. Did you ever meet him?"

"No. I've heard of him though." I see him look at me from the corner of my eye. "I've heard a *lot* about him," he says innocently.

"I'm sure," I say dryly.

"You were together for five years. That's a long time."

I suppress a smile at the casual tone that doesn't quite conceal the curiosity. "Okay, I'm not one for talking about my private life, but I suppose you deserve to know. We were together for five years and living together for two, but he never entirely settled into the relationship. His family has always had a lot of expectations of him, and settling down with a man wasn't on that list."

"Let me guess, settling down with a girl and popping out a few children was."

I shake my head. "You guessed it." I shrug. "He cheated. I found out. I expected him to be remorseful. To my surprise, he wasn't. And that's it."

"*That's it?*"

The patent incredulity in his voice makes me smile. "What did you expect?"

He shrugs. "I don't know. More."

"Why? He'd cheated. There was no way back for me after something like that, and he didn't appear to be looking for forgiveness anyway. He'd lined up my replacement before he left." I shrug. "Patrick never wastes time. He likes his life to proceed the right way and smoothly. It was never going to be that way with me."

"And yet you're his best man. Why?" He huffs. "I wouldn't have given the wanker the pickings off my nose."

I look at him curiously, wondering where this passion is coming from. Youth, I suppose. Although I can't remember being like that. My idealism left me a long time ago to be replaced by resolve. I envy him.

"Listen, Patrick is who he is. He doesn't pretend to be anything less or anything more. He's selfish and arrogant and charming. It's a slightly dangerous combination. But at one point he was my friend. I haven't got enough of those to cast one aside just because we didn't work out romantically."

"Do friends cheat on one another?"

I shake my head. "Lovers do it all the time," I say cynically. He opens his mouth, and I talk quickly because his youth hurts me somewhere in a tiny spot in my chest. "He asked. He caught me at a weak moment, and I said yes." I wonder whether he'll ask what that moment was, but to my relief he doesn't. I don't think he'd like the answer.

Instead he says calmly, "Okay, tell me about the rest of the cast."

"Frances is Patrick's fiancée. She's twenty-three, I think. The only child of very rich parents. She's charming and spoilt, but a good hostess. Her mother and father are Charles and Oona. I believe he's something big in the city."

"What does that even mean?" he grumbles. "People always say that and it conjures up an image of Godzilla shimmying up the Shard."

He surprises a laugh out of me, and I listen to it with disbelief. "It's how he describes himself. He's not known for modesty," I say wryly. "They have a huge home in St John's Wood and a cottage in the Cotswolds where they rub shoulders with the Camerons."

"Kevin and Louise?"

I laugh. "No, you pleb. David and Samantha, of course."

"Is that where we're staying?"

I shake my head. "No, we're at a country house hotel just outside Stow-on-the-Wold. It's huge and they've booked the whole place for a few days. Then in a month we'll have to go to the wedding and the party in London."

"No quick trip to the registry office, then?"

"Not for Frances. What she wants, she gets."

"Like your ex?"

I nod. "Just like him."

He nudges me gently with his elbow. "Not sure it's a prize she's got," he says softly, and I smile awkwardly.

He must sense the awkwardness. He seems to have a fine-tuned sense of what people are feeling and thinking. I've seen him turn many potentially unpleasant situations around with just a few words and a smile so the glaring people end up laughing and smiling and utterly charmed.

"So, do they know about you and Patrick?"

I nod. "I met them a few times when I was with Patrick because his dad was friends with Frances's father. We didn't particularly hide what we were to each other."

"So, how will they take to you being there?"

I smile. "They'll be very charming and welcoming, but if I cross them or look like I might throw a spanner in the works they'll unleash hell. Charles is utterly ruthless."

"How lucky it is then that you're bringing your younger and much more socially adept new partner with you. Someone who will put Patrick to shame and charm the entire party."

"Have I arranged for someone else to come with me?" He laughs, but I sober. "Patrick's parents will be there as well. They hate the gays because they think we're all prowling around waiting to find our next victim. Like some sort of glittery zoo animals. They also think I'm a sexual predator, and that I somehow tricked their son into being gay."

"How do you trick someone into being gay?" he says, and there's a great deal of interest in his voice. "Is it through card tricks or something to do with the rabbit in the hat?"

I laugh, something I never thought I'd ever do when talking about Penny and Victor. "They'd like me to disappear. Or worse."

"Lovely," he says faintly. "So a few days in the Cotswolds with a wanker. Sorry, I mean a banker. And old-aged murderous homophobes. Anyone else?"

"Quite a few of Patrick and Frances's friends, obviously, and the bridesmaids."

There's a long silence, and I'm sure he's thinking of opening the door and just walking back to London, and then he laughs.

"Well, I've always liked a challenge."

"This isn't a challenge, so much as a suicide mission," I say glumly.

The next hour passes surprisingly well. He takes control of the stereo and synchs it to his phone. I make a token protest but find that we have a startlingly similar taste in music. He loves the eighties, declaring that it's retro, which makes me wince slightly because I fucking grew up then.

With "Long Hot Summer" by the Style Council playing, we turn off the motorway and start to travel down winding roads, the trees spreading their branches over us like the world's oldest and greenest gazebo. We pass through little villages that look chocolate-box pretty with their village greens surrounded by houses made from the ubiquitous honey-coloured stone.

"Have you ever been here before?" I ask as I click the indicator and pull into the car park of an old pub. Made of the same Cotswold stone as the rest of the village, it has wisteria growing prettily up its sides and mullioned windows that gleam in the light of the sun. The pub garden has lots of benches with bright red umbrellas, and even though it's just midday, there are already a few customers sheltering under the umbrellas. Their happy voices reach us as we enter the pub and blink to clear our eyes and let them adjust to the cool dimness.

"No, I've never been here," he says. "My mum and dad spent one of their anniversaries here though. They loved it."

I wander over to the bar. "I thought we'd have lunch before we get there and our appetites totally disappear," I throw over my shoulder.

The barman comes over and I order an orange juice for myself and the cider Jesse requests. After a look at the menu we add our requests for Ploughman's, and on an assurance that they'll bring our food out to us, we head out to the garden by unspoken accord.

"I suppose we should get our stories straight," he says and I turn abruptly, almost tripping in the process.

"What?"

He grabs my elbow gently and steers me to a table in the far corner by a big lilac bush. Bees are dancing lazily amongst the flowers and the air is heavy with the scent.

"I mean," he says, "that we should work out our story. Where we met, how long we've been together. That sort of thing."

"I never even thought of that," I say in astonishment as I sit down on the sun-warmed bench.

He smiles wryly. "That's because you're very straightforward. I bet you haven't told many stories."

"Lies, you mean," I say baldly. "No, I haven't. I had enough of..." I stop abruptly, unable to believe I was just about to bring my father up.

He shrugs. "It's okay. And they're not really lies. They're more what my mum used to call fibs. Something that doesn't harm other people. We're not harming anyone, are we?"

I shake my head. "Of course not." I consider his words and find that I'm peculiarly okay with them. "Alright," I say slowly. "Where did we meet?"

"Patrick doesn't know what I look like, does he?" he asks.

I shake my head. "No, he knew your name at one point, but I don't think he'll remember it now. He doesn't retain people's names well unless he needs them for something."

"Okay then, we met at a club. I think it was Magenta," Jesse says promptly. "You spilt your drink on me and promised to pay for the dry cleaning. That's how you got my phone number."

I look at him with my mouth open. "I'm very smooth," I say slowly.

He laughs. "As butter," he says mockingly. "Now, what job should I have?" He clicks his fingers. "I know. I'll be an architect."

I blink. "Do you actually know anything about architecture?"

He grins. "I know buildings have roofs and doors and windows. And I was fucking brilliant with Lego when I was little."

I groan. "This is going to be a disaster."

He laughs. "Lighten up." He leans forward, his face alight with enjoyment. "It's a game," he says in a low, teasing voice that goes straight to my cock. "We're who we want to be and there's fun in that."

"Fun?" I echo, and he nods.

"Fun." His face becomes businesslike. "Okay, we've mentioned that we like eighties music, so that's covered. What books do you like?"

"Crime thrillers and mysteries. What about you?"

"Gay romance." I blink and he smiles. "Really. There are some brilliant books around. I'll lend you one. I've got a couple in my case."

I stare at him. "I never imagined you—"

He looks at me wryly. "Did you think I couldn't read?"

"No, of course not." My words are fast and embarrassed. "I just thought you'd be too busy."

"Shagging?" He bursts into laughter at my undoubtedly horrified look. "I'm kidding." He pauses. "Well, not about the shagging. I love that."

"Of course you do," I say faintly.

He smiles. "But I like reading too." He sits back as the waitress hands us our plates and cutlery and I watch as he charms her. It isn't a false charm. Patrick could be very charming when he wanted to, but a lot of it was only surface deep. Even while he was doing it, I'd see the thinness to the veneer covering him. Jesse doesn't have that because his charm is true. He genuinely likes people and his interest in them seems to make them come alive under those warm, twinkly eyes.

He turns back to me when the waitress disappears and unfurls his napkin with a flourish. "Okay," he says, a businesslike tone to his voice now. "Likes and dislikes?"

And so for the next hour that's what we do. We sit in the sunny pub garden working our way through a laundry list of our likes and dislikes, and I'm alarmed to find how many we have in common. Alarmed and enthralled. I sigh. That about sums up my attitude towards Jesse Reed.

CHAPTER THREE

Jesse

I continue questioning him when we get back in the car.

"This is like *Mastermind*," he grumbles, starting the engine.

I try not to stare at those big hands on the steering wheel and the veins on the back of them. However, by not staring at them I am now focusing on the scent of oranges and sandalwood. I love the smell. It's warm and rich, and underneath is the scent of his skin that makes my mouth water.

I'm beginning to think this trip might be a bad idea, mainly because he seems allergic to the slightest hint of a fib which is richly ironic as he hired me to play a part with him. However, it's a certainty that the crush I've always had on Zeb is in danger of becoming magnified the more time I spend with him.

He simply does it for me. I know he's older, but I like that. I like the way he's sure of himself and quietly confident. I like the huskiness of his voice and the way one eyebrow raises whenever he listens to me. I like how funny he is and how he can talk on any subject. He's funny and wise and more interesting than any man I've ever met, and, when I talk, he listens to me as if there's no one else worth listening to.

I'm not stupid. I know he's dismissed me over the last few years as a kid. He put me in that box the day I came for an interview, and looking back, I can see how young I was. But he doesn't seem to see me as I am now. Although why would he? I think of the funeral fight and sigh.

"You okay?"

I look up to find him watching me with a hint of concern in those bright blue eyes.

"Yes, I'm fine," I say quickly.

"You sure? We can turn round."

"You'd go back to London for me?"

"Erm, no. I'd drop you off at the station."

For some reason that makes me laugh hard, and he stares at me quizzically, that one eyebrow raised as I chortle and snort.

Sobering, I straighten up. "Well, there's no need to test my potential hitchhiking skills." I look at him and gesture down my body. "All of this says no to thumbing a lift."

He shakes his head and starts off. "Okay, what else do you need to know? Inside leg measurement?"

"Dick size?" I say, laughing as the car swerves slightly. "Only kidding. Surely no one is likely to question me about that." I tap my nail against my tooth thoughtfully. "Okay, we've covered how we met and how long we've been together. Music tastes and books. Coffee or tea?"

He looks blank. "Tea, of course."

I dramatically slump back in the seat. "Phew, I don't need to tuck and roll out of a moving vehicle. All will be well. We can settle down and have ten children now without me worrying."

"That's your yardstick for worrying? Hmm."

I laugh and he looks at me for a second before returning his serious gaze back to the road. It's empty but he still drives as if expecting a major disaster to happen any second. It's oddly endearing.

"We haven't spoken about family," he says. "That's the number one question amongst the set of people we're about to be sharing a hotel with. Would they know your family?"

"Unlikely," I say lightly. "Well, not unless they've attended Evensong at St Mary's Church in Dunsford."

He jerks. "Your father's in the church?"

"That makes him sound like a squatter. He is a vicar, but nice sexism," I say sternly. "It might have been my mum."

"I'm so sorry," he says earnestly. "I didn't mean to offend you."

I laugh. "If you knew my family, you'd be spot on. There is no way my mum could have been a vicar. She's far too impatient."

"So, your father is a vicar?" He seems oddly enthralled by this piece of information.

"Yes, you seem slightly disbelieving," I say, nudging him gently.

He scratches his chin, the intimate sound of the scrape of his stubble seeming to hit me in the back of my teeth and making my mouth water.

"Well, that's because I am," he says baldly, startling a laugh out of me. "You don't seem like a vicar's son."

"And what does a vicar's son seem like?"

"Well ..." He searches for words. "Pious," he finally says. "Quiet and studious and humble."

I start to laugh. "Well, my dad must have lucked out, then, because none of us conform to that."

"None of you? How many are there?"

"I'm the youngest of eight children."

"*Eight?*" His voice goes slightly high. He coughs and clears his throat. "Eight children," he says in a marvelling voice. Silence falls for a second until he nods. "No wonder you're so loud."

I laugh. "That's true. I had to be loud or I'd have been forgotten and left at a service station somewhere."

"Was that a thing?" he asks cautiously. "Did that happen?"

"Oh yes," I say cheerfully. "It was like *Home Alone* but with handy slot machines and a WH Smiths."

"Oh my God. How long before they realised?"

"Luckily they hadn't got out of the car park, which is a good job because it was another twenty miles before the next slip road." I sigh. "I was doing so well on those slot machines too. If they hadn't come back, I might have been a millionaire." That startles a laugh out of him and I smile. "My family is loud, gossipy, and in your face. No wonder my dad went into the church. It's the only peaceful place apart from the loo." I look over at him. "How about you?"

He jerks slightly. "Oh, there's just me," he says lightly. "My mum died having me and my father died about ten years ago."

"I'm sorry," I say, feeling guilty about mentioning my family.

He shoots me an embarrassed look. "No need to be," he says brusquely. "It was all a long time ago."

I sense there's a story here, but his voice tells me I won't be hearing it. I open my mouth to say something, but he says, "We're here" with a strong note of relief in his voice.

He clicks the indicator and steers down a long drive that weaves in and out of trees, offering occasional glimpses of a huge golden-stoned building. Finally, we enter a straight stretch and the hotel is in front of me. It's four storeys high and set in acres of landscaped grounds, including, according to Zeb, a fishing lake. It's made of Cotswold stone that glows in the sunshine and the paintwork is a soft heather grey. The leaded windows twinkle in the light.

"Wow," I say faintly.

He shoots me a glance. "I think you'll like it," he says as he pulls to a stop. "The staff are very friendly, and it's comfortable."

"You've been here before, then?"

He nods. "Patrick and I used to spend our anniversaries here."

My mouth drops open, but before I can express my amazement at the unending depths of crassness that his ex possesses, he exits the car and I see a uniformed man coming towards us. I jump out, inhaling the scent of freshly mown grass, and smile at Zeb and the member of the staff.

"Peter will take the car round for us, and they'll bring the bags in," Zeb says.

"Lovely," I say happily. "This doesn't happen at a Travelodge."

Zeb laughs, and the man smiles kindly at me.

I stand back, looking around me as Zeb slips the man some money, and the car peels away, crunching over the gravel. Zeb comes up beside me.

"Are we near anywhere?" I ask, looking out over the green fields spread before me like a verdant carpet.

He nods. "We're not far from anywhere. Stow-on-the-Wold is a few miles away, as are most of the famous Cotswold villages."

"It's really pretty around here."

He smiles. "It really is. We'll shoot off if the group gets a bit much, and I'll show you around."

I smile gratefully at him, and he must sense the slight nervousness I'm feeling because he frowns. "It must be a bit intimidating," he says. "But I'm here."

I shrug. "Sorry. I don't normally get nervous, but I don't usually stay in places like this either."

"Not even with customers?"

I shoot him a glance. "I seem to spend more time digging people's gardens and getting their shopping. I haven't done a pretend-boyfriend gig in ages, apart from the funeral incident." I narrow my eyes at the suddenly blank expression on his face. "Why is that?" A horrible thought occurs to me. "Oh my God, is it because I'm too old?"

He shakes his head, a funny smile playing on his full lips. "You're twenty-four, Jesse. No danger of a card from the Queen yet. And here you are being a pretend boyfriend. Your youth is assured. Rest easy."

I frown at him. "I can't help but think you're taking the piss out of me, Zebedee."

He glares. "Please don't ever call me that again. What the fuck?"

I start to laugh. "Time for bed, Zebedee."

"You're far too young to have ever watched *The Magic Roundabout*."

"But my eldest brother wasn't, and he had the DVD."

"I feel old," he bemoans. "I remember the original."

"Never mind, Grandpa, we'll get you a nice cup of tea and you can tell me about the war."

He shoves me, laughing, and my breath catches at how handsome he looks with that wide, white smile and the sun playing in the tangles of his hair, catching the red strands in there and seeming to kindle it.

"Zeb," comes a shout from behind us and immediately the smile is gone, replaced by his usual unsmiling exterior. He stiffens all over, and I know who it is without turning. Patrick. I rub Zeb's arm, and for a second when he looks at me it's as if he's forgotten who I am. It's surprisingly unpleasant. Then his expression clears, and he grips my fingers for a second before his hand falls loose, and he turns.

"Patrick," he says, and I turn and watch the man who was with Zeb for five years walk towards me. Viewed dispassionately, he's gorgeous. He's tall and wide shouldered with a head of blond hair which shines expensively in the sunlight. He's wearing jeans and a purple polo shirt that hugs his muscled torso.

I look at Zeb. They must have made quite the pair, I think, as Patrick comes to stand in front of him. Dark and light. The devil and the angel. I look at Patrick and mentally shake my head. No angel, this. His full mouth has a discontented pull to it, and he looks as if he could succumb to petulance at any minute. He looks spoilt and expensive.

"Zeb," he says, his voice low and intimate. "You came. I wasn't sure you would."

"Of course," Zeb says abruptly. "You invited me, didn't you, and I replied yes. That is the normal way things happen."

I bite my lip to prevent a smile as Patrick looks slightly askance. "Well, I'm glad you're here," he says quickly. He looks Zeb up and down and something kindles in his eyes. "Very glad."

I shift my position, and both men start as if woken from a deep sleep and turn to face me. "Oh, Jesse," Zeb says, sounding surprised and making me want to punch him. "Pat, this is Jesse."

"Jesse? Do I know that name?" he says thoughtfully. Zeb stiffens, but Patrick shakes his head. "Sounds a bit like someone from a Bon Jovi song."

"Rather than someone from an Irish folk song," I say very sweetly, holding my hand out and forcing him to shake it. His grip is loose and disinterested, and he drops my hand quickly and turns back to Zeb.

"I didn't realise you were bringing anyone."

"The invitation said guest," Zeb says coolly. "And Jesse is my guest."

Patrick eyes me coldly before turning back to Zeb. "I'll have to ask at the desk for them to prepare another room. We only asked for the one. You've got a lovely suite. I picked it out specially. It looks out over the lake with a balcony." He winks. "Remember it?"

Zeb stiffens, and I instantly know they've stayed in it before.

"Sounds lovely," I say happily and slide my arm around Zeb's waist. His muscles are rigid under my fingers, and I pinch him lightly. He starts imperceptibly and, obeying his cue, he slides his arm over my shoulders. "I'm sure we'll be very happy there. A balcony, eh?" I say, nudging him. "Oh, the things we can do on a balcony, lover." His eye twitches slightly, and he shoots me a quick warning glance that makes me laugh.

Patrick's eyes turn cold as he looks at us, seeming to linger where Zeb's arm touches me. I reach up one hand and tangle my fingers in Zeb's, and luckily he doesn't jump like a startled goldfish or stand like a fucking statue. Instead he seems to get with the programme and draws me closer. However, that's my undoing because now I can feel all his long warm body against mine. I can smell the faint scent of oranges. He's taller and bigger than me, heavily muscled, and somehow I feel safe under his arm.

"So you two are together?" Patrick says, gesturing at us and bringing me back to the conversation.

"Deeply in love," I say cheerfully. "You *bet* we are." Zeb tightens his grip on me, and I bite my lips to contain my smile.

"We are," he says in a very stern way. "So in love sometimes that all I want to do is spank him."

I flutter my eyelashes. "Sometimes all I want you to do is spank me too. Oh, to be in love in England in the summertime, as Robert Browning said. Or was it Art of Noise?"

Zeb shakes his head, and a laugh slips out. Patrick's gaze gets even colder and more calculating. "Really? I don't remember Zeb ever being into that. I suppose tastes change. Some for the good. Some for the bad." He eyes me up and down like I'm a piece of shit.

"They certainly do," I say sweetly, looking him up and down in return. "Still, out with the old and in with the new."

He laughs with no sign of amusement about him. "Make sure you don't toss Zeb out too, then."

Zeb stiffens, and I smile coldly at Patrick. "No chance of that. I know what I've got and I've never been one to just throw things away. I keep a firm hold of my possessions."

There's a long silence. Zeb stares at his ex, but I can't decipher his expression. He stirs. "Shall we go in?" he says abruptly.

Patrick steps back and gestures to the hotel with a flourish. "Be my guest," he says. "I'll let you go. After all, you know the way, don't you, Zeb?"

Zeb marches forward, and I skip to catch up with him. I look back, and Patrick is watching us go, standing in a pool of sunshine. He smiles at me, and there's more than a touch of shark about it. I turn to make my way up the steps, and when I look back, he's gone and the drive is empty.

Even the reception area of the hotel looks expensive, and I look uneasily down at my old jeans and battered Vans. I stand back as Zeb deals with the receptionist. He exchanges a few words with her, and I can tell from their tone that they're kind. I like that about Zeb. He's always kind and courteous. She smiles widely at him, and he turns to me with a small smile on his lips. It vanishes as he looks at me. "We're on the third floor," he says abruptly, jerking his head at the lift. *Oops!*

I follow him into the lift, which arrives with the obliging haste that life seems to arrange for Zeb. He settles his back against the mirrored wall, and I move to stand next to him, staring ahead and starting a tuneless humming which is sure to annoy him.

Sure enough, it does. "Do you have to make that noise?" he asks crossly. "Either sing or be silent."

"Are those my only choices?" I say innocently. "I'm not sure about that, Zeb. Surely life has more options for me."

"Not about humming."

I smile at him, watching the tic in his jaw get more prominent. Then I bend forward and hum straight into his ear. He jumps about a foot in the air and whirls on me. "What the fuck?" he says.

"Just making sure you're awake," I say happily as the lift dings and the door opens onto a long carpeted corridor that smells of furniture polish and money. Big oak doors are set along the wall, set far enough away from each other to denote large rooms.

He glares at me, and I follow him as he removes the key from his pocket and inserts it into room eighteen.

He swings the door open and waves me in rather like someone gesturing someone to their execution. "After you," he says tersely.

"What a gentleman," I say meekly.

I look around. I'm standing in the lounge area of the suite. There are a pair of French doors leading out onto a balcony. Two pale green sofas are sitting on either side of a long coffee table and facing a large-screen TV. One wall is entirely brick, and the other walls are painted white.

Spying a door, I beetle over and find the bathroom. It has another exposed brick wall on which the sink is set, and it's light and airy mainly because of another set of doors. Gauzy curtains blow in the slight breeze, and I eye the copper freestanding bath sitting in the middle of the room. I love a bath and constantly bemoan the fact that we picked a flat that only has a shower.

I turn round and nearly bang into Zeb, who's leaning against the wall, his arms folded and a forbidding expression on his face. I search for a diversion.

"Ooh, look," I cry out. "There's a hotel umbrella here."

"Is that so astonishing?"

"It is if you've stayed in the same hotels that I have. The closest they came to an umbrella was not getting arsy if you ripped the carpet up and held it over your head."

"Jesse," he begins, and I instantly recognise his tone of voice. It usually precedes a thoroughly good bollocking.

"Bedroom," I shout and he jumps, giving me the opportunity to get past him and into the bedroom. This turns out to be another beautiful room. The bed is huge and made up with pale blue linens and lots of cushions. A piece of artwork hangs over the bed, and it looks original. I peer at the portrait of a rather grim-looking man. "Blimey," I mutter. "That would give anyone performance anxiety. What a thing to hang over a bed."

I pace over to the French doors that lead onto the secluded balcony overlooking a wood and the lake glistening blue in the afternoon sunshine. "Room eighteen, eh?" I say, turning to find him watching me still with his arms folded. Hope they don't get stuck that way. "So, this is where the magic happened."

"Don't take the piss," he says sharply. "You're so bloody flippant all the time." I bristle at that because I know it's what he really thinks of me. It's why he hesitated over asking me to do this. "Try and take this seriously for once in your life," he snaps. "And stop taking the piss out of Patrick and trying to wind him up."

"Oh really," I say sweetly, folding my own arms, because it's obviously catching, and glaring at him. All of our happy camaraderie is gone, and I fucking hate that Patrick took it away. I try not to analyse why that is. "I'm flippant, am I?"

He stares at me, and for a second, there's a slight trace of worry on his forehead. Good. There should be.

"Yes, you are," he says. "I knew I shouldn't have done this." He rubs his hand over his hair. "You're so young, and I know that this seems like a game to you. You even told me that."

"I told you that to lighten you up." I watch as he flings himself onto a sofa and stares moodily at me. "So you didn't look constipated every time I spoke. And I'll thank you to remember that I'm twenty-four, not six. And I'm actually here doing you a fucking favour."

He stares at me and sighs. "I'm sorry," he says suddenly, his eyes looking contrite. I stand rigid, not prepared to just accept that, and he smiles. "You look like you're thinking of ways to kill me."

"I've already done that," I say tartly. "Now, I'm working on methods of body disposal."

That startles a laugh out of him, and I relent suddenly. It's hard to hold out against the power of that slightly rusty laugh. I lower myself onto the other sofa in front of him. "I'm sorry too," I say softly. "Just do me a favour and stop saying how young I fucking am. It properly winds me up. Like you think I'm a fucking child. Either that or you're using it to make sure I know my place."

"I don't think you're a child," he says slowly, and for a second our eyes meet and seem to tangle and get caught as we stare at each other. I hold my breath, but he shakes his head and looks down at the table between us. "You're right," he says reluctantly.

"I am?" I sound very startled.

"Yes, I'll note it in my diary." He smiles at me, all traces of reserve suddenly gone, melted away under the sweetness of that curve of his mouth. "I really am sorry," he offers, looking suddenly a lot younger. "I'm on edge, and I didn't need that little scene outside."

"Why are you on edge? Do you want him back?" I ask abruptly.

He looks startled and then thoughtful, and my stomach drops. "At one point I did," he says slowly. "If you'd asked me a year ago, I'd have said yes. But now?" He shrugs.

"Now what?" I ask, and he must sense the sudden passion in my voice, because he looks slightly worried. Like I'm going to leap on him with a ring, demanding to be married instantly. It itches and stings under my skin like I've grabbed a nettle with my bare hands.

I sit back deliberately and coolly. "I need to know, Zeb, because if you're making a play for the groom at his wedding, then we're edging out of romantic comedy and into something a bit darker."

He looks offended. "I'd *never* do that."

"I don't think it's entirely up to you," I say, thoughtfully watching him. "I think Patrick still has feelings."

He shrugs dismissively. "I suppose some feelings don't just go away. Me turning up with you must have thrown him. It's not easy to see your ex with someone else, no matter how much you've moved on."

"Hmm. Well, I'd watch your step with him this week because there's something a bit off about all of this."

"What do you mean?"

"I mean having it here where you used to come together, inviting you to be best man. He's either very determined to rub your nose in it, or he's got another agenda."

"What?" He sounds startled. "What do you mean?"

I shrug. "I don't know. Don't listen to me." I bite my lip. "After all, if I'm not staking ownership of the Wendy house or throwing sand at the other children, I'm having my afternoon nap."

He laughs loudly, his eyes creased. "You're not a kid," he finally says, and I smile at him.

"I promise that I won't behave like one," I say impulsively. "I don't want to embarrass you. I'll behave like an adult. I'll be reasonable and assured and a cool head in any crisis." He looks like he wants to dispute this, and I eye him for a moment. "Unless he's horrible to you," I say firmly. "Then all bets are off."

CHAPTER FOUR

Zeb

I stand outside on the balcony, the late afternoon sun laying stripes across the floor. Listening out, I can still hear the hiss of the shower where Jesse has ensconced himself. I think of that lithe form with soap bubbles trailing down it and shake my head firmly. *Nope.* I turn my attention back to the phone in my hand.

"This is a disaster," I hiss.

"I'm sorry. Is this a conversation or Chinese whispers?" my twat of an assistant whispers back. "Hang on, though. I was good at this in Cubs. I think you said that you liked James Acaster. That's fine with me. He's a very funny comedian."

"Do I pay you too much?" I wonder.

"Put it out of your head," he says comfortingly. "Now, why is this a disaster? You're away for a few days with an extremely gorgeous younger man. Were you a pessimistic child, Zeb? Because all the signs are pointing that way."

"I'm also away with my ex-lover, his future bride, and two sets of families who hate me," I mutter. "Oh, and Jesse and Patrick clashed heads earlier."

"Did Jesse actually headbutt Patrick? Because this day is getting better and better. I might buy a lottery ticket later on."

"No, of course he didn't. But he was very challenging towards him. Like two dogs fighting over a piece of bacon," I say glumly.

"Zeb, it's like the fairies sprinkled magic dust over you when you were a baby and then promptly dropped you on your head."

"I can't talk to you," I say solemnly.

"No, don't. Go and shag that beautiful man and fuck the others off. Just spend the time in bed with him."

"Goodbye," I say sadly.

I click End, aware of him laughing in the background, but all my attention is on the bathroom door which has just opened to reveal Jesse. If this were a film, triumphant music would definitely play because he's a glorious sight.

He's naked apart from a white towel wrapped around his narrow hips that accentuates the swarthy tone of his skin. I always wondered whether he used a sunbed but now I'm unfortunately aware that every inch of him is covered in olive-coloured skin. I'm also faintly surprised that he has hair on his chest. I don't know why. I suppose because he's so smooth, I expected him to be more boyish, I guess. Not very obviously a man. I swallow hard, and to my horror, I feel my cock stiffen, so I spring into action.

"Good shower?" I ask briskly.

He looks at me curiously and then gives me his wide, wonderful smile. It always strikes somewhere inside me like there's a bell that only he rings. It's full of humour, the warm, plush lips curved into a quirky tilt, and he smiles with his eyes. Very few people do. It's one of the reasons so many people warm to him. He's very puckish. Funny and kind but with a strong undercurrent of wildness about him. Like he's keeping the mischievous side of him only barely reined in.

He scrubs another towel over his hair, emerging from its folds with all that dark mink-brown hair falling over his face in silky strands.

"It's lush," he pronounces.

"Pardon?"

He smiles. "Lush. It's brilliant." He shrugs. "We lived in Wales when I was seven and my best friend is Welsh. Can't help picking up a few things."

"Oh." I'm startled. Every time he talks to me now, I uncover another fact. He's like one of those Chinese puzzle boxes that, if turned the right way, spills out its secrets.

"Did you live in many places?" I ask.

He nods. "We moved all over the country until my dad got the church in Devon. They've lived there for the last fifteen years."

He raises a quizzical brow, and I flush, realising that I'm standing staring at him. "We need to talk," I say abruptly.

"Okay," he says easily. He settles into a chair, his long legs dusted in black hair stretched comfortably out.

"Erm, don't you want to get dressed?" I say. Then I realise that I'm standing here and his clothes are here. "Oh shit. I'll go out on the balcony and–"

"Why?" He's full-on staring at me now.

"Well, because you'll want to get dressed."

"Zeb, I'm presuming that we have the same body parts. I've got changed in front of loads of people. I'm fine with being naked in front of you." He shrugs. "It's just flesh, isn't it?"

"Yes," I say slowly, my mouth watering at the scent of his damp skin. I shake my head firmly to clear it. "That brings me to another problem."

"How happy you must be," he says cheerfully, stretching his arms above his head with a satisfied grunt.

I narrow my eyes at him. I swear he's doing this on purpose. "Why?"

"So many problems. You must admit you live to sort them out. This is like Christmas and birthdays to you with all these potential areas of trouble just tumbling out around you."

I shake my head. "Jesse, you're a pisstaking prat," I say baldly, hearing the sound of his laughter with a surge of warm pleasure. Mostly everyone around me treats me warily, like I'm going to leap on them and organise their cupboards before sacking them and casting them onto the street. Jesse never has. He's always treated me with this warm friendliness, and I savour it so much more than I should.

He stops laughing and rubs his eyes. "Okay, let's have the problem."

"The bed," I say firmly.

He looks towards it and back at me. "Is it not comfortable? Are the sheets polyester?"

"No." I gape at him. "Can you really not see the problem?" He shrugs. "There's only one bed," I say impatiently. He stares at me and I launch into problem-solving. "I'm so sorry. I didn't think. But luckily there's a sofa. I'll sleep on that."

He starts to laugh again. "Zeb, it's like meeting a stranger. You didn't think *any* of this through, did you? What is *happening* to you?"

I shrug, feeling my cheeks flush to my horror. "It was a bit of an impulsive move," I finally admit.

He smiles at me kindly. "Well, luckily I excel in those," he murmurs. "I'll guide you along."

"May God help me."

He chuckles. "Listen, that sofa is as uncomfortable of a piece of furniture as I've ever sat on. There is no way you're sleeping on that while we're here." He shrugs. "There's an easy solution to all of this."

"Get another room and tell people that you're saving yourself for marriage?" I say glumly, and he laughs, his whole face lighting up and those warm eyes of his limpid and clear.

"No, silly. We'll just share the bed."

"Oh my God." I sigh and lean back, covering my eyes. "I'm your bloody boss. You can't share a bed with me."

Warm fingers cover my hands, and he prises them away from my face. I blink as I see his pretty face close up. "If it makes you feel any better," he says solemnly, "we'll put a pillow between us, each keep one foot on the floor at all times, and I promise to hide the key to my chastity belt."

I shake my head, only realising that he's still touching my face when his fingertips slide across my skin. I repress a shiver.

He smiles and steps back, adjusting the towel around his waist. "Zeb, we're both adults, and it's time you realised it. We're both perfectly capable of sharing a bed without leaping on each other the moment the lights go out."

I swallow hard. *Speak for yourself,* I think. *It's getting increasingly difficult for me to keep my hands off you.* Instead of saying the words, I send my face into its customary polite mask. It's stood me well over the years, covering up my occasional shyness and the resulting awkwardness. I found a long time ago that people largely accept the face you show to the world. I'm not sure it works with him, however, because his eyes sharpen as if he's looking inside me, and those eyes turn kind and warm.

"If this is a problem," he says slowly, all mirth gone, "I'll get another room. Fuck everyone else's opinion. You're the important one in this situation, not any of those probably snotty bastards."

I blink. I don't think I've ever heard that before.

"Oh, there's no need," I say softly, incredibly touched by the passion and heat in his voice. It's odd to have someone so focused on me and my feelings. I'm not entirely sure it's comfortable though, so I stand up. "Never mind," I say briskly. "We'll work it out. Thank you for being so patient."

His eyes sharpen as he stares at me, then, after a long second, they soften again. "You don't need to thank me for being patient. Don't ever thank me for that."

I study him, wondering what he's thinking, before realising that I probably look like an idiot at the moment. "Never mind," I say quickly. "I'm going to shower and change for dinner." I look at his current outfit. "You'll need to wear your suit."

"Never crossed my mind not to," he says glumly. "I'd probably wear court robes if I had any."

I shake my head. "Well, I'm just going to shower," I say again, slightly awkwardly, compounding my idiocy by pointing at the bathroom door as if he doesn't know where it is. His mouth twitches, and he stands up and stretches.

I watch all the muscles move languorously under his skin, sliding like silk, and feel my cock thicken. "You do that," he says throatily.

Once I'm inside the bathroom, I lean back against the door and shake my head, groaning silently. Against my will, my hand strays down to my cock which is pushing impudently against my jeans. I suppress a moan but can't help stroking along its length, the rough denim catching my nerves and making them sparkle.

Through the door I hear thumping and then the sound of "Fine Time" by New Order starting to play. I shake my head as Bernard Sumner begins to sing about age. I strip off quickly, feeling the cooler air strike against my hot skin. I start the water in the shower and step into the huge enclosure, inhaling the scent of green tea that lies heavy on the damp air.

The spray cascades over me. He has it set to a harder pressure than I normally do, and I reach out to lower it, but the water strikes my nipples at that point and the pleasure sparkling through me makes me groan low. I stiffen, but I'm pretty sure that the noise of the shower and his music is covering my sounds.

I reach over and fill my palm with the shower gel in a green bottle. It's only when the rich scent of green tea fills the shower enclosure that I realise it isn't mine but his. I bite my lip and consider washing it off, but without any thought my hand lowers to my dick, and I grasp it tightly.

The shaft is engorged, the skin tight, and just the touch of my fingers makes me jerk.

"Fuck," I gasp, and tighten my grip and shuttle my cock through it. I shouldn't be doing this here, but I'm too far gone to pay attention to the active part of my brain. *It doesn't matter,* I tell myself. *Everyone does it.* But even as I think that, an image comes into my head of Jesse on his knees in front of me, all that shiny hair wet and clinging to the sharp bones of his face. He has his mouth open and I grab his hair and push his head back, shoving my cock into his mouth. His lips are swollen and tight around the shiny length of my cock, and despite my brain screaming at me to stop this, lightning pools in my balls and I come with a heavy grunt all over the glass doors of the shower.

I lean back against the wall, panting and feeling its coldness against my hot skin as the water rushes over me, washing away the come clinging to my cockhead. I scrub my head against the unforgiving glass. *What the fuck is wrong with me?* I am a forty-four-year-old man stuck in a hotel room sharing a bed with my twenty-four-year-old employee. And with only a door separating us, I just wanked over the image of forcing my cock down his throat. I wonder wildly whether this is some sort of midlife crisis.

Jesse

I'm standing on the balcony, looking out over the lake glowing with the last threads of sunshine, when the bedroom door opens behind me. I turn and nearly swallow my tongue. I don't know which I prefer more, Zeb in a suit, or in the jeans and T-shirts I've been seeing lately.

But I have to admit that he fills out a suit like no one else. Tonight's offering is a dark grey one with a white shirt and purple tie. His skin is sun-kissed after the afternoon in the pub garden, giving him a golden glow that makes his blue eyes seem even more vivid. His grey-flecked dark hair tumbles around his face. He looks healthy. My mouth twitches. Healthy and ready to organise.

I lean back against the railing. "Okay, give it to me."

He blinks. "Pardon?"

I smile. "The lecture. I'm ready." I stretch my neck and jaw and bounce on my feet before gesturing at him. "Come on."

He shakes his head. "I never realised a man-child could be so funny."

"You think I'm funny?"

His mouth twitches. "I said I never realised it. I still haven't."

I laugh. "Come on, Zeb," I coach. "Lecture me, baby."

He sighs. "I have no intention of lecturing. That's wasted on someone with the attention span of a tree branch."

"Ouch, I am actually wounded," I try to say solemnly but spoil it by laughing. I love sparring with him. It feels like it lights me up inside. I'm never bored with him. Instead I feel alive. The times in his office when he snipes at me are something I've actually grown to look forward to over the last few years, to the extent that sometimes when I'm about to get into trouble I've actually thought, *Will this make Zeb mad?* If the answer was yes, I've swung into doing it. I will, of course, never tell him this.

He sits down on one of the chairs. "I just want to warn you that this probably isn't going to be the pleasantest evening you've ever spent." I nod encouragingly. "Both sets of parents dislike me, one to a greater extent than the others. I'm not sure who else is here out of his friends."

"Were any of them your friends too?"

He shakes his head. "No. Patrick didn't like my friends. Said they were judging him."

"Were they?"

He considers that. "Probably." He pauses before honesty obviously compels him to add, "Definitely."

"What are his friends like?"

"Like him," he says slowly, and I wince.

"Ouch. Shall we get room service?" I wink at him. "Stay in and break the bed."

I regret the last statement because a mask falls immediately over his face. "We won't be doing that," he says stiffly, and I hold my hand up.

"I'm sorry. I was joking." I wasn't, but it won't improve the situation if he knows that. I'd like nothing better than to stretch out in that huge bed and see that tanned, hair-roughened body against the blue sheets. A horrible thought occurs to me. "Are you worried that I'll embarrass you?"

I'm gratified by the confused look that crosses his face. "No. Why?"

"Because I wound up Patrick earlier."

He shakes his head. "I think that was probably justified." He pauses. "Just don't do it tonight," he adds hurriedly.

I hide a smile. At that second, a long mournful sound echoes through the room, making me jump. "What the fuck was that?" I gasp.

He bites his lip, but mirth dances in his eyes. "The dinner gong."

"Thank fuck for that. I thought it was the call for Judgement Day."

"I doubt your soul is entirely ready for that," he says primly.

He turns and walks away, and this time I don't bother to hide my smile. I follow him down the palatial staircase, through the reception area, and into a cavernous dining room. Accepting a glass of champagne with a smile from the waiter at the door, I look around curiously.

A huge mahogany table is set in the middle of the room on which glasses and china gleam. Four floral arrangements set along the table give off a pretty scent that clashes with the aftershaves and perfumes of the guests.

There are a group of people milling around in front of the stone fireplace, glasses in hand, and the low hum of slightly forced chatter reaches me. Zeb points out the prospective bride, Frances, who appears to be having a hissed conversation with an older lady who must be her mother. Frances is beautiful, with jet-black hair and a heart-shaped face. I can't see the blushing groom yet, but a man walks towards us who is the spitting image of Frances, so I presume this is her dad. He's wearing a very expensive-looking suit and his cheeks are florid. He looks like he enjoys a drink, or twenty.

"Zeb," he says expansively, offering his hand to shake as soon as he gets near. "Good to see you."

I hope his career as a financial tycoon is secure because it's a safe bet that the stage will never be an option for him.

My boss smiles calmly. "Lovely to see you too, Charles. How is Oona?"

"Oh, fine, fine. Sequestered in a corner gabbing away with Frances about wedding stuff. You know how women are."

"Not really," my boss says serenely. "Not my area of expertise, I'm afraid."

I repress a snort of laughter at Charles's nonplussed face, but Zeb must feel my vibration because he turns to me. "Charles, this is Jesse. He's my ..." He pauses. It's hardly noticeable, but to punish him I step into his body and wind one arm around his waist. His body is hot beneath my hand and for a second I almost forget why I'm doing this. Then I smile happily at the red-faced banker who is stoically trying to ignore all the gayness flying around the room. Hope it doesn't hit him.

"I'm Jesse, his boyfriend," I say, pinching Zeb, who's gone immobile and stiff beneath my hand. He instantly relaxes and slides his arm round my waist. And now I start to lose sight of the game because his arm feels so warm and just somehow right. I mentally shake my head at myself. *Get a grip, you twat.*

Charles's eyes narrow. "Is this a recent thing?"

Zeb pastes on a slightly confused expression. "Jesse?" he asks. When Charles nods his head, Zeb smiles and looks at me. "Not really. We've been going out for about ..."

"Seven months," I say, smiling limpidly at him. "The best seven months of my life," I continue in a dreamy voice and jerk slightly when Zeb pinches me.

Charles looks slightly revolted. I can't blame him this time. I'm not a fan of soppiness myself. "Well, how ... er, lovely," he says heartily. "Came as a surprise," he adds in a confiding tone. "Patrick said you were coming alone. Oona was a bit ..." He hesitates and waves his hand about. "Well, you know."

"Drunk?" I say helpfully and Zeb clears his throat loudly over me.

"I think they're about to serve dinner," he says slightly desperately.

Even Charles looks relieved, and with a final, almost desperate smile, he beetles off towards Frances and the stick-thin older lady whose pinched expression seems to indicate that she might be married to him.

Zeb clears his throat, and I turn with slight trepidation. He looks at me and sighs wearily. "Do you think you could possibly behave?" he finally says.

I bite my lip. "I don't think it would be entirely honest of me to promise that," I say slowly. "Especially if people keep treating you like you're some sort of desperate stalker. It's not fair." I frown. "You're doing bloody Patrick a favour. They should be thanking you, not treating you like an unexploded bomb from the war that might go off in suburbia and wreck someone's lavender bush."

He blinks. "Where the hell did that come from?" He pauses. "And why am I the unexploded relic from the war?"

I smile at him sympathetically. "You have a lot of pent-up aggression," I inform him.

He glares at me, and for a second he looks like he's contemplating chucking me on the fire, but then, to my amazement, he starts to laugh. I smile at the contagious, merry sound and when I look over, a few people are staring and their mouths are turned up. It's impossible not to smile at Zeb when he's like this. I catch sight of an older woman with grey hair cut into a severe bob who is glaring at my boss. *Okay, not impossible, then.*

At that point there's a disturbance at the door, and I look up to see a tall, wide-shouldered man with wavy black hair come in. He's followed by a very beautiful young man with waist-length blond hair and a very sulky expression who has his hand firmly cemented to the dark-haired man's bum.

The dark-haired man looks up and, seeing Zeb, his face lights up. "Zeb," he exclaims, coming forward and drawing my boss into a fierce embrace. I eye him dubiously, feeling something turn in my stomach. Must be hunger pains.

The two men draw away from each other. "What are you doing here, Max?" my boss says. He lowers his voice. "You hate Patrick."

Max shrugs. "Free food," he says succinctly.

Zeb shakes his head, a wry look on his face. "You came to see how I was, didn't you?"

Max appears to attempt to look guileless. "Of course not. I'm just here out of a desire to see Patrick safely within the bounds of matrimony where he can't inflict himself on any more unsuspecting men." I laugh, and he turns to me, his expression kindling into interest. "Well, hello," he says in a slightly rough but very warm voice.

I blink. He's quite potent close up. His wavy black hair showcases a beautiful face with very high cheekbones, lazy-looking dark eyes, and a full mouth which is emphasised by his grey-flecked beard. He's tall and slim with broad shoulders and very long legs.

"I'm Max," he says throatily. The blond man rouses, and, with a glare for me, he plasters himself against Max's side.

Zeb stirs. "No," he says succinctly to Max.

Max blinks. "I'm not doing anything," he says innocently. He winks at me. "Yet."

Zeb shakes his head. "No, keep away from Jesse. He's with me this week."

I try hard not to pay attention to the surge of pleasure I feel at those words. Max looks delighted. "Excellent," he says heartily.

The blond boy huffs. "I'm going to get a drink," he says haughtily in well-rounded vowels. We all watch as he saunters away, moving sinuously.

Zeb looks at Max. "And who's that?"

Max shrugs. "Fucked if I know. I picked him up last night at a club in Cheltenham and shagged him. I never got a name, and it's a teeny bit awkward to ask now."

I laugh, and Zeb shakes his head. "What would the etiquette books say?" he says in a disappointed tone.

Max laughs. He has a raffish sort of charm and an air of being on the verge of doing something either very funny or very inappropriate. Or both. He turns to me. "Zeb and I knew each other when we were kids."

Zeb shakes his head. "Is that what we're calling it now?"

Max looks me up and down slowly. "Wish you'd been around then too."

"I'm pretty sure I wouldn't have wanted that," I say sweetly. "I've watched *Jurassic Park*. Those dinosaurs were no joke."

Max breaks into laughter. It's rough and husky. "I like this one," he says to Zeb, who shakes his head. "Keep him."

"He's only mine for the week," Zeb says, and I grimace.

"I'm not a suit rental."

The blond boy comes back holding a glass of champagne in his thin fingers. He slides next to Max, looking at him hungrily. "I'm very bored already," he pronounces.

Zeb rolls his eyes. "I wouldn't feed this one after midnight," he advises, and Max laughs.

"Mal is fine, aren't you?" he says hesitantly.

The boy shakes his head. "It's Xavier actually. You should really learn to listen, especially at your age. I mean, how long will you have your full hearing?"

Max stares at him, and I break into laughter. The blond boy winks at me.

At that point Patrick comes in, and when he sees Zeb his face lights up. He makes a move as if to come over, and I watch as almost simultaneously Frances grabs his arm and the grey-haired lady who must be Patrick's mother shoots Zeb a look that suggests if she had a spell to turn him into a potato, she'd use it.

Before the old lady can get on her broomstick or call her familiar, a waiter announces that dinner is ready and we all move towards the table.

"That was a lucky escape," Max mutters. "A second longer and you'd have been bleeding on this very expensive rug. I hope you haven't given a damage deposit for this week. Nina looks like she's contemplating disembowelling you before she really gets around to torture."

Zeb shakes his head repressively and takes my arm gently to steer me down the table. There are cards stuck at the place settings, and I'm relieved to see that Zeb and I are together, and that Frances and Patrick are at the far end of the table. I'm less relieved to find that Max and Xavier are sitting at the other end and sitting opposite us is the homicidal old lady and her husband who looks like he's contemplating throwing himself under a bus. I sneak a look at the old lady again. I wouldn't blame him, really.

Amidst the bustle as everyone sits and snaps their napkins out, I lean closer to Zeb. "Is that Patrick's mum?" I ask.

He blanches slightly. "That's her. Nina and Victor."

"And you were with Patrick for five years? Weren't you afraid that as the offspring of a witch he'd eat you in your sleep?"

He shakes his head and fights a smile. "Be nice," he warns me. He looks at her, and at that point she looks up and catches his glance.

"Zebadiah," she says in a glacial voice.

He nods at her. "Nina."

She sniffs haughtily. "I'd like to say this is a pleasure, but I'm afraid it's not. I'm amazed you have the nerve to attend this joyous occasion."

I open my mouth to speak but Zeb grabs my knee under the table and squeezes. Hard.

"Ouch," I mutter.

"Behave," he says tightly.

"I can't promise anything if you happen to move that hand a couple of inches up."

"A couple of *inches*? You've got a comfortable self-image."

I shrug. "I work with what I've got."

A waiter inserts himself between us to position tiny plates before us. Each plate has a piece of meat on it with an inch of sauce curled round it. Zeb's hand falls away. I look down at the plate gloomily. "Is this it?" I ask sadly, and the waiter snorts before resuming his stately procession down the table.

Zeb looks at me and his mouth quirks. "I'd say that was a mouthful," he mutters. "For someone who hasn't got a mouth the size of yours."

"Zeb, I am a growing boy. I'm hoping they serve more food than this over the next few days or you'll have to take me to hospital for a drip."

"You're exceedingly dramatic," he intones. "I'm guessing it's because you're the youngest of eight children. You must have had to work very hard for your voice to be heard."

"Not really," I mutter, downing my starter in one sad bite. "It was never a problem."

"Quelle surprise."

I nudge him. "I like a man who's lingual."

He stares at me. "I have never met anyone who manages to turn such an innocent sentence so dirty."

"So." Nina's voice cuts through our quiet talk. "This is your latest, then, Zebadiah?"

He turns to her, and my heart clenches as he smiles kindly at her. "He is. This is Jesse."

She grimaces. "Of course it is."

My eyes narrow at her. *Old cow.*

She looks me up and down as if I'm a piece of dog shit he's managed to bring in with him. "He's very young. But I don't know why that should surprise me. You obviously like them that way."

"But surely the whole world is younger than you," I mutter. Zeb lowers that hand to my knee and squeezes again, but I ignore him in favour of smiling coldly at the woman.

"I beg your pardon," she says in a low voice.

I lean forward. "I said how young you look," I say in a clear, loud voice, like I'm talking to someone deaf.

She glares at me but turns back to Zeb. "Did I say how glad I was that you and Patrick split up?"

"Quite a few times," Zeb says wryly, and I snort.

She looks at me again. "This man is a serial predator. I'd get away from him if I were you."

I inhale sharply, feeling rage sear me as Zeb stiffens all over.

"Nina," her husband says in a resigned voice.

I lean forward and smile sweetly at her. "Predator, eh? The last time I heard that used was on *Planet Earth*." I tap my finger on the table. "Is this a dinner-party game? Are we naming the animal that's most like us as people? If we are, I'm trying to think what animal is most like a rude and excessively bad-mannered woman."

She breathes in sharply, rage clouding her face. "I have never been so insulted."

"You do surprise me," I say sweetly.

I think it's only the fact that the waiters start to clear the table that saves me from total annihilation. I shoot a quick glance at Zeb who is staring hard at me with an inscrutable look on his face that doesn't promise good things. *Something to look forward to,* I muse gloomily. My gloom intensifies as a plate with more small food is placed before me.

I turn slightly desperately to the woman on my other side in an attempt to avoid Nina. "So, what do you do?" she asks cheerfully.

Why do people like this always ask that question? Why don't they ask someone's favourite colour or what music they're listening to at the moment?

"I'm an architect," I say brightly. Zeb jerks and gives a desperate sort of groan, but the woman immediately sits forward.

"*Really?* My son wants to do that. Do you have any career advice for him?"

"*No,*" Zeb says in a very loud voice and we slowly turn to face him. He looks slightly panicked. "I mean no," he says in a lower voice.

"Oh no, not … trifle. It's trifle for dessert," he finishes somewhat lamely, and I bite my lip.

"He's very passionate about his food," I confide in the woman. "But it's nice to have strong feelings about things." I catch Nina's eye. "Unless they're homicidal ones, of course," I finish robustly.

"Career advice for my son?" the woman reminds me.

"He should be very enthusiastic about buttresses," I say seriously.

Zeb leans forward. "I'm so sorry," he says very charmingly to the woman. "Could I just borrow Jesse for a minute?"

He then forces me to listen to a conversation he's having with an old man about stocks and shares. I muse rather sadly on the fact that I wasn't able to spin my architect story. It would have been a hell of a lot more interesting than what the city closed at today, which I'm pretty sure has nothing to do with when they all clocked off and went to the pub.

Towards the end of dessert, which is basically one mouthful of peach juice and a bit of cream smeared on the plate, Nina leans forward again. Her expression doesn't bode well.

"I was very sad to see your eye."

"My eye?" I stare at her and then realise that she's gesturing at the remnants of my black eye. "Oh, thank you," I offer.

"I have the number of the domestic-abuse hotline if you'd like it," she says in a very sweet but carrying voice.

"*Mother*," Patrick says in a loud voice, but she just smiles at me, widening it to include Zeb.

A startled silence falls over the table. I stare at her. *What a fucking horrible bitch.* "Oh, there's no need," I say loudly. "Zeb didn't punch me, if that's what you're thinking. That *is* what you're trying to imply, isn't it?"

"Jesse," Zeb mutters. I smile at him before reaching over and pressing my lips to his. It's a soft kiss, and, to my regret, I have to pull back immediately before I really have time to register the soft plushness of those lips under mine. I turn back to Nina.

"They can get you help," she says smugly, raising her glass to take a sip of wine.

I wait until she's taken a sip. "No need," I say cheerfully. "Well, not unless they employ an exorcist or the *Most Haunted* team. A dead woman did this when she hit me in the face with her shoe."

To my satisfaction, that sort of kills the conversation around us for the rest of the meal.

CHAPTER FIVE

Jesse

After dessert, people start to drift away from the table. To my relief, Zeb grabs my hand and steers me out of the dining room and away from the witch. I offer her a casual wave over my shoulder while she looks thoughtfully after me as if calculating how many hours it'll take to disembowel me.

"Phew," I say. "Another five minutes and I'm sure she'd have brought out her flying monkeys."

He shakes his head and picks up his pace. I follow obediently instead of pulling my arm out of my socket, and we're practically moving at a jog as we hit reception.

Patrick appears in front of us. "Zeb, have you got a minute?"

"No, sorry," he says tersely, seeing the lift doors open ahead of us. "Things to do."

"That's me," I whisper as I pass Patrick. "I'm the thing he has to do."

I catch his frown and offer him a sweet smile before Zeb yanks me into the lift. The doors close behind us, and I watch him as he leans back against the lift wall. His face is closed but something is working over it. *Is it rage?* I squint to check, but I can't be sure, so I launch into speech.

"I promised I'd behave if people were polite to you. And I kept my word," I say loudly as he lowers his head into his hands and his shoulders start to shake. "She was fucking awful to you, and I won't have it." I pause and amend my sentence quickly. "In my position as your fake boyfriend, I wouldn't have stood for someone talking to you like that." I huff indignantly. "She's the rudest person I've *ever* met. I am quite frankly astounded that nobody has murdered her. If this was an Agatha Christie mystery there'd be no bloody mystery because we'd all have done it." I pause. "I think that's been done," I say slowly. "Although if it was *Murder on the Orient Express* someone would have just chucked her under the train as it set off."

I pause as he makes a faint sound. *Oh shit, is he crying? Have I broken him?* Surely not. If anything was going to break him it would have been the time I crashed my old Fiat into his new Mercedes. Nevertheless, I move closer.

"Erm, Zeb," I say consolingly, moving to him and patting one very wide shoulder. "Please don't be upset. I'm sure it's not you and I'm really positive it's her and—"

I break off as he raises his face. His eyes are wet, but he's laughing, almost silently heaving with the chuckles, and when he sees my face, he bursts into peals of laughter. "Oh shit," he gasps. "I couldn't have held that in a moment longer."

I fall back against the wall. "Oh, thank God. I fucking thought you were upset." I smack his arm. "Give me some sort of sign next time." I watch him laughing, my own mouth tipping into a smile. It's so rare to see him uncontrolled. He looks young and untroubled.

The lift dings and the door opens, and he tries to sober up, but chuckles burst out as we walk towards the door of our room. I take the card he offers me and insert it into the slot. "You okay now?" I ask. "I can't believe you're not mad at me."

"How could I have been mad at you? I haven't seen a takedown like that since Marquez and Pacquiao."

"I'm Marquez though, aren't I?" I say, shrugging off my jacket and slinging it over a chair before hastening over to the balcony doors to open them. Fresh air scented with the fragrance of freshly mown grass hits my face, and I sigh happily and stretch. "That's better." I turn only to stand still, caught in his fixed stare. "You okay?" I ask.

He jerks and looks slightly awkward. "Yes, I'm fine," he says hurriedly.

"Okay." I wander over to the table where the room service info is. "I'm going to order some food."

"You've just had a meal."

I fix him with a hard stare. "Zeb, that wasn't a meal, it was an amuse-bouche in four fucking courses. That wouldn't have filled me when I was ten, let alone now." I look down at the menu and smile contentedly. "I'm having a burger and chips. What do you want?"

He stares at me for a second. "Eating a huge meal after what we've just eaten is guaranteed to give you heartburn." I gaze at him and deploy the big eyes, and he sighs. "Okay, I'll have a salad."

I make a moue of disgust, and he shakes his head. "I'm going to get changed," he says, moving towards the wardrobe. I place the order on the phone while watching him open the doors and look at the neat row of his clothes hanging inside. I look guiltily at my suitcase which hasn't been unpacked yet. Instead I'd dug through it earlier and now it looks like a very small bomb went off in it, strewing clothes around the vicinity with abandon.

Zeb takes his jacket off and hangs it neatly in the wardrobe, and I watch idly as he takes off his tie and coils it into a drawer before unbuttoning his shirt. Then I watch not so idly as the hairy planes of his chest appear. He's muscled and the skin glows golden in the low lamplight. I think what I like best is that he's not perfect. He doesn't have a perfect six pack. He's muscled but it lacks the definition of the gym junkies I've slept with lately. He looks more real somehow and all the more desirable for that. I study the way his trousers hang loosely from his narrow hips and the way the skin shines soft and warm there.

Realising that I'm watching him and getting the beginnings of a stiffy while he's not paying any attention to me makes me feel a bit pervy, so I adjust myself quickly and turn my back on him, putting my phone down and making my way over to the fridge set under the polished table. I open it and wave some small bottles at him. "Which goes best with burgers? Jack Daniel's or gin?" I shake my head. "We'll have all of them. I can never understand hotel fridges. They're either intended for alcoholic pixies or the manager is a half-hearted member of the temperance society."

I hear a laugh and look up as he comes towards me. He's wearing blue checked pyjama shorts and a white T-shirt that makes his face glow with his tan and his eyes seem very blue. I swallow hard and pass him the bottles. "There's some ice in there too," I instruct him. "You do the drinks while I get out of this suit." I pause as he obeys me. "I must say I'm enjoying this new dynamic where I tell you what to do."

"Don't get used to it," he advises me, and I sigh and slink over to my case. I rifle through it, pulling out my pyjama shorts and a T-shirt, and then seeing his jaundiced gaze fixed on the clothing spilling everywhere, I huff and start to hang everything up. The food arrives as I'm putting the last bits away, so I cram the rest of my clothes in higgledy-piggledy, and after a short battle with the wardrobe door I manage to force it closed.

I eye it dubiously and then shake my head. *Food.*

When I walk out onto the balcony, I find Zeb laying the food out neatly. Glasses full of ice and alcohol are set meticulously in the correct position and the cutlery is set neatly on the other side. I shake my head fondly. It's burger and chips, but it looks like we're expecting the queen.

He looks up and I don't miss the way his eyes flit down my body. It's a quick but comprehensive glance, and by the time his eyes raise up to my face again I'm half hard. Our eyes seem to meet and catch for a lovely, sleepy moment full of promise, but then he clears his throat and shutters his expression.

"Come and eat," he says, his deep voice slightly roughened. "Before you faint away."

"You joke," I say judiciously. "But it's a real threat."

"Okay, Camille."

I eye him as I lift my burger up and take a huge bite. "You think I don't know who that is but you're wrong," I say indistinctly.

He shakes his head. "Isn't it rude to talk with your mouth full?" he observes, shaking out his napkin daintily and forking some lettuce up.

I swallow the food. "Depends what you've got in your mouth," I say cheerfully, watching happily as he checks slightly before giving me a glare and starting to eat his own food stoically and with little obvious pleasure. I wait a second and then sigh and cut my burger in half and slide it onto his plate.

"Oh no, I can't take that," he immediately and predictably protests.

I wave my knife at him. "I can't tolerate watching you force that down. It's like I've taken you to Rosies for the twink parade and you've settled for cleaning the tables."

"There's a twink parade at Rosies?" he says faintly. "Do they wear costumes?" I open my mouth but he shakes his head forcibly. "No, don't bother explaining. I think it's probably better that way."

Despite his protestations, he eats heartily and with every sign of enjoyment, and I watch him contentedly. He had hardly anything to eat tonight, even with those meagre portions, and I know it was because he was tense in that social situation. It's one of the reasons why I was so mad at the old cow. Zeb needs to eat properly. He quite often looks tired and worn.

I shake my head at my thoughts and fall on my own food like a starving dog. Finally, when my hunger is appeased, I sit back and watch him eating the salad.

"I always wondered who ate that," I observe, and he shakes his head.

"I suppose it's useless to ask if you eat five a day."

"Not at all," I say primly. "I had a Fab lolly earlier on. That's got strawberry and milk in it, so I've had my fruit and dairy."

He shakes his head. "I'm amazed you can manage to walk and talk at the same time. Not that you make any sense while you do it."

"Zeb," I chide. "Give in to my charm. I know you feel it. The force is strong in me."

"And so is the bullshit," he observes, a small smile tugging at his lips as I roar with laughter.

When I sober up, I stare at him. "So, Max?" I say. "An old friend?" He looks at me with one supercilious eyebrow raised and a small smile on his lips. "Have you fucked him?"

He blinks. "I often wonder if you'll ever lose the ability to ask inappropriate questions." He shrugs. "Today is not that day."

I look hard at him and he shakes his head. "No, of course I haven't."

"Why do you say of course not? He's gorgeous."

A shadow crosses his face almost too quickly for me to notice, but I do. "You think he's good-looking?" he says in a voice wiped clean of expression.

"Good-looking and like a very loose cannon," I observe and he laughs, the shadow falling away.

"You'd be right. And in answer to your question, I haven't slept with him because he's my stepbrother."

For some reason that takes me completely by surprise. "Your stepbrother?"

He looks amused. "His mother was my father's last wife." He considers. "That sounds as if he'd found the one. Regretfully, it just meant he died before he could trade her in for a newer model."

"How many did he have?"

"Seven," he says almost reluctantly, looking out towards the wood.

"*Seven.*" My voice is high and loud and a pigeon who'd alighted onto the balustrade gives a startled flutter and flies off.

Zeb shakes his head. "Max's mother was the seventh. He was fourteen when they got married, and I was twenty."

"And you've kept in contact? Were you close?"

He shrugs. "Not at first because that's a big gap at that age, but he's one of my best friends now. Somehow he just held on." He looks almost bemused at the concept and my heart twists. Then he shrugs. "I do keep in touch with all of my stepmothers though." He looks suddenly awkward. "It wasn't their fault the marriages failed, and they were very kind to me."

I study him, feeling a rush of something push through me. I don't know what it is, but it's strong, and accompanying this rogue feeling is an urge to comfort him. Why, I don't know. He's the most confident and sexy man I've ever met, but for just a second he looked so vulnerable. I think of all those stepmothers and my own family where my parents have been married for thirty years. I open my mouth, but the moment is lost as he stands up and reaches over to the small table at the door.

"This came with the food," he says, brandishing a leaflet. "It's the itinerary for the week."

"Itinerary? That sounds ominous," I say slowly, reeling a little at the abrupt change of subject.

He shoots me a wry look. "Frances is a planner. She loves social occasions and is under the impression that her guests should be organised to within an inch of their lives. This is nothing. The last itinerary I had from her was two A4 pages long."

"Lovely," I mutter. I wipe my fingers on my napkin and reach out to take it from him. "Let's have a look." I read quickly down the list and then more slowly, my heart sinking. "What the fuck?" I say, looking up at him where he's leaning back against the balustrade, his eyes alight with mirth. "Watercolour painting, brass rubbing. I bet that's not half as dirty as it sounds." He laughs, and I carry on reading. "Cordon bleu cookery lessons and clay pigeon shooting. I wish I'd seen that earlier. If I'd known there was a gun on the premises, we could have shot our way out."

"Like Bonnie and Clyde," he says lightly.

"No, that ended badly," I chide him. "And double-breasted suits don't flatter me."

I look down at the list again and shake my head. "Fuck," I grumble and he laughs.

"That's one way to put it."

"I'll tell you another. This week is going to be torture."

An hour later and I know I spoke the truth. We're lying in bed. It's quiet with the only sound that of the breeze in the trees outside the open balcony door. The room is washed in moonlight, giving me just enough light to see that he's sleeping peacefully with no sign of agitation. I shoot a glare at him which is obviously wasted but makes me feel a bit better. *How can he sleep?* I'm wide awake, mainly because the sheets smell of him, and I can feel the heat of his body even with the foot of space between us.

He sleeps on his side facing me. In deference to the heat, he stripped off his top earlier, so I get a good view of that glorious hairy chest and wide shoulders. His hair is tousled and his arm is flung out with his hand palm up and looking somehow vulnerable. His lips are softly pursed, and he looks delicious.

I roll onto my back and sigh before scrubbing my face with my hands. My cock is throbbing like a fucking toothache. I want to slide in next to him and fit my body against his. I want him to strip me naked, and I want him to fuck me. Unfortunately, none of that is going to happen because I'm apparently too young and chaotic. I huff. Maybe if I walked around with a bar chart and a protractor he'd want to sleep with me. Maybe if I was distinguished and kept my paperwork organised he'd stick his cock in me.

I lower my hand and push it against my dick. It's rigid in my shorts, and there's a damp spot. The pressure feels good, and I arch my groin into my hand for a brief moment before I realise that rubbing one out next to my boss is not a good idea. He wouldn't approve. Well, not unless I cleaned myself up with the correct day-of-the-week hanky.

I snort and force my hand away from my cock before rolling onto my side and facing him. I can't stop looking at him. He looks so different from the awake Zeb full of purpose and drive. Now he looks like he's having sweet dreams, and it makes me happy. I don't want to know why that is, so instead of thinking about it, I watch his peaceful face until sleep steals over me.

Zeb

I come awake slowly the next morning in a puddle of sheets warmed by the sun. The window is open, letting in the sound of birdsong. I stretch, enjoying the moments before I have to get on with the day. Then I register that the bed is missing a person, and I'm abruptly awake. *Where the fuck is he?* The suite is quiet. *Has he gone downstairs for breakfast?*

I groan and sit up, scrubbing my hands down my face. What is he saying to everyone? What ridiculous thing is going to come out of his mouth next that will make me want to gag him and kiss him at the same time? I think of Nina's face last night at the dinner table, and unbidden, a snort of laughter escapes me. I don't think I've ever seen her speechless. It was a rare and beautiful thing. She's always been so poisonous and controlling. It's one of the reasons I cut Patrick so much slack. Who could turn out as a well-rounded individual with that as their role model?

I slide to the end of the bed and zip into the bathroom for a piss. Wandering out a few minutes later, I look around for my phone. I contemplate how he's going to react to me summoning him back to the suite. I shake my head. *Not well.*

Seeing no sign of my phone, I hurry out into the lounge and stop dead. He isn't downstairs regaling the table with more quirky conversation. Instead, bare chested and dressed only in his shorts, he's sitting at the table on the balcony in front of his laptop. He's tapping away furiously with a frown of concentration on his face, occasionally pausing to look at a huge textbook sitting to one side of him. A cafetière sits on a tray at the table filled with cups and saucers and plates and a big basket with a napkin over it.

I blink at the sight of the tortoiseshell glasses he has on and his air of quiet determination. It's such a radical sea change from the way he normally appears in my office, dripping laughter like water after a refreshing shower.

He curses slightly and taps crossly on the keyboard. Something makes his head shoot up, and he stares at me for a long second, his face cloudy with concentration. Then it clears, and he smiles delightedly. I shift awkwardly. He always looks at me like that, as if he's discovered something wonderful that pleases him tremendously.

"Zeb," he says happily. "Did you sleep well?"

"I did." It's more of a question than I'd like because at three in the morning I was awakened by the fact that I was tucked up tight behind him, my cock snuggled happily in the crease of his arse and my arm slung over his narrow waist. I'd shot straight over the other side of the bed so fast I'm sure I left scorch marks on the cotton. It had taken me ages to get to sleep again. Luckily, he hadn't woken.

"Come and sit down," he urges, kicking out a chair for me. "I ordered some breakfast. There are croissants and pastries in the basket and a pot of tea here for you. It should still be warm."

"I usually just have muesli," I say doubtfully, and he groans.

"That does not surprise me."

"I thought you might have gone downstairs," I murmur, taking a plate and the croissant he hands me.

He grimaces. "No, I thought it would be much more pleasant sitting up here away from everyone."

The croissant is soft and warm in my hand, and I'm suddenly starving. I don't normally eat much in the morning as my stomach twists and hurts until I've got some work done and off my mind. But it seems different today, sitting on the sunlit balcony with him smiling at me. I spread damson jam over the pastry and look at him as he pours me a cup of tea. I'd love to know how he knows how I take it.

I pull myself back to the conversation. "It's clay pigeon shooting today," I say through a mouthful of food. "God, this is lovely."

He looks absurdly pleased and starts to spread jam on another croissant. "Here," he says.

"Oh, I shouldn't."

He shrugs. "Not sure why not."

"Well, they're a bit fattening."

He looks me up and down. "You're in fantastic shape," he says in a low voice. "I think you can spare the time to spoil yourself."

I'm absurdly pleased and immediately seek to divert the conversation. "What are you doing?" I ask, nodding at the computer.

"Oh, it's my last paper." He stares at the laptop. "Once I've finished this, I'm done."

"Done with what?"

"My degree."

"Your *degree?*" I hear the note of complete astonishment in my voice and try to dial it back. "I mean, sorry, I didn't know you were at university."

His lip twitches. "It's not a secret."

"Yes, but surely I should have known." I'm as shocked as if he'd suddenly declared he was running off with Camilla Parker Bowles.

He looks down at the computer as if avoiding my eyes. "I think it might have interfered with the box you put me in," he says, looking up abruptly and spearing me with the sudden clear and direct challenge in his eyes.

"I didn't put you–" I start to say and slump. "Okay, I might have put you in a small one."

"More like a packing crate," he says almost sympathetically.

"I'm sorry." I lean forwards. "I've known you for all these years and I never realised. I'm your boss."

He shrugs. "Would it have made a difference to your opinion of me?"

"Of course," I say and hesitate. I can't for the life of me think of what to say next. It's a novel situation.

He takes pity on me. "Well, never mind. Now you know."

"So, what are you studying?"

"Social care. I'm going to be a social worker."

I stare at him. "Well, of course you are." I smile. "How absolutely perfect."

He looks startled. "Why?"

"Because you're kind and interested in people but don't take any shit. You really care and you're prepared to go to great lengths to help them." I sit back and look at him. "You'll be wonderful."

A faint flush hits his high cheekbones, and he fiddles with his pencil before shooting me a quick, almost furtive look. "Do you really think so?"

I nod emphatically. "I wouldn't say it if I didn't mean it. You know me." I shrug. "Probably better than I know you." I think back to Felix's smug smile in the office before we left, and I know if he was here he'd be laughing at me. Of course he'd known about the degree and I would never have listened until now. This is somehow the perfect moment to peel another layer off Jesse.

A slow, glorious smile fills his face. "Thank you," he says. He sniffs. "Just so you know, you're excused for the packing crate."

I smile. "Well, that's a relief." My smile drops away as the ramifications suddenly hit me. "You're going to have to leave the agency, aren't you?"

He sighs, and there's a wistful look on his face. "Yes. I have a job that starts next month." I sit back in a stunned silence, and he smiles coaxingly. "Look at it this way, at least there'll be no more fights at funerals and bad gardening decisions."

"No," I say slowly. As it occurs to me what life will be like without him, suddenly the time ahead looks dull and dreary, as if the sun's going in on a wonderful day. Without the merry smile, the sassiness, the kindness of him. It's only as I face the prospect of him not being around anymore that I realise just how much I've treasured the time he has been. The emptiness inside me is sufficiently alarming to straighten my back.

"Well, I'm sure we'll all miss you," I say briskly, and I'm saddened to see the smile fade slowly from those full lips.

"I'll miss you too," he says, and it's not until I'm in the shower that I realise he mentioned only me.

CHAPTER SIX

Zeb

An hour later finds me on the field next to the hotel. I look around to see Max sauntering towards me. "You shouldn't have dressed up," I say wryly, looking at his jeans and red T-shirt.

"I didn't." He looks me up and down. "Although why would I when you look so spiffy?"

I shake my head. "It's navy chinos and a shirt. Frances wanted everyone to dress up for this in historic costume, but this is as far as I can go without getting heatstroke."

"My outfit is historical. These jeans are at least eight years old."

"Why am I explaining this to you? You read the itinerary, didn't you?"

"Read it and mourned the fact that I've probably misplaced a precious childhood memory to retain that information." He looks around. "Is that man wearing plus fours? I didn't think anyone made them anymore."

"Shh!" I hiss. "Someone will hear you."

"Then maybe they can explain people's attire this morning. We are actually shooting bits of pottery, aren't we, not stalking pheasants?"

"You know Frances," I say out of the corner of my mouth. "She watches a lot of *Downton Abbey*."

"I watch a lot of porn. Doesn't mean I corral people into wearing bad underwear and having very stilted conversations." He pauses as he sees Nina. "Brilliant. Now I need mental bleach."

"It's your own fault," I say serenely. "Where's your boy toy this morning, anyway?"

"Resting up," he says with a wolfish grin. "When I left, he was sunbathing on the balcony wearing the smallest pair of briefs I've ever seen."

I shake my head. "And when do you move on to the next one?"

He shrugs. "When I feel like it." He nudges me. "Don't give me that disapproving look. You've brought your own diversion this week."

"Distraction, more like it," I say glumly and groan when I see his delighted expression. "Please don't matchmake," I say imploringly.

"Why not?"

"Because you're not very good at it, which goes a long way to explaining your single status too."

"I'd be very good at matchmaking if I actually believed in love," he says crossly.

I lower my sunglasses and stare at him. "Putting you in charge of my love life would be like making Felix the boss of Manchester United."

Hesitation crosses his face which is so alien to his normal confidence. "How is he?" he asks in a low voice.

"Fine," I say tersely.

He scuffs his foot across the grass. "Is he still dating that wanker?"

"Do you mean Carl, who is lovely and polite and worships the ground he walks on? That wanker? Yes, he's unfortunately still with him." He opens his mouth and I hold my hand up. "I don't want to know." I turn to him. "Do you remember when all the shit kicked off and you told me to mind my own business?" He nods, looking surly.

"Well, this is me. Minding my own business. Behold. See how good I am at it."

"I just want to know if he's okay," he says, and his air of quiet desperation stops me in my tracks.

"He's fine," I say quietly. "Max, I–"

"Oh look," he says with a determined cheerfulness. "We're about to start."

I let him pull me along as we move further onto the field next to the car park. The sun is blazing hot now, burning down on our heads and dancing dazzlingly over the cars. I accept the cold lemonade that a waiter hands me and listen as the man in charge of the shoot gives his safety talk.

After ten minutes he waves up the first person to shoot and I look idly round at the group. Most have obeyed Frances's instructions to the letter, wearing various versions of shooting gear. They look quite hot and bothered and rather like extras from an historical drama. I brighten slightly. If Richard Armitage strides through the crowd, all bets are off.

The bangs from the gun are loud and the cheering and banter get louder and louder. I turn to Max to say something just as he laughs and his whole face lights up.

"Don't talk about my trouble," he mutters. "Yours is sauntering towards us now and he's got it written all over him."

I turn and shake my head even though my heart is pounding. "That is *not* on the dress code," I say disapprovingly.

Jesse is wandering lazily towards us. His dark hair shines in the sun, the loose strands pushed back by a Union Jack bandanna. He's wearing cut-offs that show off the tanned length of his hairy legs and old checked Vans, but my attention is on his T-shirt. It's a bright green *Sesame Street* T-shirt with a picture of the Muppets on it along with the words in big type: *Hi, my name is Jesse.*

As he nears the crowd, it parts and the man in charge calls to him and offers the gun.

Jesse looks slightly surprised but takes it and goes to stand next to the man as he talks and nods. I look at the group who are, by and large, staring condescendingly at Jesse, apart from a group of women who are eyeing up his long legs and small arse. Frances's father shakes his head as he looks at Jesse and says something to the group of men he's standing with that makes them break into laughter.

I bristle and only realise that I've tightened my fists when Max reaches down and separates my fingers. "Okay, Rocky," he hisses. "They're just your ordinary garden variety of arsehole. No need for fisticuffs."

I shake my head. "Pricks. He's better than any of them."

I can feel his stare on the side of my head like a sunburn. "Hmm," he says contemplatively.

He opens his mouth to say more but at that moment one of Charles's group shouts out, "Hard to hold a shotgun with a limp wrist, son."

I move a couple of steps forward but Max grabs me and pulls me back just as Jesse turns and smiles cheerily at the man.

"Are you speaking from experience?" he asks happily. "You'll have to give me some tips." Then he turns and shouts "pull" in a way that inexplicably makes my balls tighten. He shoots the clay pigeon into smithereens. The first person to manage it so far including all of Charles's group.

He gives the gun back to the man and smiles warmly at the crowd. "It's all in the wrist action," he says loudly, and a few of the girls giggle.

I shake my head as he comes towards me. "When did you learn to shoot?"

He shrugs. "One of my brothers fancied a girl who was into it. We went every Saturday."

"One of them?" Max says. "How many have you got?"

"Five, and two sisters."

"Fucking hell, it's like meeting one of the Waltons."

Jesse laughs. He turns to me, smiling, and I shake my head. "What *are* you wearing?"

He looks down. "Is there a problem?" he asks mildly.

"Is that a child's T-shirt?"

"Of course not," he scoffs. "You might not have noticed, Zebedee, but I'm a big boy now." Max snorts, and he grins at him before turning back to me. "Although I did have one like this when I was little," he says consideringly, looking at his name in bold letters. He grins. "It helped in our family to wear something identifying yourself at all times. My friend Eli bought this for me for my birthday."

"And you are wearing it because?"

He blinks. "Well, because the itinerary said to come in period clothing, although that's a slightly vague request." He waves his hand downward. "Anyway, you can't get much more period than *Sesame Street*." He looks around. "Oh, you can," he says in a disappointed voice.

I open my mouth to speak but Nina strides across to us.

"Nina," Jesse exclaims as if she's his long-lost family. "How are you doing this fine morning?"

Nina ignores him. It's a neat trick and one I wish I could learn, but here we are with no sign of that happening yet.

"Well," she sneers. "You've managed to make quite the spectacle of yourself today, Zebadiah."

I blink. "Have I?"

She waves her hand at Jesse. "Your companion is making a total fool of you. If you must pick up very young men, at least make sure you pick a classy one."

"Now, you wait a minute," I hiss, seeing her look of surprise. In all the years I've known her, I've never risen to her rudeness, having been taught to be polite at all costs to women. But I'm not having her talk like that about Jesse. "We really shouldn't talk about classy behaviour, Nina, because you're not exactly displaying it yourself. You're acting like a fishwife." I pause. "Why do we say fishwife?" Jesse grins delightedly and I shake my head. "Never mind." I look hard at her. "I'm here because your son asked me to come. The same way he asked to live with me. I spent five years looking after him, and

I'm glad to rest the burden on someone else's shoulders. However, I promised him I'd be here, and I keep my word. But I detest pettiness and rudeness. You don't know Jesse, and I won't have you talking to him like that. He's a wonderful young man with a big heart. I'd explain what that means because you patently don't have one, but I'd lose the will to live, and we're out of time anyway as I have to shoot pottery now."

Nina stares at me. For once she's speechless and I give thanks.

Jesse breaks the silence as adroitly as ever. "I think your cauldron's bubbled over," he says helpfully to her.

She grimaces at him and stalks away.

"Did you know her husband was in the SAS?" Max says.

Jesse looks thoughtful. "If you were trained to kill in twenty different undetectable ways, wouldn't you have knocked her off at some point?"

"Bloody old bitch," I say forcefully and Jesse and Max turn to stare at me.

"Not now," I say wearily. "I've got to go and shoot an imitation pigeon. Fuck my life," I bemoan. I stalk off just as Patrick says "Zeb," and comes towards me.

Jesse

Max and I stare after the stiff back of Zeb as he marches towards the man holding the gun. The man looks rather hesitant which might have something to do with the way Zeb is scowling, but he still bravely hands over the gun.

"Well," I say slowly, and Max gives a sudden bark of laughter.

"You can say that again."

"I don't think I've seen him that cross since I spilt Tipp-Ex down his new Tom Ford suit."

He smiles at me. "You seem to bring it out in him."

"Is that good or bad?"

He hums and looks at Zeb. He's talking to the organiser and has a frown of deep concentration on his face.

"I think a good thing," he says. "He's too fucking buttoned up for his own good."

"He does like order," I say, looking at Zeb as he smooths a hand over his navy and white checked shirt as if searching for wrinkles.

"He's had to."

Something about the grim tone catches my attention, and I stare at him. "Why?"

He hesitates for a long second and then comes to some form of conclusion. "This is very private," he warns. He pauses. "But for some fucking reason I'm still going to tell you."

"I won't tell anyone else," I promise, and he examines my face intently before nodding.

"His father wasn't exactly known for steadiness," he says slowly, his eyes going unfocused as if he's remembering something. Then he smiles. "Eddie was one of the most charming men I've ever met. He was funny and loud and kind and very charismatic. When he came into a room, you knew it."

"Are any of those things bad?" I look over at Zeb. The sun is kindling the waves of his hair, and everyone is watching him. "Zeb's got the same charisma. People notice when he walks in a room."

He smiles a little sadly. "The difference is that Zeb has willpower. He had to develop it very fast because Eddie didn't have any. He was everyone's friend and no one's enemy and he loved a good time. Unfortunately, that good time meant womanizing and gambling."

"Oh dear. I have a horrible feeling about where this story is going."

He nods, staring at Zeb with a deep fondness in his eyes. "Eddie had a knack for making money, but he had an equal talent for losing it. Like the fairies at birth gave him too big a gift and had to hastily counteract it. He was exceptionally generous and lived like a king when the money was in, but then the next day he'd be dodging creditors and bailiffs. By the time he married my mother he'd had six wives. And the remarkable thing is they all loved him even after the divorces. There was something very lovable about Eddie." He shrugs. "Even when you hated him, you still liked him."

"Did Zeb hate him?" I ask tentatively.

He shakes his head. "God, no. He idolised him at first, by all accounts. By the time my mother and I came along, that idolisation had faded and there was something almost weary about his love for his dad. He'll never speak badly about him, but Eddie's the reason he is the way he is."

"Organised and serious," I say with realisation.

He nods. "He had to be. By the time he was nine, he was organising Eddie's chequebook and squirrelling away any spare cash he could find in the house so they'd have something for what Eddie called rainy days." He shrugs. "It was England. Of course there were a lot of those. He went to ten different boarding schools. He'd last a couple of months there and then he'd be leaving because Eddie couldn't pay the school fees. I don't think he had friends because they never stayed anywhere long enough for him to make them. But he loved Eddie, and Eddie loved him."

I sneak a peek at Zeb, and it's as if I'm looking at him with new eyes. He's always been far too organised and wears responsibility like it's his underwear. Unseen and unnoticed. But to know what's made him like that makes my stomach hurt. To think of a young and probably stoical Zeb packing up from another school and moving on with only Eddie for company makes my eyes burn.

Max smiles fondly as he looks at Zeb. "He still looks after all his stepmothers, you know?"

"I got that impression from the way he spoke."

"He talked about them?" He sounds startled, but when I nod, he smiles. "He's the best man I've ever known," he says quietly. "He was immensely kind to me when his dad married my mother. I was young and probably really annoying." I grin, and he winks. "I know it's hard to believe." His grin fades to a soft smile of remembrance. "He looked after me and made sure I was okay, and even after his dad died and his responsibility could have ended, he kept it going. He'd come to my sports days and wrote me letters every week when I was at boarding school and sent me treat boxes. Then when I was old enough, I decided he was my best friend, and I made him agree." He chuckles. "It's the best thing I ever did. He's kind and fiercely loyal. When you're in with Zeb, you never really leave."

I look at Patrick who is staring at Zeb and oblivious to his fiancée's glares. "Does that apply to Patrick?"

He shrugs. "We're here, aren't we?"

My stomach twists and something must show in my face because he grabs my arm lightly. "I like you," he says quickly as Zeb turns and comes back towards us. "You're good for him. Don't let Patrick wind you up."

"Am I good for him?" I say, startled. "I irritate him mostly. I'm too young for him, apparently, and too chaotic. He's obviously looking for someone older and responsible."

"He's more alive this week than I've ever seen." He shakes his head. "Zeb doesn't know his arse from his elbow sometimes. He's infuriatingly blind to what's under his nose."

"What are you two talking about?" Zeb asks as he comes up to us.

"What a terrible shot you are," Max says, releasing my arm as Zeb glares down at it. He holds up his hands in defence. "We weren't doing anything."

Zeb shoots me a look as if to see if I'm okay, and I see now what Max was talking about. He wears that responsibility like Superman wears a cape. I smile at him. Some superheroes never get recognised, I suppose.

He looks a little startled at the warmth of my smile, and then his gaze focuses behind me, and he blinks a few times. I turn and start to laugh.

Xavier is walking towards us with a sheet wrapped around him.

Max groans. "What the hell are you dressed in?" he mutters as Xavier saunters up to us as cool as an ice cream.

He looks down at his outfit and up at Max as though he's a moron. "A toga."

"I can see that," Max murmurs. "I should have actually said *why* are you wearing that?"

"It's period dress," he says, frowning at Max.

"*Thank you*," I say triumphantly. "I told you that invite was badly worded."

"Zeb?" comes a tentative voice from behind us, and as a group we swing round to face Patrick who is standing with a warm smile on his face. His blond hair glows in the sun and he looks unspeakably beautiful. My heart sinks a little from where it had been buoyed by Max's words. Why on earth would Zeb look at me when this man was obviously his taste? I look at Zeb who is staring hard at Patrick as if analysing him and my heart sinks further. *Still is his taste.*

"Can I help you?" Zeb asks. "Should I be doing something? You never gave me any tasks this weekend."

I smile a little. I'm sure mentally he's cursing that he hasn't got his diary on him. It's huge and held together by bands because it bulges with paperwork and lists.

"Oh no, I just wanted you to have a good time," Patrick says, drifting closer to Zeb and nudging me subtly out of the way. I open my mouth to object, but shut it as the two of them stare at each other like they're mesmerised.

Max coughs and elbows Zeb who jumps.

"Sorry," Max says cheerfully. "But I think the man heading towards me with the gun is indicating it's my turn to shoot." He winks at Patrick. "Unless he's on a homicidal rampage, in which case I'm volunteering you to take one for the team." He looks him up and down. "You're so very good at that, after all."

"*Max*," Zeb warns, and Patrick bristles.

"Oh don't bother, Max," he says spitefully. "If I wanted some dinosaur of a reporter to cast judgement on me, I'd have gone to Piers Morgan. At least he's famous."

"You wound me," Max says cheerfully. "I'm literally bleeding on the ground from your sharp words."

"Better than bullet wounds because you couldn't duck quickly enough," Patrick says sharply and I gasp.

Now, I remember who Max is. He's a famous reporter who quit after he was taken hostage in Syria. He was shot in an escape attempt but still managed to make his way through the country on his own until he reached safety. I hadn't recognised him at first because his hair is longer now, and he's grown a beard.

I glare at Patrick but Max just shrugs. "The bravest thing you ever did, Patrick, was to leave the house not wearing underwear. You'll excuse me if I don't take your words to heart."

I laugh, and Patrick flushes and edges into Zeb's side. I narrow my eyes, and Max stares at the two of them.

Then he takes the gun the man gives him, steps up to the line and calls, "Pull." In one smooth motion, he turns slightly to the right and fires. A second later there's the sound of breaking glass and a car alarm starts to blare.

"That's my fucking Audi," Patrick exclaims, and Max shrugs.

"Oops! Butterfingers," he says casually.

Xavier starts to laugh.

CHAPTER SEVEN

Jesse

Patrick's temper tantrum over his car rather puts the mockers on the shooting party, and people start to drift off back to the hotel, declaring their intentions of having a drink. Finally, there's just Zeb, Max, Xavier, and me left standing by the field.

"Well, you know how to help a party along," Zeb says wryly, and Max smiles happily.

"I think I might need my eyes tested."

"Why? You hit his windscreen head on."

Max shrugs. "I was aiming at the bonnet."

The two men laugh before Max cracks the gun and wanders over to the man in charge, who looks like he's preparing to give him a lecture. Zeb trails after him.

I turn to Xavier and smile. "Are you enjoying yourself?"

He scrunches his face up in concentration. "We've had some good times in bed, but this party is fucking shit."

I burst out laughing. Zeb shoots me an intense glance before he turns back to answer something Max is saying. When I look back at Xavier, he's smirking at me.

"So, you and Max?" I say quickly.

He looks blank. "What?"

"Will you keep seeing him?"

He scoffs. "*No.*"

"Why not?"

"Because we're not about that," he says simply. He shrugs. "Don't get me wrong, he's an amazing shag, but he's entirely wrapped up in someone else."

"Who?" I shoot an uneasy look at Zeb, and Xavier laughs.

"Not him. Even I can see that. No, I think he fucked up something good and blah blah blah according to the semi-coherent conversation I had last night with him. And now he just fucks around." He smiles affectionately. "That's my gain because he's *very* talented in the bedroom."

I blink. "Well, that's good, I suppose."

He smiles sunnily. "All good." He whistles and waves at Max. He and Zeb amble back over. I blink at the sight of them, all dark hair and long legs. But Xavier just continues to smile. "I'm going tonight," he says to Max. "So if you want a last go at my arse you'd best get moving."

Zeb blinks. "It's like pure poetry. Someone contact Goodreads and get them to write it down."

Max laughs and slaps him on the back. "Got to go and burn the sheets up."

"Do that afterwards," I advise. "He looks strenuous."

Zeb laughs and then Max and Xavier walk away, leaving us standing alone. The sun beats down on my head, and all I can hear is the sound of a wood pigeon cooing from the shade of a tree. I love that sound. It reminds me of summer.

I stir and look at Zeb. "What next?"

He smiles almost cautiously at me. "I think we now have a few hours free. Want to go explore the villages?"

I grin at him. "I'd love that." It's a little more enthusiastic than I'd like, but it's too late to call it back now, so I settle for smiling innocently.

For now, though, he doesn't get that worry frown he always gets when I'm being flirty. Instead, to my surprise, he grins happily. "I'll get the car."

I look down at my outfit. "I'll get changed."

He stares at me. "Why? You look fine."

"Won't you be embarrassed? I don't exactly dress like–" My words trail off before I can mention Patrick, but I know he knows who I'm talking about. He draws me to a halt, holding my arm loosely, but I can feel his skin against mine and the slight roughness of his fingertips. His isn't the hand of someone who sits in an office full time, which makes me curious.

"Do you want to dress like Patrick?" he asks baldly.

I consider him. "No, but you obviously liked the way he looked."

He looks suddenly awkward. "Jesse, I chose to be with Patrick and lived with him, so that was a very different–"

"Oh no," I break in quickly, feeling my heart flop and sink. He couldn't have made it clearer if he'd written it in the sky that he doesn't consider me a viable proposition to date. "I just don't want to embarrass you," I finish lamely, feeling my face burn.

He stares at me and a kind look crosses his face. "You couldn't," he says staunchly. I raise an eyebrow at him, and he smiles. "Come as you are."

"Well, thank you, Kurt Cobain," I say tartly.

He laughs. "I like the way you dress."

"Really?" I say doubtfully. I pull myself together, still thinking of that almost pitying look in his eyes a few seconds ago. "Well, that's good, I suppose," I finish coolly. "But I think I'll still get changed."

The outfit that had seemed okay a few hours ago now feels like a red flag. As if I've embarrassed him in front of his peers by dressing like a kid. I think of the story Max told me, and all of a sudden I feel small. This kind, gentle man asked me here to help him. He trusted me to do that, and all I've done so far is muck about and make passes at him that obviously make him uncomfortable.

He hesitates like he wants to say something and then settles for looking worried. The silence stretches, and I watch him. "Okay then," he finally says. "I'll be in the car."

I nod and walk away and give myself a talking to in the lift. By the time I get to the room, I've settled my mood. Just because I fancy him doesn't mean he has to fancy me back. This isn't a rom-com. It's real life, and in real life he's a wealthy older man who probably has far too many well-groomed men throwing themselves at him to be interested in a walking disaster of a twenty-four-year-old undergraduate who still dresses in *Sesame Street* T-shirts and doesn't keep enough control of his mouth in social situations.

I change into smart grey chino shorts, a pale pink shirt, and leather deck shoes. I look in the mirror and decide I definitely look more suitable now.

"At the end of the day, I'll be gone from his agency soon," I say out loud. "And I'll become that funny story he tells about his old member of staff at dinner parties he throws with his very perfect boyfriend."

The thought is peculiarly painful, so I do what I always do. I push it to one side and focus on being friendly. I'm going to make him happy this week.

"I'm going to behave and not let him down so I'll be more of a pleasant memory to him," I say solemnly and my face looks back at me carefully. I let that settle, and by the time I reach the car and hop in, I'm smiling more or less naturally.

Zeb

I watch him worriedly as he gets into the car. I don't know what happened earlier. One minute he was full of life, fairly glowing with fun and a simple sort of joy that seems to hang around him like glitter. Then he visibly shut it down, and I can't work out why. Catching hold of him is like trying to cup water as it runs through my fingers.

The only thing I can think of is his peculiar insistence on getting changed. I'm slightly disappointed in this buttoned-up version of

Jesse in perfectly ironed shorts and shirt. I preferred the earlier Jesse with that shiny hair held back by a bandanna and that ridiculous T-shirt. It was so him. So vibrant. Now, he seems almost colourless.

I can't say anything, though. *I'm his boss,* I think desperately. It seems like I'm clinging onto that lately like it's a raft that's slowly disintegrating underneath me.

"Where are we going?" he asks, thankfully interrupting my thoughts.

"Bourton-on-the-Water." I steer the car down the drive. "It's pretty, especially in the summer," I say somewhat desperately.

"Sounds lovely," he says politely.

I shoot him another quick glance and open my mouth to speak but he reaches over and quickly switches on the radio.

I fall back into silence broken only by his increasingly cheerful conversational asides.

He brightens up, however, when we get to Bourton-on-the-Water. It's a pretty, quintessential Cotswolds village with beautiful golden-bricked cottages and little stone bridges that span the River Windrush that runs all the way through the village. And tourists. Hundreds and *hundreds* of tourists.

"Why is everyone in the world here today?" he marvels as we step around what feels like twenty thousand pushchairs and wandering children to get out of the car park.

"It's pretty," I say, grabbing his arm to steer him around an old couple.

"Even so, there are just too many people here," he grumbles. Then he pauses. "Oh, it is pretty," he says in a delighted voice. Ahead of us the river moves past old houses with mullioned windows looking down on it. Paths branch off, leading to shops and more houses. "It's like the Lego village," he says delightedly. He pauses, shooting me a sideways look, and I see the flush on his cheeks.

What the fuck is going on here? I open my mouth to ask, but he diverts me by pulling me along. I realise he's deliberately avoiding talking about whatever problem he currently has about the same time that I realise we're now holding hands.

He pulls me down the sun-dappled path, pointing out houses he likes, and I nod and smile and I must make sense when I talk because he displays no sign of unease. That's good because inside I'm a turbulent mess. I can't focus on anything. It's like I've been blinded by the sun and can't see anything apart from snapshot impressions. Like the sun on the mink-brown strands of his silky hair, the brightness of his eyes, the long length of his legs and the feel of his hand in mine.

I try to remember when the last time was that I held hands. It must have been with Patrick, but I can't ever remember feeling like this before. I search my memory banks for a name for it, but I can't find it. It leaves me uneasy. I don't like uncertainty. I like to be fully prepared at all times. But nothing prepared me for him.

When we get into the village with its shops and cafes, the crowd disperses a little and I watch him as he looks around with those bright eyes of his. He's still holding my hand, and I'm aware of several disapproving looks. However, they don't motivate me to drop his hand at all. Instead I tighten my grip as he pulls me along.

He stops, looking up at a house that has scaffolding all over it. "What do you think they're doing to it?" he asks.

I send a cursory glance over the building. "New roof, from the looks of it, and they're repointing some of the brickwork."

"How do you know that?" he asks, his bright eyes set on me.

I shrug. "I told you my dad was a property developer. He didn't just buy houses. He did them up too, and I helped him. By the time I was fifteen, I could do most stuff." I look up at the cottage. "It's a good feeling to renovate old properties and see them come back to life."

"Why aren't you doing it, then?"

The question is stark, and I flounder slightly. "Erm, well, I suppose that was just something I associated with my dad." I come to a stop, unable to explain how, for some ridiculous reason, doing up properties seemed to edge too closely to becoming my father in my mind.

He cocks his head on one side and looks intently at me. "Shame," he says quietly. "You need a challenge." He walks slowly away, examining another house while I stand struck dumb. Coming to my senses, I bolt after him.

We pass an ice cream parlour, and he nods to himself and smiles. "We need ice cream," he decides.

I shake my head. "You're such a child," I laugh but it falters as I catch the shadow crossing his face. "Hey," I say. And suddenly I've had enough. I look around and pull him down a side street. It's quiet in the morning sunshine and the only sound is the chuckling water running near us. "Okay," I say abruptly. "What's the matter? And tell me the truth."

"I'm not sure what you mean," he says evasively, and I pull him to face me.

"Yes, you are. Why the sudden bouts of quiet? You're not quiet. It's a completely unnatural state of being for you."

He half smiles. "I think I need to work on that. I'm a bit loud."

"Who said that?" I say fiercely.

"Erm, you."

I hesitate. "Oh, well." His lip twitches, and I shake my head. "I was wrong."

He tips his head to one side, the shiny brown strands moving silkily against the tanned skin of his neck. "Really?" he asks mockingly. I shoot him a warning glance, and he chuckles. "Sorry. But I think Noah might have been building a boat the last time you said you were wrong."

"It doesn't happen often," I say slowly. I smile at him. "I like the sound of your voice. I like listening to you talk."

"But you like quiet too?"

"I admit I'm not loud. But that's why it's so good to be with you. You're funny and quick-witted, and you liven things up around me."

"But you're used to older men." He hesitates. "More sophisticated men."

It hits me like a thunderbolt. "*That's* why you changed into that outfit that makes you look like you've been body snatched by Ralph Lauren." He glares at me, and I reach up and cup his shoulders, looking into that lively face of his. "You don't need to dress like Patrick. You don't need to be silent, or discuss politics in a very loud voice. You don't even need to smoke a pipe and wear a cravat or whatever idea you have of someone who is with me."

"But that's what you're used to. I don't want to embarrass you. You think I'm a kid."

I stare at him. "I have never thought of you as a kid." He looks at me with one eyebrow lifting slowly, and I smile. "Okay, I tried to think of you as one."

"Why?"

The question is bald and not one I'm prepared to answer. It'll lead to things that really can't happen no matter how much I'm growing to want them. I want his hand back in mine, I want to kiss those plump, puffy lips. I want to fuck him. But as he's my employee, and happier and twenty years younger than me, I'm not going to do any of those things.

"Sometimes habit is not a good thing," I say. I shake my head. "I was with Patrick for a long time but that doesn't mean it was good. Max is right. I do feel more alive with you around. I don't want you to change. I like that you're inappropriate sometimes. I never got the chance to do that, so it's nice to listen to."

"I don't want to be a clown to you."

The statement is quiet and firm, and I look at him in amazement. "You could never be that, Jesse." I hesitate. "I guess the truth is that I admire you."

"You do?" The astonishment is palpable in his voice.

I sigh. "I do. You're so full of life. You take chances and throw yourself into things. You care about people."

"You care about people too. You care about far too many people, if you ask me."

I shrug, suddenly becoming aware that we're standing very close to each other. His eyes examine my face and his full lips are so close. I let my hands fall and step back slightly, seeing the faint look of disappointment he can't hide. Fuck, this is getting into quicksand territory very quickly.

"I do care," I say slowly. "But sometimes I don't want to. Sometimes I'm tired of problems and solutions." I shrug awkwardly. "My father was a bit of a character." He tries to look surprised, but he's not a good actor, and I sigh. "Max told you, didn't he? I saw him talking very intently. Interfering wanker."

He steps close again, and I inhale the scent of green tea on his skin. "He wasn't being disloyal."

"Of course he wasn't. He's my family." I sigh again. "Oh well, at least I don't have to go into the nitty-gritty."

"You can though," he says softly. "I'm sure your nitty-gritty is very different from his."

I stare at him, wanting suddenly to talk to him, to tell him about my childhood. I wish I could describe the man my father was and how our relationship epitomised confusion, how I'd learnt at an early age that it is possible to love someone very deeply and still want to hit them over the head with a chair.

Instead, I smile and shake my head. "Not now," I settle for saying, and he smiles with understanding written in his eyes. Over the last few days it's amazed me how attuned our moods are. He seems to sense mine and steer around or through them in the same way I do his. It's an astonishing feeling to someone like me who's led a very self-contained life.

"Okay, then," he says calmly. "Let's have a wander."

"And an ice cream," I say sternly. He looks at me, and I nod. "Ice cream and when we get back you can burn that fucking outfit and put your *Sesame Street* T-shirt back on."

"That'll put the cat amongst the pigeons at the formal dinner tonight," he says demurely.

"Will the cat eat the Nina pigeon?"

"Not unless it wants severe heartburn. That woman has indigestion written all over her."

My laughter is loud on the quiet street.

Jesse

We eat ice creams and wander the pretty village, following the river, crossing bridges and finding ourselves in little roads filled with gorgeous houses. I spin fantastical stories about who the owners are, becoming bold again under that warm gaze of his that looks at me so attentively.

As we walk, I lean closer, feeling the occasional brush of his hand against my leg and inhaling the scent of oranges and sandalwood on him. It used to epitomise the distant glamorous figure of my boss, but these last few days have given me a different view. Like I've shaken up a prism and seen different colours and patterns. Now, he's still glamorous but he's not distant anymore. He's the kind, funny man with tired eyes that still show a faint hint of the self-contained boy he must have been, striving to take care of people in a world filled with ever-shifting priorities.

I still see the perfect good looks and charm but they're buttressed by the way I now know that he's secretly a little awkward in social situations. I can see past the shiny exterior to the way his back gets stiff and a faint furrow appears between those pretty eyes when he's having to make polite conversation. It gives me a heady thrill to have this secret knowledge.

I shake my head as we stop outside an art gallery. I don't know what to do with this new knowledge of him that I have. I watch him looking at a huge watercolour with lively appreciation. In a month I'll probably never see him again.

The thought makes me flinch. Where once I couldn't wait to start the new job and begin my life properly, now I just think of how much of a fucking hole he'll leave in my life.

"You alright?" he asks, staring at me with a look of concern.

As much as I love that he seems to see me now, I also hate to be yet another person that he has to worry about, so I smile brightly and convincingly, pleased to see the shadow leave his eyes.

"I'm fine. Do you want to go in?"

He shoots a longing glance towards the door. "I'd love to. Would you mind?"

I stare at him. "Why would I mind?"

"Well, I can get a little lost in these places. Patrick always used to moan about it."

"Remind me not to let you go to Waterstones with me," I say, nudging him towards the door. "You can lose me for hours in there."

"Oh, me too," he says eagerly, a wide smile on his lips. "Especially with the sofas."

"And the coffee. I could live there."

We smile, and I follow him into the shop. It's filled with light, and Zeb immediately makes a beeline for a group of pictures hanging near the front of the shop. They're bold and vivid abstract paintings that would look amazing in the high-ceilinged rooms of his flat.

I study him for a second. He looks as if he belongs somewhere like this in those chinos that cling to the long muscled length of his legs and the checked shirt that makes his eyes look very blue. An assistant brushes past me, making hasty tracks to someone who obviously has deep pockets, and I turn away and wander further into the gallery. It's quiet and has a very expensive atmosphere, and I walk from one exhibit to the next undisturbed by assistants or other customers.

There's a lot of stuff from local artists, but it isn't until I'm making my way back towards Zeb that I spy something I like. It's a huge canvas filled with pink peonies painted on a black background and it seems to glow against the white walls of the gallery. The passion and talent in every stroke of the paintbrush is mesmerising. It's part of a group of paintings, all obviously from the same artist, and I move from one painting to another but always come back to the original one.

I'm looking at it when I catch the scent of warm citrus and feel

Zeb come up next to me. "You like this one?" he asks, standing next to me staring at the art. I nod thoughtfully, looking at the painting again.

"It's beautiful. I'm not one for flowers at all, but–" I hesitate, afraid of looking stupid, but he just looks at me enquiringly, and I know suddenly that he'll never laugh at me. With me, yes, but never *at* me. And something in me relaxes instantly and unfurls a little bit. "I get the impression that it's about more than flowers," I say slowly. "It feels full of emotion somehow."

He grins. "Probably is. That's Ivo Ashworth-Robinson's work. He's slightly temperamental, so I'm sure it's absolutely chock full of very loud feelings."

"You know him?"

He shrugs. "Vaguely. He's one of Max's best mates. They were apprentices at a newspaper together and then worked together a lot. Ivo was a war photographer but he's a full-time artist now."

I turn back to the picture, admiring the colours. "It makes me feel happy," I finally say judiciously, and when I look at him, he has a look of almost astonishment on his face. "You alright?" I ask. "Did you buy that picture you were looking at? Do you need a sit down now? We can catch the moths that flew out of your wallet later on. You're my priority at the moment," I finish solemnly.

He frowns at me but it doesn't work and he bursts into laughter. It's loud and almost shocking in the cool, quiet room.

"Cheeky twat," he says almost affectionately. "I've bought it. It'll look amazing in my bedroom."

"Better than your etchings," I say slyly.

"Come on," he says, ushering me out of the gallery. "We'll go and grab some lunch. There's a lovely fish restaurant here that has a nice view of the water."

"Have you eaten there before?" I ask reluctantly.

He nods, looking suddenly awkward. "Patrick and I used to eat at the restaurant." He stops suddenly. "Shit, I forgot to give the sales assistant my mobile number for the delivery driver. I won't be a minute."

He vanishes back into the gallery, and I wander over a little bridge, stopping in the middle to stare down at the water running busily over the stones. It glitters in the sun, nearly hurting my eyes. I lean my elbows on the balustrade and sigh. I hate the fact that he's been here before with Patrick. It feels like everything we do has his perfect shadow falling over it.

But what worries me most is that I shouldn't feel like this. Zeb hired me to do a job, and throughout my time with the agency, I've prided myself on being able to care about the clients but still be able to leave them behind once the job is done. I know I won't be able to do that with him.

I look up and see him walking towards me. I watch the long length of his legs and the sun shining on the messy waves of his hair. He smiles, and I groan under my breath. "I'm fucked," I say out loud. "Sorry," I mutter to the old couple who just heard me. "But it's the truth. Fucked," I say sadly.

CHAPTER EIGHT

Jesse

When we get down to dinner that night, I stop dead.

"What is it?" Zeb's hand comes to rest at the small of my back. He's probably unaware of the gesture, but it feels like he's branded me. I can feel the heat of his hand at my back, his fingers spread. It's almost possessive, which is completely ridiculous, but I can't deny that he's seemed softer with me in some way since we got back from our afternoon out.

I sneak a look at him as he stares at the table, a small frown on his face. *Probably looking for potential problems,* I think affectionately.

He looks back at me. "What's the problem?"

"The seating arrangements." He looks at me in incomprehension. "They haven't changed. I was hoping we were sitting next to Jeffrey Dahmer tonight rather than George and Mildred."

"Nina and Victor," he says in a measured voice, but the tug at his lips betrays his amusement. "And you'd probably have been better off with Jeffrey Dahmer because at least you could have had his share of the dinner menu."

"I'm not sure who told you that you were funny, but I'd get a second opinion," I inform him haughtily, and we both grin at each other like idiots until a throat clears. When I turn, I find the whole table watching us. Max has a grin on his face, but Patrick's face is poisonous. Frances looks at him, and becoming aware of her glance, he rearranges his face hurriedly. I look at him thoughtfully and then obey Zeb's urging and sit down at the table. I smile at everyone until I get to Nina, and the smile slides slowly off my face.

"Jesse," she says in a glacial tone.

"Please don't hurt me," I mutter and then say "ouch" as Zeb kicks me.

She ignores me like the Queen of the Angry Dead that she undoubtedly is, and I settle down for what promises to be another fun-filled evening of food that wouldn't fill a chihuahua, and conversation with Nina and Victor that runs the gamut of stocks and shares to icy digs at Zeb.

After one particular humdinger, I inhale sharply and open my mouth, only to shut it quickly when he grabs my thigh and squeezes. When I look at him he mouths, "Leave it," and, endeavouring to keep to my plan of making him happy, I subside.

"Thank you," he whispers into my ear, and I shudder. It isn't inconspicuous, either. It's a full-body judder, but I can't help it. He's so close to me, his hand warm on my thigh and his warm breath playing across my ear. To my horror, I feel my cock stir, and he goes completely still as if sensing it.

I look determinedly down at the table but when his grasp doesn't ease up, I sneak a glance at him. He's staring at me, his eyes dark and peculiarly intent, seemingly focused on my lips. As an experiment I run my tongue over my bottom lip and feel his hand tighten. I can't help my gasp this time because he's about two inches away from my cock, which is rock hard now. His gaze shoots up, and for a long second our eyes tangle.

Then Nina says something in a querulous tone, and the intimate bubble pops. His hand moves away from my leg, and he faces forward, talking to her, but I can see that his breaths are fast and unsteady. *Like mine. Shit.*

When dinner is finished, which is considerably before my appetite is satisfied, Frances stands up. She's dressed in a black cap-sleeved dress and looks poised and attractive. She claps her hands to get our attention. "The older members of the party are going to the Blue Room to carry on their evening. We've got something different planned for everyone else," she says.

"Will the older people be eating?" I say hopefully to Zeb. "Because I vote we go with them if that's the case."

He rolls his eyes and focuses on Frances.

"The rest of us," she's saying, "are going to play a game."

"I'm not sure about this," I hiss. "I've read books about the upper class and their parties. I don't wish to be corrupted."

He turns a gaze brimming with mirth on me just as Frances says excitedly, "We're going to play hide-and-seek."

I make a moue of disappointment, and Zeb chuckles. "I'd love to live in your head," he mutters and pauses. "But only after I've taken Valium."

I nudge him, trying not to laugh as Frances carries on talking, giving us an incredibly long list of rules that seem to go on forever.

"This is like the Geneva Convention version of hide-and-seek," I whisper. "I vote we go and do something else."

"And," Frances says excitedly, "the prize is an all-expenses-paid week in the Caribbean."

"Oh, well now, that's different," I say hurriedly. He raises an eyebrow, and I shake my head. "We should endeavour to take part in this wonderful event," I say piously to him. I grab his hand. "Come on. Get up quickly because we need a fucking great hiding place. We're going to win that prize."

"Competition brings out a very unexpected side of you," he muses, getting to his feet and following me as I tug him along.

"You have no idea," I mutter. "Now, where's the best place?"

We look in cupboards and rooms on the ground floor and every-where is the sound of excited laughter. Then, all of a sudden, the lights go off.

"What the fuck? Is it a power cut or have they not paid their electricity bill?" I breathe, and he chuckles. It sounds rich and warm in the sudden darkness.

" They switched the lights off on this floor to make it more difficult. You weren't listening to the rules, were you?"

"Pshaw! Rules are for people who don't win a week in the Caribbean." I exclaim in triumph as I open a door. "Perfect. Get in here."

"What the hell?" he says as I pull him in and shut the door. "Where are we?" His voice is suddenly at my ear and I jump.

"Jesus, warn a bloke, will you?"

"Oh, I'm sorry, Jesse. Did I not warn you where I was when you thrust me headfirst into a cupboard?"

"You're so dramatic, Zeb," I breathe admiringly. "I love this unexpected side of you."

"Don't get used to it. It doesn't appear very often."

"Lies," I say blithely. "Very big lies."

He chuckles and shifts position. I can feel his body all against my side, and I still suddenly as I realise how very small this fucking cupboard is.

"What are we hiding in?" he asks, and I shudder as his breath washes across my ear.

"Oh, erm." I stop to clear my throat. "It's a storage room for luggage. I found it when I got lost going to the shoot today."

"Surely it's completely in the wrong direction."

"Not if you're acquainted with this party." I shift position, trying to lean a little bit away from him before I lose my head and grab him. He's just so close and hot. I squeeze my eyes closed, which makes it worse as his scent fills the small cupboard. It's so warm and sexy. Like him.

He chuckles, and I suppress a groan of despair as my cock fills until it's almost uncomfortable. I shift my feet again.

"You okay?" he asks.

"Fine. Just that this cupboard is very small."

"Are you claustrophobic?" I can hear the concern in his voice. He fumbles, and I want to moan as he cups my face in his hands. "Say the word and we'll fuck the game off," he says, and I wonder if I'm imagining things because his voice sounds thick, and his hand is shaking with a tiny tremor.

"No," I say, turning into him. His fingers brush my mouth. In a state of almost suspended animation, I feel them slowly sweep across my mouth. His thumb catches the lower lip, and I hear a hiss, and then he pushes down slowly, the wetness there touching his thumb.

I can hear panting breaths in the dark, and I don't know whether it's him or me, but I abruptly lose my control and take his thumb into my mouth, sucking it slowly and thoroughly.

His breath catches, and I hear a rumble before suddenly his thumb is gone and his hands are at my shoulders as he pushes me into the back wall. "Jesus," he says, his breath harried and heavy. "Jesus, Jesse. We shouldn't be doing this."

"No," I moan, and I lift my arms and tangle my hands behind his head, bringing it down until his lips graze mine. We stay there for a long second and then I swear I can literally feel his control snap as he lowers his mouth and takes mine in a deep, wet kiss.

I moan in my throat and pull his hair in an attempt to get more of his lips. He obeys and we sink into the kiss, tongues tangling and rubbing.

I pull my head back to take a breath and promptly lose it when he sinks into me, his body pressing mine into the wall. "Oh God, yes." My voice is slurred and fucked up. "Get on me."

He moans a wild sound and then he's kissing me again, his cock a hard and heavy pressure against my own. He ruts against me and lowers his hands to grab my arse and pull me into him so he can get closer. It's a desperate, unchecked gesture, and it turns the heat up for me even more. I cant my hips and rub on him, feeling my balls bunch and press into the seam of my trousers. It's a sharp, bright pain and I kiss him deeper and wetter, our teeth clashing.

When he pulls away, I open my eyes blearily. "What is it?" I mutter. "Come back."

He stands back, but I'm reassured by him keeping a hold of my arms. I look at him in the dim light now that my eyes have adjusted. He looks astonished. As if I've punched him in the face. "Zeb?"

He gives a sudden, sharp bark of laughter. "What am I doing?" he mutters.

"Not enough," I observe and try to tug him back.

"I want you so much," he says. "I don't want to stop."

"Stopping would be very bad. For my cock," I add in case he didn't get the memo.

He shakes his head, and grabbing my face between his palms, he kisses me slowly and so thoroughly that, when he draws back, I'm an inch away from coming.

"Come upstairs," he whispers. "I need to be inside you so badly."

I grab my cock and squeeze hard. "Fuck yes," I mutter and follow him out of the cupboard. I can't believe this is actually happening.

We somehow manage to make our way back to our floor without meeting anyone which is probably a good job as we can't keep our hands off each other. We can't even manage to make it into the room as he seems to lose patience and slams me into the wall by the door.

He takes my mouth with a low groan and I arch back off the wall, grinding my cock against his and moaning low. When he pulls away, I slur a protest, but he holds me against the wall with one hand while fumbling with the room card. It takes two tries but eventually the light glows green, and he opens the door, pulling me in after him and slamming it shut.

I start to laugh but it dies in my throat as he pushes me against the door and kisses me. He sucks on my lower lip, sending his tongue over it afterward to ease the sting as he pushes me into the hard surface, fitting his hips into mine. I pull my mouth away and groan at the feel of his cock against mine, fumbling with my hands at his hips, trying to pull him closer so I can grind harder against him.

His hands are rough as he pushes up my shirt, sending his palms over my chest and tweaking my nipples. Pleasure sears through me, and I cry out. He looks up with an evil expression.

"You're sensitive here, aren't you?" he mutters, rubbing the pad of his thumb over my nipple before he pinches it between his thumb and forefinger. The pain is sweetly sharp and I grunt, grabbing his head and pulling it towards me so I can kiss him. We get lost in this for what feels like a long time. The light is red behind my eyelids, and I tangle my tongue with his as his finger rubs ceaselessly against my nipples. First one then the other.

When he pulls back, my eyesight is blurry and my cock is throbbing almost painfully.

"Where are you going?" I slur as he stands back and weaves slightly. His face is set and intent, his eyes lowered to half-mast and his mouth swollen. His hair is sticking up in a messy tangle, and his shirt is half out of his trousers. It's hard for a second to believe that this is buttoned-up, in-control Zeb, and it's a dark thrill.

"I'm not going anywhere," he says hoarsely. "I need your clothes off."

"I'm happy with this plan," I mutter, pulling my shirt up and off and faltering slightly as I forget to unbutton it and get it caught on my head.

"Somehow this is not surprising," he says, and I can hear the amusement in his voice as his hands help me off with my shirt. When it clears my head, I glare at him. Control is coming back into his face, and I'm not having that, so I kick off my shoes and slowly unzip my trousers, the hiss of the zip loud in the quiet suite. I push my fingers into the gap as he stares with hot eyes at the strip of pubic hair now showing above the fabric. I'm relieved to see that the humour is gone again.

My trousers fall to the ground, and he grunts, looking me over where I stand. His eyes are avid and hot on my chest and the narrow strip of fabric that's all that stands between me and nakedness.

"Get on the sofa," he orders.

"Why? What about the bed?"

"The sofa's closer," he barks and starts to strip off his own shirt, revealing that wonderful hairy chest of his. His nipples are pale brown discs and his hips narrow. His trousers fall to the floor, leaving him in a pair of navy boxer briefs that do little to hide the bulge of his erection.

I lie back hurriedly on the sofa and cup my cock as I watch him stride towards me. It's hot and hard in my briefs, and I can feel the spot of wetness growing.

"Hand off your cock," he mutters, and all I can do is gasp as he lowers himself over me, giving me all of his lovely weight. I can feel the sharp dig of his hipbones, and his chest rubs against my swollen nipples, sending sparks of pleasure through my body.

He slides over me sinuously, his hands gripping the armrest behind my head as he starts to undulate against me, his cock rubbing against mine. I moan and he draws in a sharp breath before lowering his head and taking my mouth again.

He pulls back, and for a long second we stare at each other. Long enough for me to wonder whether he's going to back away. Instead, he smiles almost tenderly and brushes his fingers down my face, lingering over my cheekbones and the tip of my nose before he rubs them over my lips. I kiss the tips, and he stares, before bending his head and kissing my sternum, tracking kisses in a row until he reaches my nipple. He pulls it into his mouth and suckles it, and I cry out, grabbing his head and forcing it against me. He laves and sucks, and when he pulls away, it's only so he can do the same to the other one. When he sits back and starts to kiss downwards, I can barely remember my own name.

He nuzzles into the hair around my belly button, darting out his tongue to rim it, and I wriggle protestingly. "Ticklish," I murmur, and he smiles up at me. His eyes are a startling blue in the light, and for a second I want time to stop so that I can stare at him. Then he begins the descent towards my groin, and I abandon the idea of stopping time. How stupid would that be when I want him to hurry up and get to my cock?

He spreads my legs further with a demanding shove that makes my cock even harder, if that's possible, and then nuzzles into the space where my leg meets my groin. He inhales deeply and when he looks up his eyes are bleary. "You smell so good here," he says gruffly, and I can't help arching my pelvis towards him.

He hovers over my straining cock, his warm breath brushing hot over the sensitive tip. Reaching out one long finger, he tracks over the sensitive skin of my hipbones and down the groove in my pelvis to where my dick is waiting. I shudder as he traces his finger over it, the pressure a taunt when I need a hard touch.

"Touch me, for fuck's sake," I groan desperately as he hovers there, watching the damp spot grow on my stripy briefs. "Zeb," I moan, and something in the desperation seems to snap his control. He removes my briefs with a sharp tug and throws them over his head before bending and taking my cock down his throat.

"Oh shit," I shout out far too loudly and then fall back, staring blindly up at the ceiling and panting as I feel the wet, suckling pressure on my dick. It's pushed halfway down his throat and I feel his lips press against my pubic hair. This immediately makes me struggle up onto my elbows so I can see it. When I do, I groan loudly at the sight of his lips stretched tight and swollen around my cock and those blue, blue eyes staring at me intently.

He sucks hard, his mouth a heated seal round my cock, before letting me slip almost free so he can lick and suckle the sensitive head. He licks at the drops of precome on my cock and gives a pleased grunt that causes my balls to draw up.

"Shit, no," I say, pulling back and grabbing the base of my dick. "God, that was too close," I mutter, trying to get my breathing under control. He levers off me in a flurry of movement, and when I look up, he's standing by the sofa stripping off his underwear. He tosses the fabric somewhere. It could be Outer Mongolia for all I care because I'm staring at his cock. It's huge, the head angry and red-looking with moisture beading the top. His balls are big and hairy, swinging lower than mine, and my mouth is watering with the desire to suck him.

"Come here," I say throatily, and he shakes his head, his cheeks ruddy and his eyes laser focused as he gropes for his trousers on the floor. When he comes back up with a tube and a gold packet, I shudder, and he smiles darkly.

He sits on the floor, leaning back against the sofa and chucking the lube next to him. "That sofa is like a torture instrument. Get down here," he says, fisting his cock and starting to jerk himself lazily as he eyes me.

I get up and stand over him as he runs his hands up my legs. He cocks his head, watching as I shiver when his fingers touch my hips. Obeying the sharp pull of his hands, I lower myself to sit in his lap. We both groan as I settle, and his cock rubs against my hole as if demanding entrance.

"Come here," he says gruffly, and I lower my lips to his. We both let out a sigh as they touch, gently at first but then harder as we sink into the kiss. I press down, groaning as my cock rubs against the hair on his stomach and sends bright sparks behind my eyes. We kiss hungrily, and I shudder as his hands leave my hips where they've been rubbing circles, and I hear the snap of a bottle opening.

I fold my arms behind his head and kiss him harder, only to pull away as he pulls my cheeks back to expose my hole. For a second I feel cold air and then the touch of wet, slippery fingers as he rubs over my entrance, gently flirting with the wrinkled skin.

He plays there for a second as he takes my mouth again in long, slow kisses before I feel one finger slide in. I tense for a second, and he stays still, watching me carefully, his eyes like neon in the dim light.

"Okay?" he whispers and I nod, easing down on the digit.

"God, yes," I moan, feeling pleasure race through my passage. "Fuck, that's good. More."

One hand holds me firmly by the hip while the other plays, adding another finger and then another, the lube making an obscene noise in the still room. Our panting breaths are loud as I start to ride his fingers, forcing them in further and crying out as he crooks them and massages my prostate.

"Oh shit," I gasp, pressing my forehead into his shoulder. "That's so good." I look up at him to find him examining me. His colour is high, and his eyes are almost dazed. "Want you to fuck me, Zeb," I whisper and his eyes flare.

He pulls his fingers out slowly and I moan at the loss. He hitches me up slightly, and I hear the snap of the rubber before he lowers me again, and his cock nudges my entrance. For a second, I blanch at the thought that it's much bigger than his fucking fingers.

"We'll go easy," he says hoarsely as if he's read my mind. "Tell me to stop and I will, darling."

For a second we both still at the endearment. He looks shell-shocked, while I feel a wide surge of pleasure. I want him to call me that again and again in that hoarse voice. I wriggle, bringing his mind back to the task, and then I feel his cock start to enter me.

It hurts. More than usual, but then he's big. However, I'm one of those men who love the burn. I like to feel the pain as I stretch around him because the pleasure afterwards always feels more intense.

I grit my teeth and bear down on him as he slides slowly into me until finally my backside meets his lap, and I feel the crinkle of his pubic hair.

We hang there for a second panting and twitching. I wriggle experimentally, and he groans.

"Alright?" he asks gutturally, and I nod, too overcome to find my words. Instead, I pull his head towards me and kiss him feverishly. At first, he stays still, apart from the movement of his mouth, and then gradually he starts to thrust upwards in gentle movements like the tide. I'm sitting on him, my backside tucked neatly into his lap and stuffed full of cock, and it's almost overwhelming,

Then his cock bushes my prostate, and I shout out loud, which acts like petrol on the fire for him. He seizes my mouth in a fierce and dirty kiss, our teeth clashing. He pulls back. "Okay?" he asks through gritted teeth, and I nod furiously, starting to ride him, lifting up so that his cock almost comes out and hovering there, feeling it stretch my rim and then pushing down so it tunnels back in.

His hands bracket my hips, digging in so hard I know I'll have bruises tomorrow, and I revel in it. He pushes upwards, a powerful movement that makes me cry out and writhe in his lap, and he begins a series of punishing thrusts. His cock feels like a steel pole in me, and my own dick lets out a spurt of liquid, painting his stomach as he hits my prostate almost continuously.

The room is full of the sounds of grunts and moans and the scent of sex is heady in the air. I grab my cock and start to jerk it, feeling the tingle in my balls. "Fuck, I'm close," I groan. "Oh shit. I can feel it."

I cry out as he suddenly grabs my hips and levers me up so that he slips out of me.

"What are you *doing*?" I moan. "I need you in me."

"Get up," he grits out. His eyes are blind and sweat drips down his face. "Bend over the sofa. I need to pound that arse."

"Oh God, yes." I jump up frantically and bend over the sofa, burying my face in the cushions. My scream is therefore buried in them as he pushes back into me. He pistons in and out, starting up a punishing rhythm with the only goal being for us to come.

I hang over the sofa, my hair in my face and sweat stinging my eyes as the cushions rub against my cock.

"I've dreamt of doing this," he whispers hoarsely. "Seeing you bent over like this."

"Me too," I whimper. "Oh shit, Zeb, touch me."

He sends one arm over my chest, pulling me up and bracing me against him as he fucks into me in fierce choppy thrusts, while the other slides down and his rough hand circles my dick. I'm leaking a lot now, and he groans as the liquid coats his palm. I cry out as his fist forms a tight slippery tunnel, and he shoves into me hard.

I don't even have time to say anything. Instead, I cry out and, feeling my balls draw up, I shoot over his hands, spurts of come filling his fingers and slicking his palm. He moans as the sharp scent rises between us and he gives one thrust, two thrusts, and a third. Then he goes rigid, pushing his cock up so far it's like he's trying to climb inside me. He lets loose a guttural shout, and I feel warmth flood the condom inside me.

For a few minutes, we hang over the sofa panting. His hips move in tiny thrusts, as he rides out his orgasm, and we both twitch occasionally as pleasure flares and burns away.

Eventually, he sighs. "Holy fucking shit."

Incredibly, I start to laugh, and he grunts as it tightens my passage around his cock, probably painfully.

"You can say that again," I mutter. "Did you pay a damage deposit? Because I think this sofa needs reupholstering now."

He starts to laugh and we stay there for a second, his arms warm around me and his laughter like bright spangles in the dark. It's oddly wonderful.

Eventually, we half walk and half stagger to the bed and collapse into it without saying another word, but the silence is somehow comfortable. He pulls the covers over us and I take the opportunity to snuggle into him. For a second, he's rigid as if surprised, and then I'm gratified to feel his arms tighten around me.

He kisses the top of my head, and we lie quietly, neither of us seemingly inclined to question what just happened. Suits me because a reckoning is no doubt on the horizon.

Zeb's phone beeps, and I groan as he removes his arm from around me and reaches for it amongst the tangle of clothing I threw by the bed. Looking at the screen, he huffs. "Jesus Christ."

I raise my head from its spot on his hairy chest. "What?"

"We won the hide-and-seek competition." I start to laugh, and he grimaces. "Apparently, we couldn't be found tonight."

"Because we've been fucking in our room." I snort. "We were playing a different game of hide-and-seek. One that Frances never considered in her *War and Peace*-sized list of rules."

"They want us to go to the library to collect the prize."

"No."

He cocks one eyebrow. "Why?"

I send my hand down and cup his cock, which stiffens in my hand. "Because we're going to carry on our winning streak. I want you again."

"Aren't we going to talk about this?" he says breathlessly as his hips start to churn, pushing his cock into my tight fist.

"No, the first rule of Shag Club is we don't talk about Shag Club."

"That is *not* a thing, and what a disgusting name for a club," he pants, his voice catching in a moan.

"It's definitely a thing." I bend to lick up the length of his dick before suckling on the head, digging my tongue gently into the slit. I pause and look up at him. He's watching me intently. "Oh, I'm sorry," I say innocently. "Would you like me to stop so you can collect our holiday to the Caribbean?"

"Fuck the Caribbean," he says hoarsely, lying back down on the pillows and throwing his arm over his eyes. "The Shag Club is in session."

"That's the spirit," I say approvingly and bend back to my task.

CHAPTER NINE

Zeb

I wake up in the morning slowly and the first thing I realise is that I feel warm and lazy. That's sufficiently unusual for me to crank my eyes open. When my gaze drops on the man lying next to me, I jolt upright like I've been electrocuted.

My first thought is *Sweet Jesus, what have I done?* Actually, that's a lie. My actual first thought is *Holy shit, he looks amazing.* Jesse is lying face down on the bed, his dark brown hair a silky mess around his face and his full, pink lips slightly parted. His olive skin is dark against the blue bedlinen, and I'm now in a position to know that he's that colour all over apart from a pale strip around his arse. The reason I know that is because said arse is exposed, as I've pulled the sheet off him in a panic.

He starts to stir and panic fills my head. *What the fuck am I going to do?* Thoughts swirl around my brain. *He works for me. I'm his boss. He's so much younger than me. God, he's lovely. What about that thing he did with his tongue last night?* To my horror, I feel my cock fill. Images of last night flit lazily past my eyes.

He opens his eyes to cast a bleary gaze over me, and he smiles. It's glorious, full of sleepy happiness, and I panic. I totally panic.

"This was a mistake," I blurt out. Loudly. I watch the sleepy happiness fade to confusion and feel my heart sink. *What am I doing?* I'm not sure, but as a testament to my stupidity, I carry on doing it. "I'm so sorry," I say hoarsely. "We shouldn't have slept together."

The confusion melts to something dark before he shutters it, leaving him with a blank, cool expression that doesn't sit well on that lovely, mobile face.

"Bit late for that now." He sits up, completely unfazed by the fact that he's stark naked, while I have the sheet wrapped around me like I'm Doris Day in one of those old films with Rock Hudson. I wish I was as cool, because just the sight of his cock lying semi hard against his thigh makes my mouth water.

I become aware that I'm staring at his dick, and it appears to be equally interested. I drag my gaze up to find him watching me with one eyebrow raised. I clear my throat and try to gather my composure. Remembering that I'm old enough to be his father helps.

"I'm sorry, but we can't do this again. It would be wrong," I say awkwardly. Unfortunately, the awkwardness comes across as cold, and I wince as I watch his face harden.

"Oh, how did I know you were going to say that?" he says, sliding out of bed and striding over to the wardrobe. He grabs a pair of faded old jeans and pulls them up. I watch that tight, round arse disappear and have a sudden flashback to seeing the cheeks spread as I eased my dick into his tiny hole, watching as it closed around my cock. I blink. *Oh my God, I'm having sex-related flashbacks.*

His expression is blank when he turns round, and much as I try to search his face, I get nothing because he's locked down tight.

"Jesse," I say, hating the begging note in my voice but unable to hide it. "I'm—"

"There's *really* no need to say sorry again," he says coldly. "I knew this was going to happen." He gives a humourless laugh that really doesn't suit him. "Maybe I should start predicting the outcome of the World Cup, seeing as I've been gifted with foresight. I'm much better than an octopus."

It's his first display of emotion since that lovely smile when he woke up. I watch a muscle tic wildly in his jaw, belying his flippant words as he drags a white T-shirt over his head and disappears into the bathroom. I get up from the bed, still clutching the ridiculous sheet to myself.

"Can we just…" I manage to get out before he shuts the door in my face. To add to the cold feel of the room I hear the lock turn.

"Jesse," I say softly, banging my head against the door, wishing I could do it hard enough to smash some sense into my head. My brain is whirling with confusion. "I'm so sorry. I just don't want to see you get hurt. You're so wonderful. You're funny and beautiful and brave and so full of life. There is no way as an adult that I should in good conscience damage that. And I will damage it. I'll hurt you, because I'm too closed off." I think of all the things Patrick had thrown at me. "I'm cold and obsessed with order and way too regimented for someone as full of life as you."

The door opens, and I sway before regaining my balance.

"That's the trouble, Zeb," he says icily. "You're talking to me like an adult to a child. I'm twenty-four. I'm an adult too, but I'll never be one in your eyes because you categorised me three years ago and filed me in the wrong fucking place. But you're too stubborn to admit that you made a mistake, so here I am. Still on your shelf with the wrong label."

"I didn't mean to hurt you."

"You didn't," he scoffs.

"But I was rude," I persist diligently. "I just panicked."

He laughs, and there is none of the usual rich humour about it. It sounds horrible. "Why the fuck would you panic, Zeb? We slept together. That's it. Panic should be reserved for running away from tornados or erupting volcanos. Not sleeping with the office joke who will be forgotten as soon as he leaves."

"Where the hell did that come from?" I say angrily as he marches towards the door, grabbing an amber-coloured jacket as he goes. "No, you wait a fucking minute. You're not going to be forgotten like that and who the fuck ever called you the office joke? Wait, where are you going?"

I follow him into the hall and he whirls to face me. "I am going to breakfast. *Alone*," he says as I open my mouth. "I don't want to speak to you for a while, Zeb, because I've just realised that you're a bit of a fucking cunt." The door slams behind me and his mouth quirks. "And you're going to be super busy soon anyway. You're in the corridor naked apart from a sheet, and now you're locked out of our room." He shrugs. "Still, as you're such a fucking grown-up, I'm sure you've got a spare key somewhere on your person. See you later."

He gives me a casual wave of his hand and disappears down the stairs. A door opens behind me and I turn and sigh. "Oh, of course it would be you."

"Good morning, Zeb," Nina says icily. "Nice to see you taking your messy private life onto the hotel corridors."

"Fuck my life," I groan and bang my head against the locked door. It hurts and maybe it should.

Jesse

I make my way quickly downstairs and out towards the lake. I need to be outside where I can pace and try and get rid of this tight feeling in my chest. My eyes feel hot, and I rub them briskly until the moisture goes away. I knew this was going to happen. I bloody knew it. So why did I do it? I shake my head. Because I want him. I want him all the fucking time and that was my chance to have him.

I rest my back against a tree and look out over the lake. A storm is threatening and the sky is a heavy golden-grey colour, infusing everything with that strange glaze. The water reflects the sky back, making it look somehow magical like a portal into fairy land. I bite my lip. If I had the chance, I'd fuck off to fairy land straightaway. Never mind the enchanted food and drink. Just the chance not to have to face Zeb would have me signing up for wings and a wand.

I pull my coat around me because it's noticeably cooler now and tap my fingers on my knee, hooking my nail into the slight rip there and tugging on the loose fibre. It unravels slightly and a bigger hole appears in the denim. Sort of appropriate for the way I feel this morning.

Voices sound in the distance and I push myself closer to the tree. I don't want to talk to anyone at the moment. But then equally, I sort of do. I want to talk inanities so I can push away the look on Zeb's face when he woke up this morning in bed with me. The shock and shame were written all over him, and, for a minute, I'd wanted to shrivel up and die. Was he wishing I was Patrick or just wishing I was anyone but me? The thought makes bile rise in my throat. I'd gone to sleep so happy wrapped around him, and to be cast aside like this is startling.

My phone vibrates, and when I look down I can see a message from Zeb. Actually, I can see five messages from him. I wonder if he's managed to get back into the room without embarrassment. I hope he hasn't.

Having the phone in my hand, though, reminds me that there is one person I can always talk to, and I pull up his contact details. The ring tone sounds and then the call connects, and I hear the lovely Welsh tones of my best friend.

"Jess?" he says. I can hear what sounds like cutlery and the radio in the background, so he and his boyfriend are probably having breakfast.

"So, hypothetically if I'd gone away for the week with my boss to pretend to be his boyfriend and ended up sleeping with him and then falling for him, would you say that was wise?" I say in a jumble of words.

There's a long silence. "And how hypothetical would that be?" he says slowly.

I hum contemplatively. "Yeah, no, not at all hypothetical now that I come to think about it."

There's a longer silence and when he speaks next, he sounds

incredulous. "Your boss being Zeb?" His voice goes high. "Oh my *God,* you fucked Zeb."

"Yep," I say glumly. "And it was bloody amazing, but I think he's still in love with his ex and his ex is definitely in love with him, but he's committed to marrying this woman so he can have children and please his parents and so he wants Zeb for a bit on the side."

"Have you wandered onto the set of *Downton Abbey* and just not realized?"

I snort out a laugh. "Eli," I say in a warning voice.

"Well, sorry but really?" He pauses. "And you fucked Zeb and it was brilliant?"

"The skies opened and the angels wept."

"*Zeb?*" he says again.

"Yes," I say crossly. "*Zeb.* You seem rather stuck on that one point. What about the incredible mess I've made of my life?"

"Well, at least you can say you fucked Zeb Evans. That's a bloody major win in my book."

Someone says something in the background and he laughs. "Now, boo, you know you're my one and only."

"Excuse me. Can you maybe stop flirting with your hot actor boyfriend and incidentally sounding like a complete douchebag and concentrate on my pain?"

"Sorry, sorry." He pauses and his voice gets suddenly serious. "And you think he's in love with his ex?"

"I'm pretty sure of it," I say glumly. "He binned me off this morning."

"Babe." He sighs loudly. "Well, that's just fucked up."

"*That's it?*" I say incredulously. "Well, I must say, don't ever write a problem page. You'd be shit."

He laughs but then goes quiet. When he speaks next his voice is firm. "Okay, so let me get this straight. He fucked you and now he's having regrets and you have feelings for him?"

"*So* many feelings," I say dolefully.

"Jess, you must have known this was going to happen. He wears responsibility like it's a fucking hair shirt. I don't know what happened to him, but he's as buttoned up as if he's in a straitjacket."

"I do know."

"Was it bad?"

I shrug, forgetting he can't see me. "Bad enough that it's completely understandable why he is the way he is."

He sighs. "Shit, that makes it worse. You can't even hate the fucker."

"I think I'm managing quite well with that at the moment," I say glumly. "And if I waver, I just have to remember the way he looked at me this morning like he'd tracked dog shit over the carpet."

"He did *what*?" His voice is low and dangerous.

"Eli, calm down."

"No, you calm down. He gets to sleep with you and bins you the next morning. You, who's so lovely and fucking gorgeous. The man's a total fuckwit."

"He says I'm too young for him. I'm too wonderful and he's too old. He'll drag me down and I deserve everything in the world. And blah blah more lovely stuff blah."

"Jesus, I *hate* that wanker," he hisses. "He can't even be a complete bastard to make us feel better."

I laugh and there's silence for a second. "What am I going to do?" I say softly.

"Babe." He pauses. "You still want him, don't you?"

"How did you know?"

"You've wanted him for as long as you've known him. That doesn't wear off with one shag." There's a silence, and I listen to him breathe on the line. In my mind's eye I can see him standing in his kitchen with that wild mess of blond hair and kind face. "Okay," he says finally. "I want you to go and have breakfast first. You're awful when your blood sugar goes down."

"Such a nurse."

"You know it. An exceptional nurse in this case. It is, after all, how I landed my sugar daddy."

Gideon, his boyfriend, says something indignantly in the background, and Eli laughs. "Go and have breakfast, Jess, and then I want you to clear off somewhere for the day."

"Why?"

"If I know Zeb, he'll be looking for you."

"Why?"

"Because just as I know you've always fancied him, I equally know he's always fancied you."

"Really?"

"Yes, really. Whenever we've been at parties, you're the first person he seems to look for, and he watches you when you don't know it."

I feel warmth fill my chest. "So, how is going out going to solve it?"

"He won't know where you are, and that'll drive him mad. Let him have a day of having to ponder what he's done. It'll do him good."

"But what about when I get back?"

"Well, that's up to you. You can collect your stuff and fuck off because you'll be leaving the agency soon anyway, or–"

He pauses. "Or what?" I ask, not liking the first option.

"Or you can fuck his brains out and see if he can replace them with enough common sense to know what he's going to lose if he carries on being a twat. And Jesse, whatever you do, you know you're always welcome here, don't you?"

Gideon says something in the background, and Eli mutters a reply. Then he comes back on the line. "Gid says for you to come and stay with us for a while. Get your head on straight. We'd love to have you."

"Won't that interfere with your twenty-four-hour-a-day sex fest?"

"Nah, Gideon really needs to find a hobby apart from my arse." I can hear Gideon say something, and Eli laughs. It's the same laugh I've heard most of my life that got me into trouble constantly. "Come to Fowey if you're sad," he says. "I miss you loads."

"I miss you too," I say, touched by the conviction in his voice. "Thanks, babe."

"Anytime. You know that."

I end the call and stare at the lake, contemplating my options for a few minutes. Then an evil smile crosses my face. I'm not a quitter, so that really leaves me with only one option.

Zeb

It takes me an hour to get back in the room, during which I'm humiliated by the receptionist's smirk when I have to descend to the lobby dressed only in a sheet to ask for a spare key.

However, after grabbing a shower and dressing in jeans and a dark green T-shirt, and sending at least ten messages to Jesse which are ignored, I finally make my way into the breakfast room and look around anxiously for him. I slump as I realise he isn't here.

"Can I get you a table, sir?"

The voice comes from my side, and, as I turn to the waitress, I spot Max. "No, it's okay," I say quickly, giving her a weak smile. "I'm going to sit with him."

"He's a popular man this morning," she says, smiling.

"Oh, erm. Oh," I say in dawning realisation. "Was my friend sitting with him, by any chance? Tall with brown hair."

"You mean Jesse?"

I smile because that's so him. Everyone always seems to know him, wherever he is. "That's the one."

"Yes, he sat with the other gentleman before he left."

I toy with the idea of asking her where he's gone, but abandon it as a couple come in behind me. Leaving her to seat them, I walk quickly over to Max.

He looks up and smiles coolly. "Ah, here's Casanova. I'm surprised you could walk this morning."

I groan and throw myself into the seat opposite him. "I take it Jesse told you, then."

He shakes his head. "Zeb, you're a bloody fuckwit."

I blink. "Please don't hold back."

He leans forward, pointing his fork at me in quite a threatening manner. "I don't know when your brain vaporized but it must be a recent thing. What the hell were you thinking of?"

"Thank you," I say in vindication and then I sigh. "It was such a stupid thing to do. I just got caught up in the heat of the moment and the next thing I knew we were in bed and... Why are you looking at me like that?"

He shakes his head in apparent disbelief. "That's not the mistake I was referencing. I'm not talking about you sleeping with him, for fuck's sake."

"Then what are you talking about?"

"This morning's behaviour," he says loudly and then lowers his voice as some people at nearby tables turn to stare at us. "I'm talking about you acting like we're in the plot of *Poldark*, and you've just despoiled a virgin."

I shoot a quick glance around, but everyone has gone back to their breakfasts. "I panicked," I mutter. "It wasn't the best thing I've ever done."

"You're telling me. It was unkind."

"Oh, I see you got the full story," I say, stung because Max doesn't look like this at me. He's always looked up to me. "Jesse didn't waste much time."

He looks even more disappointed, if that's possible, and my stomach churns. "He hardly said anything. I just got the whole picture from a few words and his general air of being kicked in the fucking teeth."

I sigh and scrub my hands down my face, digging my palms into my eyes. "Shit, I knew I hurt him. I handled it so badly."

"Yes, you did, and that should tell you something right there."

"What do you mean?"

"I mean that you *never* handle things badly. You're always

perfect. Perfect dress. Perfect manners. Perfect way to deal with every situation."

"Nice to know you noticed."

He doesn't take the bait. "And now look at you running around the foyer in just a sheet, offending Nina and Patrick at every turn."

"Who told you that?"

"I'm a journalist," he says primly. "I'm an expert at getting information."

"It's not Iraq." I pause. "So, you're agreeing with me, then?" He stares at me, so I elaborate. "I'm behaving very foolishly. The whole thing is a big mistake, and after I've apologised to Jesse, hopefully we can go back to our own lives and..."

"No."

I nod. "Exactly. Wait. What? What do you mean no?"

"You're missing my point, Zeb. Those things aren't bad. They're actually good." I stare at him in absolute confusion. "Zeb, I love you. You're my brother in all but name. But Christ, you're buttoned up. You're such a fucking grown-up." I draw back, stung, and he seizes my hand. "I know what your dad was like and much as I loved him, it wasn't easy living with that." I stiffen, and he lifts my hand and kisses it swiftly. "Babe, you're wonderful and one of the most important people in my life, but you've worried me over the last few years. You hardly laugh anymore. You've become obsessed with keeping things on an even keel."

"There's nothing wrong with that."

"There is if that's all there is. You only appreciate an even keel when you've been through a few storms. You steer away from them, Zeb, and sometimes you shouldn't." He sighs as I stare at him. "Life shouldn't always be pleasant. It shouldn't always be nice. Life should be lived to the utmost, and you're just not doing it anymore. Do you know what I've seen this week?" he says fiercely. I shake my head, a little afraid to provoke him at the moment. "I've seen you laugh."

"I do that all the time."

"Name the last time, and it can't be if it was just a polite response to someone's joke so you didn't make them feel bad."

I think hard and finally shake my head. He nods in satisfaction. "Exactly. Zeb, you're a snarky, sarcastic bastard but you conceal it with mostly everyone apart from a few." He lifts his fingers and counts. "Me, Felix, and Jesse."

"Max," I say on a long sigh.

"No," he says passionately. "You're more alive with that boy than I've ever seen you before. You laugh and you're animated and just here. In the present with the rest of us mortals. I don't want you to lose that and go back to being responsible Zeb who's too bothered about other people rather than himself. You put yourself too much in their shoes when you should be kicking your own footwear off and dancing on the odd table."

"I can't help being responsible," I protest. "That's a good thing. And my responsible boring side tells me that I shouldn't do this with Jesse. He's lovely, Max. He's warm and kind and funny. He's quick-witted and clever. Why should someone like that be saddled with me? I'm forty-four. I'm twenty years older than him, for fuck's sake. Any glamour he sees in me at the moment will have long worn off by the time I'm sixty and he's only forty."

"Or maybe it won't," he says quietly. I stare at him, and he gives a small sigh. "Maybe it will never wear off. You don't know that, Zeb. You're so focused on what's going to happen down a long road that you don't stop to look at the scenery around you." He pauses before shooting me a quick intense glance. "He could die tomorrow, you know. I've seen death." His eyes darken. "Far too many times with people I've cared about. Jesse could be knocked down by a bus or have a heart attack or fall down some stairs or—"

"Shut up," I hiss. "Don't say that."

That dark gaze of his sharpens and a look of astonishment comes over his face. "You care about him?"

"Well, of course I do," I say desperately. "He's my employee and—"

"Shut up, fuckwit. You actually care about him." I open my mouth and he makes a sharp gesture with his hand. "Oh my God, this is better than I thought."

"How is it better?" I say fiercely. "Nothing can come of this."

"So you admit it?"

I stare at him for what seems like an eternity. Then I give up because Max has always won a stare-out. Even as a teenager he had preternatural patience. "I do care for him," I say slowly. "I want the best for him, and the best is going to be someone younger and less damaged." I think of all the things Patrick flung at me in our last major row when I'd come home and found him in bed with his best friend. Hours of shouting. Mainly by him. I remember the criticism and steel myself.

"It's good you know what's best for everyone, Zeb," Max says, popping the last piece of toast in his mouth. "Maybe you should give the Tory party a ring and see if you can sort out Brexit. Or maybe ring up the Kardashians and ask them to stop taking pictures of themselves."

He sits back, obviously abandoning the argument of how good I am with Jesse. As much as I wanted him to shut up, I now immediately want him to start again and list more reasons why I should be with Jesse.

Instead I make myself relax. "Maybe to the first, but the second is hopeless. Mankind was doomed as soon as the first camera was invented."

After breakfast, I wander the hotel looking in every room downstairs, but Jesse is nowhere to be found. Max had refused to tell me where he'd gone and said I deserved to wonder because I was a shithead. He'd then informed me that he wasn't stopping at the hotel any longer because he couldn't bear to watch me being a twat and stated his intention of buggering off home. I'd given him the two-finger salute, and we'd parted with a fierce hug as normal.

When I come to the function room, I find twenty people standing by easels in front of a huge floral display. I look around but don't spy Jesse. It doesn't surprise me, as he'd come out in hives if he had to spend this long standing still. However, I still slump in disappointment.

"What are you doing?"

I spin round when I hear Patrick's voice and sigh inside. I could do without this. "Just looking," I say slowly. "You not painting?"

"Not fucking likely. I'd rather eat my own testicle with a rusty spoon." I shake my head, and he looks around. "Lost your little twink? Need a hand looking for him?"

"I don't need your hand with anything," I say evenly. "And please don't call him that in such a derogatory tone."

He laughs incredulously. "What the hell is the matter with you? You need to chill out, Zeb. You've got even more uptight, if that's possible, since you've been with him."

"Don't be ridiculous."

"Oh, *I'm* ridiculous," he says, still giving me that smile that makes him look like a tosser. "I think that title might belong to the middle-aged bloke sticking it to a twenty-something."

I spin round and something in my face must warn him, because he steps back quickly. "You need to shut the fuck up," I say quietly but so forcefully that he blanches. "I'm getting very fucking tired of the way you're talking about Jesse. He's my guest, and if you don't like him, then there's a simple solution. We can both fuck off."

"You'd go with him? You're my best man."

I stare at him. "What bit about him being my date are you getting confused about?"

"Please. He's like a fucking chip wrapper. Easy to dump."

I open my mouth to say something I'm pretty sure I won't regret, and then we both turn as Frances comes up next to us. "What are you two boys talking so intently about?" she asks with an edge to her voice.

I smile innocently at her. "Patrick was just saying how he really wants to do some painting."

Patrick scowls at me but immediately pastes a smile on his face when she turns to him. "That's wonderful, darling. I'll put you next to your mother."

"Ouch," I mouth and then smile at both of them. "Well, I must be going," I say cheerfully and make my escape.

I stop outside the function room. Jesse isn't coming here, so where to next? A sudden horrible thought occurs to me. *Has he already been back and collected his stuff? Maybe he's caught the train home.*

Once that occurs to me, I'm consumed with the desire to know. I bolt up the stairs and let myself into the room. It's filled with the eerie murky gloom of a summer storm, the light turning everyday objects almost extraordinary. The wind blows outside, flinging the first few drops of rain at the window.

The room is tidy because housekeeping has been in. I rush over to the wardrobe, flinging it open and then subsiding with a sigh of relief when I see his clothes jammed in there in a disorganised mess.

A crack of thunder shakes the air and a few seconds later there's a flash of lightning. The room fills with the intense sweet scent of rain on dry earth.

I look around, filled with sudden despair. *Where is he? What if this is it? What if last night's wild events are the only time that I'll ever be with Jesse?* It's only when I think it's over that I realise how much it meant. I shake my head. I'll go downstairs and wait in the foyer. Lunch will be served soon, and he won't miss that.

I turn, and it's only then that I notice the steam coming from the bathroom door that's slightly ajar.

"Jesse?" I call but it's drowned out by another crash and rumble of thunder. The lightning follows quickly after, so the storm must be overhead. I push the door open and promptly lose the power of speech. All I can do is stare.

The French doors onto the balcony are open, letting in the scent of the storm which mingles with the green tea aroma from the bath. The wind blows the gauzy curtains back and rain patters onto the balcony, encroaching into the room and dampening the tiles. The huge copper freestanding bath glows in the strange storm light but no more than the man inside it.

He's on his front, his arms holding onto the edges as he stares out of the window. All I can see are his wide shoulders and the sleek muscled planes of his back leading down to the globes of his arse which are just above the waterline. All that sleek olive skin glows in the light, so for a second my fanciful mind passes me visions of the way the gods used to come down to Earth to tempt mankind.

He turns to look at me, and I dismiss the notion. No god ever used that cross expression to tempt someone.

"Here you are," he says almost casually. "I wondered when you'd turn up."

I lean back against the sink and cross my arms over my chest, trying to conceal the fact that they're shaking slightly. "I've been looking everywhere for you."

He shakes his head, the ends of his hair spraying water over high cheekbones that have become flushed. "And yet here I am."

"Well, I never thought you'd be in the suite."

"Why?" He laughs. "Oh, because you binned me in here this morning."

"What a terrible expression. And I never binned you. I just said it was a mistake that couldn't happen again."

My words trail off, and he shakes his head again. "Like I said. Binned."

I'm trying valiantly to pay attention to his words but all I can see are those tight arse cheeks, and my head is filled with the sounds of the sex last night and the way he felt when I pushed into him. It was sex unlike anything I've had before. A connection that I've never shared with another person.

I realise that he's watching me with a sardonic expression, and I open my mouth, but he shakes his head.

"Here's what's going to happen, Zebedee."

"Do not call me that," I say faintly, but he talks over me.

"You are going to take all your clothes off, and then you're going to grab the lube and condom from where I placed them earlier, and then you're going to fuck me in the bath. After that, we're going to bed where I'll probably fuck you. Next, we'll order some proper food from room service, and then maybe we'll fit another round in." He looks me up and down challengingly. "If you've got another one in you when I've finished with you."

I actually don't know what to say. My cock unfortunately knows who its boss is, because it stiffens immediately. I find my voice. "But what happened to me hurting you and you storming off?"

He shifts position and turns around, leaning his elbows back on the bath so his body is a glorious golden arch. His prick is hard and visibly throbbing.

He raises one wicked eyebrow. "I decided I wasn't ready to stop having sex with you." I blink, and he gives an evil sort of smile, and I just know that this is Jesse unleashed. "I figured we've done it once, so why not be hung for a sheep as a lamb. Whatever that means."

He frowns for a second as he thinks about the idiom, and I want to get down on my knees and thank someone because there's my Jesse peeking out at me.

Then he shutters his expression. "Time's a-wastin', Zebedee. Strip and get over here and fuck me before I find someone else to do it."

"I know you think you've won," I say darkly, starting to take my clothes off despite my brain trying to shout a deterrent.

He shrugs, his eyes running over me like a brand. "You're about to be naked. I think that's done it."

I feel ridiculously flattered as I look down at my body. Last night we'd tumbled around the bed under the sheets, but he'd seemed to spend the night surgically attached to me. This is different, and it feels like being under a spotlight. However, when I look at him, I can see the way his pupils have expanded and his breathing has picked up, and I take heart from it.

The thunder crashes and the room is filled with the sound of the rain as I strip the last of my clothes off, throwing them to the floor in a careless abandon that's never been me. I grab the condom and the lube, noticing with a corner of my mind that it's waterproof, and step into the bath. The water comes up to my shins and the scent of green tea is rich on the air. The wind blows through cold on my skin, and I shiver slightly, watching him as he lies back against the glowing copper of the bath. It makes his skin shine like he's an otherworldly being.

I look at his face as he stares at my cock and hide a smile. He's firmly of the earth, my Jesse. Lusty and so real. I still for a second. *My Jesse?* Where the fuck did that come from? Then he slowly sits up and rolls over onto his front and scatters my thoughts.

"Do get on with it," he says in a bored voice that's slightly ruined by the hoarseness he can't conceal.

I swallow hard at the sight of the taut globes of his arse glistening with water. "Stop issuing orders," I say thickly. He wriggles his arse and I give in to temptation and slap the cheeks. He stiffens as if outraged and shoots me a fiery glance back.

"Fuck off," he mutters.

"I don't think you want that," I whisper. Setting the condom and lube on the side of the bath, I kneel down behind him and fold myself over him, not even attempting to conceal my groan as I feel his buttocks cradling the weight of my cock. I look down, grabbing his hips, and push my cock up and down through the clench of his cheeks a few times. It looks so dirty and hot, a visual I know I'm going to store in my head forever.

He gives a low wild moan and pushes back against me so for a second my bare cock catches on his hole. "Oh fuck," I gasp as the sensitive skin of the head pushes into the wrinkled skin and nudges him.

He throws his head back, his knuckles whitening on his grip of the side of the bath. "Yes," he gasps. "Fuck me."

"Not like this," I say, hearing the hoarseness in my voice. "You're not ready yet, love." He stills for a second, but I don't give him chance to think. Instead, I lean down and, parting the cheeks of his arse, I snuggle my tongue in behind his balls. Pushing against the sensitive skin there, I listen to his loud shout with satisfaction before licking up along his taint until I come to his hole.

I trace my tongue over the wrinkled opening, feeling a tiny flutter there and noting that he's starting to pant. Using my hands, I push his cheeks apart and blow cool air across his opening. It clenches and I chuckle, feeling it deep in my stomach, before leaning in and starting to suckle the little hole.

He cries out and pushes his bum demandingly towards me, and I go to town on him, exchanging long licks of my tongue with sucking, biting kisses and then pushing my tongue inside him as the hole slackens.

"Ungh," he shouts, and I inhale greedily, taking the smell of him into me. It's Jesse at his basest – clean skin and a dark scent that makes my mouth water and my cock throb almost painfully.

He lowers one of his hands and I reach round and slap his wandering hand. "That's mine," I say hoarsely, looking up. "You don't touch yourself. It's my job." I return almost frantically to fucking my tongue inside him, listening to his cries and sending my hand down to encircle his cock. It's hard and wet and he shuttles through my fist with a desperate gasp. His movements get more frantic until I realise almost too late that he's about to come.

"No, you don't," I gasp, reaching down and grabbing his balls and pulling them gently. He subsides against the bath, his head down, panting. And suddenly I need to see him.

"Out," I bark. "I need to fuck you."

We tumble out of the bath and, pausing only to throw a bath sheet onto the tiled floor near the window, I take him down onto it, rolling him onto his back and coming down over him. He makes a move as if to roll over and I shake my head. I'm shivering as if I have a fever. "Need to see you," I gasp.

He stills, his chest rising and falling as he drags in air. "Why?" he gasps.

I shake my head. *How can he not see what he does to me?* "Jesse," I say hoarsely. "It's you."

"A mistake." The bitterness is obvious, and I blanch.

"*No*," I say fiercely. "The mistake was mine."

"I don't want to talk," he says petulantly. "I just need fucking."

I stare down at him and know I'm onto a loser at the moment. "I'll do that," I say, holding his face gently so he's forced to look at me. His eyes are dark and almost lost. "But we're talking after that," I say softly. "I'm so lost in you, Jesse."

He stares inscrutably back at me for a long second and I wonder what he's thinking. I still. *When did this become so important to me?* The thought vanishes into vapour as he reaches one long arm up and knocks the condom and lube onto the floor by the side of me.

Movement catches my attention, and I turn my head and still when I see that we're lying in front of the huge floor-to-ceiling mirror. He catches my gaze and looks beyond me before smiling wickedly. "Hot," he says and, grabbing my head, he pulls me forward and kisses me, and I lose my mind.

I don't think anyone would do differently. My arms are full of his hot slippery body, and I kiss him wildly, eating at his mouth with choked gasps and twining my hands in the soft dampness of his hair almost as if I want to be absorbed into him. I rut against him, sending my cock over the sharp groove of his iliac muscle and feeling his cock rubbing against me, leaving a trail of wetness.

It doesn't take long for me to feel my balls draw up and I pull back, clenching the base of my cock tight to stop myself from coming. He stares at me in the dim storm light before opening his legs wide so I can see him. I grasp his knee and look to my side, seeing us in the mirror's reflection. I almost don't recognise myself. My hair is wild and my expression wrecked. I'm flushed and lust-struck, staring down at him sprawled in erotic abandon, his legs open and his arms flung wide.

I grab the bottle of lube and pour a stream onto my fingers, rubbing to warm it before placing one finger at his entrance. I'm still staring at the mirror as my reflection slowly inserts it into him and he throws his head back, his face flushed and his eyes dark.

He grabs my hand as I go to insert another finger and shakes his head. "I don't need any more," he pants.

"Sweetheart, I'm not hurting you."

Again the endearment. But I don't think he even hears it. "I don't need it," he says again. "I like the burn." He shakes his head violently. "Please, Zeb. Don't look at me."

He throws his hand over his face as if to hide, and I pull it back gently before reaching down and kissing him. I suck on that full lower lip before pulling back. "You think that I'm so controlled?" I say hoarsely. "You think I have the power?" He stares at me, and I shake my head. "*You* have the power, Jesse. You always have."

Something alters in his face, but instead of saying anything, he lifts his legs and pulls his knees up, holding himself open for me.

"Shit, that's so hot," I breathe and reaching out, I grab the condom. I fumble with it as he watches me with dark eyes.

When it's finally on, I lower myself over him, positioning my dick against the small hole. I open my mouth to ask again, and he shakes his head crossly, so instead I push in. It's hard going, as he's still tight, so I go gently, pausing often, but I'm relieved to see the pleasure in his face, the almost blind look in his eyes as he focuses inward on the feel of my cock in him.

Finally, I bottom out and I groan helplessly at the feel of that tight sheath milking my prick. For a wild moment I wonder what it would be like to be bare in him, to feel him burn me from the inside and to spill in there feeling it hot around my cock. I moan at the thought, and he lowers his legs to twine them around my hips as I start to thrust.

I piston into him, slowly at first, alternating deep thrusts with shallow ones, hearing his groans in my ear as I watch our reflection in the tarnished depths of the mirror. It's like we're one body joined as we grunt and heave together. I watch his arms and legs band around me and the blind joy in my expression.

I'm broader than him and I look almost protective as I hover over him, forcing my cock into him. My tanned skin shines in the low light, darker against the olive tones of his. His dark hair gleams in the light as he throws his head back and moans long and low. His mouth is open and his eyes clenched shut. I stare again at that reflection as my hips sling back and forth. *We look beautiful together,* I have time to think.

Then the pleasure seizes me in its grip like the storm overhead, and I start to thrust deep and hard, grunting each time I bottom out. He cries out, lowering his hand to grab his cock as he writhes under me, the thunder crashing overhead. I can feel the spray of the rain from the open balcony doors cold on my hot skin and the ticklish sensation as the gauzy curtains blow over our bodies.

Then the lightning flashes, lighting the room, and he screams and arches up. I lower my head to watch come shoot from his cock, jerking in creamy spasms over the taut skin of his abdomen and chest. My balls draw up, and I gasp before feeling the come shoot out of me hot inside the condom as I batter into him, riding out the most intense orgasm I've ever felt, inside the tight clench of his body.

I don't know where I go, but when I come to properly we're lying on the bed, our bodies still wet and the sheets damp beneath us. The storm has moved away, and there's just the gentle patter of the rain on the balcony outside. I look down and smile at Jesse. He's curled into my side, his head resting on my chest and his arm and leg flung over me almost as if he doesn't want to let go. The thought warms my chest.

His eyes are closed, showing off how ridiculously long his lashes are. Like black feathers. As I watch him, his eyes open and I find myself speared by the chocolate-coloured depths. For a long second, we study each other. All the fire he greeted me with has gone now and in its place is what seems to be confusion.

I'm instantly seized with the fierce desire to ease him. I think it's always been there, to be honest. It's in the way I took him off the jobs with younger men and made him dig gardens for old people, the way I've always watched out for him and tried to smooth his way. *A bit like an aging Walter Raleigh*, I think wryly. *Trying to spread my cloak on the ground so he doesn't get soaked by life's problems.*

"Alright?" I ask quietly.

He nods solemnly, his eyes fixed on mine.

"What are you thinking?" I ask, suddenly seized with this huge curiosity about how he thinks and feels. It's at this point that I should back away, because that's always been my launchpad in the past to becoming fascinated by someone. I wait for the panic to hit that I'm feeling it towards this beautiful boy, but for some reason it doesn't come.

"I'm thinking I like this," he finally says, and my heart clenches at the courage it must have taken to say that when I'd treated him so badly this morning.

I dive straight into speech. "I like it too." His eyes widen in surprise for a split second before he conceals his gaze, his lashes swooping down to cover that bright gaze. "Oi," I say quietly and he looks at me again. "I am *so* sorry about today," I say firmly. He opens his mouth, and I shake my head. "Please let me say it." He nods, and I take a deep breath. "I never should have reacted like that. It was horrible, and I was unkind because I panicked. And that was because I am older than you, Jess. You deserve a lot more than some middle-aged bloke who's too scared to try." I look at him as he watches me from his spot on my chest. "But I'm not too scared now," I say softly, and he jerks slightly.

"What?"

I huff. "I think you might have noticed that I can't keep my hands off you."

I grab his hand, examining the long slender fingers and bitten nails, and, seized with a stupid tenderness, I bring it to my lips and press a kiss into the palm. He folds his fingers over it reflexively, as if holding the kiss, and stares at me, still silent as I speak.

"I've had all day to think about this, and I don't *want* to keep my hands off you. I want you more than I've ever wanted anyone, Jess. I don't know where it's going, but I know I don't want to stop now. I want to–" I hesitate. "We're going back tomorrow, and I want to see you again. Not just for sex," I say quickly as he stares at me, his eyes as bright as a penny. "I want to get to know you."

"Are you saying you want to go out with me?"

I feel my cheeks flush. "What a terrible expression. No, I'm not doing that."

"Would you rather pay your addresses to my father and arrange to court me? I'll make sure my mum's got a good book for when she's sitting in the same room chaperoning us."

"You're hilarious," I try to say and then just give up and laugh. Sometimes it's easier to cut out the middleman and head straight to Jesse Land. And it's such a relief to hear his humour again after what I did.

I sober. "I can't promise forever like those books you read," I say softly. "I mean–"

He stops me talking with the simple move of putting his hand over my mouth. "No one can say that at the beginning of a story," he says quietly. "It's always saved to the end of the book." He smiles calmly at me, and I feel moisture in the back of my eyes at his trusting expression. "I want to try that too, Zeb. I really want to."

I draw him into a hug, squeezing him until he wheezes and starts to laugh. When I let him go, his merry face is front and centre again, and I smile helplessly back. "Then let's try," I say.

And that's how simply we start our story.

CHAPTER TEN

Jesse

The knock at the door of the flat interrupts my nervous pacing. I race over to the door and then stop, reminding myself that I don't want to look too keen. I shake my head. I'm sure I'll give that away at some point. I take a deep breath and rub my damp palms down my jeans before flinging open the door. Zeb is leaning against the wall outside the flat with a very quizzical expression on his face.

"I was wondering whether you'd changed your mind," he says. There's a wry note to his voice, but for some reason I'm sure there's a bit of truth in that statement.

"Not likely," I say briskly. I wink at him. "I just had a bit of a job navigating my way around the huge parcel that arrived today."

For a second he looks mystified and then I watch in fascination as a tide of red floods over his face. "Oh erm," he stammers, and I take pity on him.

"Do come in. Watch out for the gigantic expensive picture though."

He edges his way into the flat, and I shut the door behind him, suppressing a smile as he tries to look anywhere other than at the six-foot picture of pink peonies that's propped against my lounge wall. Ivo Ashworth-Robinson's work looks rather incongruous in my drab lounge with the peeling paper and beanbags. Like a very expensive racehorse sitting in a cow shed.

I fold my arms and look at Zeb. He's wearing white jeans with a faded denim shirt and leather deck shoes, but I'm particularly loving the way he's accessorised with a severe case of the fidgets.

"It looks very nice," he finally says in a slightly high voice.

"It certainly does," I say blandly. "Not *quite* the setting it's used to though."

For a second we stare at each other and then he breaks. "I'm sorry," he mutters, running his hand through his hair. "It's just that you loved it so much in the gallery, and I wanted you to have it."

"I love Ryan Reynolds too. When is he arriving?"

"Not for a while. We ran into problems with Customs." I laugh, and he shakes his head. "He couldn't cope with you anyway," he says dryly. "He'd be checking in for mental health care within twenty-four hours."

I laugh again and tug on his shirt to pull him closer. I can see the flare of nerves in his eyes, and I welcome it because they're a twin to the flutters in my belly.

"Thank you. I love it so much. It's the nicest present I've ever had," I breathe and bridge the gap between us to kiss him. For a second he's still and our mouths rest against each other almost in astonishment that we're here. Then he's in movement, pulling me close, his hands on my lower back as he licks into my mouth. I open my mouth, moaning under my breath as his hands slide lower, grabbing my arse and tugging me sharply into him so I can feel the weight of his big cock against mine.

He moans, and I push my hands under his shirt, feeling the satiny hot skin underneath the sun-warmed denim. I rub my hands there, and I'm just pushing his shirt up further when I hear a key in the door. We break apart almost guiltily as the front door opens and Charlie appears.

"Afternoon," he says. He looks between us. "Oh sorry, have I interrupted a work meeting? Are you having an appraisal?"

Zeb looks at me in a panicked way, and I try to stop myself but burst out laughing anyway.

"He's joking." I snort. "Your face."

Zeb sags. "You know?" he says to Charlie, and Charlie shrugs.

"The expensive artwork kind of gave the game away," he says, smiling. "The last gift he got off a bloke was a voucher for a McDonalds breakfast."

"Nice to know the bar is set low."

"It's buried so far beneath us the kangaroos will find it soon," I say slightly mournfully.

Zeb looks at Charlie. "Well, I'm pleased to meet you properly," he says, holding his hand out to shake, and we both stare as Charlie immediately backs up.

"Better not, mate," he says. "I've got cat piss all over my hands."

"Ugh," I say, and Zeb blinks.

"How lovely," he says faintly.

Charlie shakes his head crossly. "A customer brought her library books back today covered in it. Then she had the nerve to say she shouldn't have to pay for them because they were still readable."

"What did you say?" Zeb asks, staring fascinated at Charlie.

He shrugs. "I told her just because you can, doesn't mean you should. I mean, I'm dateable, but it doesn't automatically follow that Henry Cavill is going to take advantage of that."

"*Henry*," I say slightly longingly, and we both sigh before recalling ourselves. Zeb is watching us with a wry look on his face.

"So what happened?" he asks.

"She paid. But one of the volunteers then spent the whole afternoon trying to sponge the books clean so we could use them again." He pauses and shrugs. "Council cuts," he says to Zeb, who nods. "Anyway, to cut a long cat-pee-scented story short, she failed, but not until everyone smelt like an old lady's front room."

"Is that a euphemism?" I enquire, and Charlie winces.

"Fuck off. Don't be disgusting."

"The last librarian I saw was in *The Mummy*," Zeb says. "That sliding ladder always fascinated me."

"Trust me, I'd rather tackle Imhotep than old Mrs Saunders who keeps Tipp-Exing the swear words out in the large-print books."

Zeb laughs and Charlie looks at both of us, his eyes bright with curiosity and a hefty dose of amusement. "So, you're going out, then?"

"We are," I say grandly. "*I* am planning our afternoon and evening entertainment."

"Shit," Charlie mutters. He smirks at Zeb. "It's not too late to run. The last time he organised anything we ended up in Dover."

"Was that bad?"

"It was, considering we were supposed to be in Edinburgh."

Zeb laughs and smiles at me. It's more, somehow. Still tinged with amusement but there's something extra in that smile that makes my heart beat faster. "I'll take the gamble," he says softly.

Charlie grins. "Well, I'm off to remove the stunning fragrance of Moggy Number Five. Have a good time."

He disappears, and Zeb looks at me steadily. "You ready?" he asks, and something in his eyes tells me that he half expects me to run away.

I nod and step closer to him. "For anything," I say deliberately, and he swallows and nods.

"Let's go, then. Show me this date, Casanova."

An hour later he looks up at our destination and blinks. "So, our date is Stanfords, the bookshop?"

I nod happily. "The *travel* bookshop," I emphasise. "Have you ever been in here?"

He shakes his head. "No, I haven't travelled much." He looks almost shamefaced. "I always wanted to, but there was never enough time. My dad was too busy to travel when I was a kid," he finishes almost inaudibly, and my heart twists. His dad was probably too busy getting married. He seems to have been the Zsa Zsa Gabor of London.

"Well, can I just say that I'm profoundly grateful to have discovered somewhere that you haven't been with Patrick yet," I say tartly to cover up his embarrassment.

His face clears. "There are a lot of places I didn't go with Patrick, and a bookshop would be number one on the list."

"Did he read much?"

"Only his horoscope."

"Did he believe in all that?"

He shrugs. "Only in so far that it suited him. If he didn't like his own forecast, he'd take one from another star sign."

"He cheated at astrology?" I say and my voice is far too delighted.

He shakes his head. "I'm getting the impression you don't like Patrick."

"I can't imagine where that comes from," I say innocently, and when he shoots me a glance, I smile brightly. "Luckily, I have been here before, which is why I am such an astounding guide for you."

"So, our date is in a bookshop?" he says again.

I nod happily. "Not just any bookshop, though. This one was frequented by people like Florence Nightingale, Captain Scott, and Ernest Shackleton. Oh, and Jesse, Eli, Misha, and Charlie for the Amsterdam trip that shall forever be remembered for Charlie falling in the canal and being rescued by a man wearing leather chaps." He laughs, and I grin back at him. "We do have a mission though," I say solemnly as he goes to open the door. He pauses and steps back to allow a couple behind us to go through, and we move to the side, out of the way.

"A *mission*? What sort of date is this?" he asks.

"The best. Our mission is to each choose a travel guide to a country that we'd like to visit."

"Why?"

I nudge him. "Were you an unusually curious child, Zebadiah? Because all the signs are pointing that way." He opens his mouth to answer, and I hold up my hand. "We are doing this so we can get to know something about each other. This is how people date."

He shakes his head. "It's how *you* date. I'm not sure about anyone else. What happened to dinner and drinks?"

"Zeb, Zeb, that's other people, baby."

"Please don't call me baby," he says in a slightly anguished voice.

"What shall I call you, then? Bunny? Pet? Lovie? Princess?"

"No," he says in a revolted tone of voice.

"Anyway, Mr Evans," I say loudly. "That sort of boring date is not for us."

"It isn't?"

"Nuh-uh. No. We are going to do dating a different way."

He folds his arms and grins at me. His smile is wide, his eyes very blue, and for a second I lose my train of thought.

I shake my head to clear it. "I was thinking about this last night, and I came to an executive decision." I wink at him. "I put the word executive in there. You should be thrilled."

"Ecstatic," he drawls, and I snort.

"Okay, you dated Patrick for five years during which you no doubt alternated periods of being extremely bored with the odd bit of wanting to murder him." His mouth twitches. "You probably did lots of really boring stuff. While you were doing that, I didn't so much date as just try to keep up with whatever criminal impulses my dates had towards my money." He straightens, looking cross, and I wave my hand. "Never mind," I say airily. "The point is that you and I are different."

I sober quickly. *Are we, though? Are we different or am I just an amusement and he'll go back to what he knows?*

"We are different," he says quietly, his eyes steady on mine. "Don't ask me how, but we are."

I smile gratefully at him. "So, we're each going to come up with dates that are different. Something a bit quirky. Something that shows the other person something about us." I wave my hand at the bookshop, its windows shining in the sun. "This is mine. I love travelling. I've been all over the world, usually on a very small budget. This is always my first port of call." I pause before looking hard at him. "But absolutely no sex tonight."

He blinks and an old man huffs disapprovingly as he walks past us.

"Thank you for broadcasting that to the entire street," Zeb says dryly. "You know I live to share my personal life with complete strangers."

I smile somewhat nervously. "I don't think we should have sex while doing these dates," I say softly.

"Why?"

The bald question surprises me, and for a second I fumble with an answer. "Because we know we're good in bed together." I pause. "We're actually epic in bed." He smiles slowly with heat in his eyes, and I shake my head. "But if we're trying this, I don't want to get waylaid by that. Because otherwise that's all we'll ever be." I look at him nervously. "What do you think?"

He's silent for a long second, his eyes examining my face as if he's thinking of picking me out in a line-up. Then he smiles. "I agree."

I sag. "You do?"

He nods. "I want to get to know you, not just your arsehole."

There's a horrified gasp behind him and he sighs and closes his eyes.

I laugh and grab his arm. "We'd better go inside, Zeb," I say in a loud voice. "You really need to learn some discretion."

I usher him into the bookshop, inhaling the scent of the books greedily and looking for the wall of globes which has always fascinated me. When I look at him, he's doing the same thing. When he meets my eyes, we smile at each other in perfect accord.

"Okay," I say. "We're going to split up to make our choices. We'll meet when we've chosen and discuss our books."

"You're so bossy," he murmurs.

I wink at him. "And you like it."

"Only in the way I like it when the tap stops dripping."

I shake my head but can't stop my laugh. It's far too loud and a few people turn to look at us "Go on," I say, pushing him gently. "You're a bad influence on me."

He grins, and I watch as he moves away. I can't take my eyes off him, normally, but there's something extra about him today. I study him as he moves to a shelf, running one long finger along the spines of the books, and I suddenly realise what it is. He's open and welcoming. Usually, he's sardonic and closed off, but today all that has softened. His face is alive and engaged as he pulls a book down and leans against the shelf to flick though it.

Something in me twists because this man has the capacity to really hurt me. The pain I felt when he binned me was just an early warning sign. There have been other warnings too. The way he closes himself down like a hedgehog at the first sign of trouble, the fact that he seems to think he's an OAP, and his conviction that I'm too young for him. However, I've casually blitzed through all of these warning markers.

I could be heading straight for a lot of heartache, but somehow, as I look at his absorbed face, the tangle of his hair, and his beautiful face, I can't bring myself to step back.

I watch him for a few precious seconds more and then, smiling, I wander along to make my choice of travel guide and then over to my favourite set of shelves that contain the maps.

Half an hour later, I'm happily ensconced in one of the very comfortable leather chairs when I smell oranges and sandalwood. When I look up, he's leaning against the shelf watching me with a smile tugging on his lips.

"Did you get something?" I ask, grinning up at him.

He holds up a guide to Rome. "I've always wanted to go there," he says. I start to laugh and he stares at me. "What on earth is so funny?" he asks, looking slightly upset.

I fumble with my carrier bag and then pull out the book I bought. A travel guide of Rome. "Snap," I say, and he looks astonished.

"Really? You've never been?"

I shake my head. "It's the sort of place you want to go with a partner. Someone who you can really share things with. Not with a group of lads more interested in finding a bar."

He stares at me for a long beat, and I wonder whether he too is hoping that we'll go there together because I can imagine Zeb and myself in Rome, wandering the streets, holding hands and eating in little street cafes.

He straightens up and predictably changes the subject. "I was standing here for a few minutes. You were very absorbed," he says and pauses. "In the ordnance survey map." He shakes his head. "Jesse, you're a never-ending source of surprises to me."

I grin at him. "Is it the map? Did you expect me to be dancing around a glitter ball in my go-go shorts?"

He snorts. "Not in the place where Florence bought her maps," he says in an outraged tone which is spoilt by the laughter in his voice. He edges closer. "Why are you reading that?" he asks, lively interest in his eyes.

I stand up and move next to him, unfolding the map. "I love these things," I say, feeling almost embarrassed. I've never shown this geeky side of myself to anyone before.

"Why?" he asks, his eyes intent on my face, which I'm sure is slightly flushed.

"It's like finding treasure," I say slowly. "Most people only look at a road atlas, if they look at all, because now the first instinct is to check your phone." I shrug. "A road atlas is fine, but it doesn't tell you anything interesting."

"What do you mean?" he asks, genuine interest in his voice.

I give him the edge of the map to hold and move my finger along the lines. "Look. A road atlas would tell you that this road in Yorkshire leads to this town. But *our* map tells you so much more. It tells you that there's also a footpath that leads you to a small war memorial and then, further along, the remnants of an ancient barrow. If we move west, we'll also find some abbey ruins." I shrug. "Treasure. There's something wonderful about walking along one of the ancient roads in the sunshine, tracing the path of people who walked there thousands of years before."

I look up and go still at the intent look on his face. "What?" I start to say, but he shuts me up with the simple act of leaning forward and kissing me. It's an innocent kiss with no tongues and no touching anywhere apart from our lips. But his lips are soft and plush, and even though there's an inch or two of space between our bodies it feels like he's surrounding me. When he pulls back, I blink, and he smiles. It's wide and so warm that it makes my heart beat faster.

He looks down and a smug expression crosses his face. He taps my hand. "I think you'll need to buy that map now," he says happily.

I look down and see that it's now creased in my hands. "Gah," I mutter, and he grins, looking impossibly young somehow.

"Maybe it's a good thing," he says softly. "I'd like to visit that barrow one sunny day."

"It's a date." His smile widens, and my heart skips a beat. "Come on," I say. "We have the first part of the date down. Now we need to get to the second part."

He follows me like an impossibly hot shadow as I pay for the map, and we emerge onto the bustle of the street.

"This way," I say, tugging his arm and feeling the muscles and heat of his skin. I pull him along the road past the small street market that is always here on a Friday. We walk past an old book stall, and we both automatically slow to examine the covers on the shelves. It makes me smile. I can't walk past books, and it appears he can't either.

Then he exclaims and darts over to the stall, plucking a book from the pile. "I'll have this one," he says to the woman behind the counter, and she smiles at his look of excitement.

"What did you get?" I ask as we move away.

"Here," he says, pushing the paper bag at me. "It's yours."

"What is it?" I pull the book from the bag and stare down at it. "*A Child's Garden of Verses* by Robert Louis Stevenson." I look up at him. "Why?"

He shrugs. His eyes are very bright, and he's actually blushing. "The point of this date so far is to get to know each other through a book. This was my favourite book of poetry when I was little. I had the version with these amazing pictures and I read it over and over again. I'm sorry. It's silly." He goes to take it back, and says "*oof*" as I elbow him in the ribs.

"Fuck off," I say indignantly. "You just gave it to me."

"It was a silly idea. The poems are very lame now."

"It's the best thing anyone has ever given me, and no poetry is ever lame." I stare at him, clutching the book to my chest protectively. "Your present means so much more. It lets me see inside you. My travel book idea seems really silly now. They didn't show you anything about me."

"On the contrary, you've shown me so much more than you think." I open my mouth to ask what that is, but he pushes his hands into my hair and brings me forward into a hard kiss. When he pulls back, I blink at him, and he smiles. "Jess, you didn't need to show me much anyway. You're an open book in yourself. I don't need a contents list or a glossary for you. You're just you, and it's wonderful."

I shake my head and put my book carefully back into the paper bag and then into my carrier bag. "Well, I have to say that I need some Cliffs Notes for you," I mutter and he laughs, slinging his arm over my shoulders and turning us to start walking.

"I'll buy you one," he says. "But I need to see what's next on this date of yours."

I eye him. "Are you enjoying yourself?"

He smiles at me. "So much. This is the best date I've ever been on."

I shrug. "Well, I am pretty epic." His laughter fills my ears, and I smile because in the walk to the next part of the date his arm stays over me, warm and solid and somehow wonderful.

When we get to our destination, he looks up. "Lick the Bowl," he reads. He turns to me with one eyebrow raised. "We're going in here?"

I nod. "This is a restaurant that serves only two things."

"And what are they?"

"Desserts," I say, smiling at him. "We're having dessert for dinner." I wink. "We're breaking all the rules here, Zebedee."

He shakes his head. "What if I don't like eating pudding?"

"I'm sure you're not quite that strange," I muse. He laughs, and I grin and tuck my hand into his arm and pull him towards the door. "If you don't like desserts, I know you'll like the other thing they serve here."

"Which is?"

"Cocktails." I smile happily. "They have over *one hundred* cocktails on the menu."

"And I suppose you've sampled all of them," he says, holding the door open for me.

I shake my head sadly. "Charlie, Eli, and I tried one night. I tried really hard, but it was no good."

"What happened?"

"I fell off my stool and had to be helped to a taxi." I look around and then sigh in relief. "Phew, the waiter isn't on tonight. He wasn't particularly happy when I threw up on his shoes."

"What a strange person," he drawls.

We give our name to the waitress who's dressed like a schoolgirl. She zips off to get our table ready, and Zeb looks after her in confusion for a second and then leans back against the wall and stares at me. "So," he says slowly. "Who's Eli? Is he an old boyfriend?"

I stare at him, flabbergasted at the level of jealousy in his voice. I don't know whether he's aware of it or not, but it's definitely there and it sends a thrill running through me.

"No," I say. "Eli's been my best friend since childhood."

His expression clears. "The Welsh one you mentioned?"

"Yes. How did you remember that?" I ask, amazed.

He shrugs. "It helps that I listen to you." He pauses. "Well, it doesn't help my mental health, but c'est la vie."

"You're so cosmopolitan, Daddy," I say, nudging him and listening to his throaty laughter with pleasure.

The waitress returns to guide us to the table, and it takes a few minutes to settle down. He looks around with interest. The restaurant is set up like a classroom with educational posters on the walls, a blackboard with the specials on it, and desks for tables.

We order our drinks and desserts. Zeb chooses a peach panna cotta while I go for the popsicle cheesecake and we both opt for Irish coffees. When the waitress leaves with a smile, he sits back and looks at me. "So, back to Eli?"

"What?" I say innocently and then laugh. "He's my best friend. Never been anything else and I think his boyfriend would have something to say if there was." I pause. "Although I'd pay to hear him say even horrible things."

He looks at me quizzically and I smile. "Eli lives with Gideon Ramsay."

He whistles. "The actor who came out last year? Eli is the nurse he was seeing?"

"Living with," I say. "And I fully expect they'll get married."

He sits back as our drinks are delivered. "So, Eli is taken," he says happily, and I grin. He shoots me a look. "Do you miss him?"

I take a sip of the hot drink, tasting the rich cream, and sigh contentedly. I nod. "A lot. I miss sharing the flat with him and so does Charlie. But he's happy and that's the most important thing. I can't see that ever changing. He and Gideon go together like toast and marmalade."

"Can you imagine doing that?"

I flick a look at him. "Of course," I say simply. "I want that. Not all of it," I add quickly. "I mean, Gideon and Eli want kids. That's not me."

"*Really?*" He sounds startled. "You don't want children?"

I shudder. "Never. No, thank you. I grew up in a family with children seeming to come out of the fucking walls. My sisters spent five years dressing me up like a goblin and pushing me around in a fucking toy pram. My brothers meanwhile either sat on me, locked me in wardrobes to see if Narnia was real, or dobbed me in."

"It's like *The Lord of the Flies*," he says wonderingly. "Do you still speak to each other as adults?"

"Of *course*. I speak to a member of my family every day. It's a red-letter day when I manage five minutes on the loo without a phone call interrupting me and giving me bossy instructions about what to do with my life." I shrug. "I'm the youngest. They all think they know better than me."

He looks almost wistful and I remember that he was an only child. "Do you wish you'd had brothers or sisters?" I ask abruptly.

He shakes his head, looking thoughtful. "No, never. It would have just meant another person who..."

He trails off. "Who what?" I ask.

He smiles almost sadly. "Another person I'd have had to be responsible for," he finally answers, tapping his fingers restlessly. I reach over and stay his fingers by squeezing his hand, and he looks surprised and grateful. It makes my throat tighten.

"So, do you want kids?" I ask.

He shakes his head. "No. Don't get me wrong, if my partner has nieces and nephews, I'd love to spoil them. But I don't want any myself."

"What do you want?" I ask impulsively.

He smiles in a soft way. "I'd like to travel. Go to all the places I've heard about." He pauses. "I'd like to do that with someone. Being on your own isn't much fun when there's so much to share."

I nod enthusiastically. "That sounds amazing. That's me too. I want to travel the world, not be tied by kids. The only person I want to be tied by is the man I end up with." I pause. "Obviously by tied I don't mean in a restrictive fashion," I say quickly. "I'm not into that. I whinge if I get a paper cut."

He bites his lip, the smile deep in his eyes. "You'd make a disgustingly bad sub anyway. Although the gag is a very appealing thought."

I laugh and drain my drink, motioning to his. "Come on. We're going to order some more drinks. We might even order another dessert just to be really decadent. And for each cocktail we drink, we have to share an embarrassing story from our past."

He groans but the twinkle in his eyes gives him away. So that's what we do. We eat and drink and laugh until the waitresses are yawning and putting up chairs on tables. And I'm never once bored. The thought scares me because my feelings are already so strong for this man. Although looking at his face full of laughter, those kind eyes, and his hot body, I know I'm going to go full steam ahead anyway.

CHAPTER ELEVEN

Zeb

The knock on the door makes my stomach fill with butterflies but it doesn't make me slow down in my rush to answer it. Just the knowledge that Jesse is on the other side makes my pace pick up.

I fling open the door and grin at him. "Somehow I thought that when I specified thirties dress you'd still come in that *Sesame Street* T-shirt."

He grins at me, his smile wide and white. "*Sesame Street* wasn't around in the thirties." He pauses. "Or was it? You'd know, being a child of that era."

He saunters past me, squawking when I grab and kiss him. He relaxes against me and for a few minutes I lose track of time. When I put him away from me, his eyes are heavy-lidded, and I can feel my lips tingling. "Hello," I whisper.

He steps closer and hugs me. "Hello," he says with a smile. It's powerful at such close range, and I swallow hard before stepping back.

"You look great," I say hoarsely. He's wearing a white shirt with a dickie bow, grey flannel trousers, and braces. His hair is pulled back loosely in a high topknot.

He grins. "Do you like the shoes? Charlie and I found them in a vintage shop in Islington."

I smile down at the two-tone brogues. "They're fantastic."

"Never mind me," he says slowly. "Look at you."

I shrug, feeling suddenly awkward. "You like?"

He nods, slowly walking round me, examining the pinstripe suit, white shirt, and black tie.

"You look gorgeous," he says and unselfconsciously rearranges the bulge in his trousers. "Tell me you've got a hat."

I grin and reach for the black fedora on the side table and put it on, tilting it at a rakish angle.

"If I hadn't instituted a no-sex ban, I would so fuck you right at this moment," he breathes.

I grin at him. Somehow it's become second nature to smile at him. He brings them out of me like the sun brings out the daisies.

"I could always alter the stupid parameters," he suggests. "Fit in a blowjob."

"I am not *fitting in* a blowjob," I say indignantly. "They should be slow." I wink at him. "And savoured." He swallows hard, staring at me as if hypnotised, and I laugh. "As much as I hate to say it, there's no time for sex, Jesse Reed. We've got a secret date to go to."

He grins at me and then cocks his head, listening to the music drifting through the flat on the speakers. "What's this song you're playing?"

"Tim Booth and Angelo Badalamenti. It's called 'Fall in Love with Me'." I swallow hard, hearing the words fall into the air between us.

He listens for a few seconds. "I like it."

"My life is complete." I laugh and edge out of his way as he pinches me. "Okay, are we ready?" I pick up my phone. "I've given the secret code, and they've sent me a location."

"Are you intending to sell me or my organs?" he asks, and I choke on my spit.

"Not really," I say mock apologetically. "I don't think I'd get much cash for you, and I'm pretty sure you should maybe look at paying money for other people's organs given your drinking history."

He laughs. "Okay, not that. How about a secret sex den?"

I make a buzzer noise. "It's not very often you're right, but you're wrong again." I hold out my hand. "Come on. I'll tell you in the taxi. He'll bugger off if we don't go down soon."

Once we're in the taxi, I hold out my phone. "That's where we're going."

He looks at the address. "That doesn't tell me much."

"Well, to be honest, you know as much as I do. I only get the address and a secret word to share to get in."

"Is this like one of those films where foolish teenagers go somewhere to play a game and get picked off one by one? In which case I'm done for. I'm pretty, and I've had sex with you. I obviously therefore deserve to be struck through with a ship's anchor."

"I don't think there are many of those in South West London," I say dubiously.

He edges closer, and I feel my arm go up so he can lean into me. I hug him tight and marvel at the fact that he smells so wonderful and that my body is also operating completely independently of my brain nowadays.

"Tell me," he whispers.

"I joined this club. It's huge. Each month they hire a location and you have to put in your code to get the address. They send it to you and you have an hour to get there."

"This is like being spies," he marvels, and I kiss the top of his head, inhaling the faint scent of eucalyptus that clings to the shiny locks. "So, what happens when we get there?"

"I'm sorry," I say smugly. "You don't have the code. I can't tell you. You'll have to guess."

His guesses get wilder and wilder, and I'm laughing as we get out of the taxi. "No to naked camel racing. Jesus Christ."

He looks around. We're standing outside what was obviously once a huge ballroom. Its Art Deco exterior is still beautiful despite the faint air of neglect clinging to it. His eyes sharpen as he looks at the queue of people waiting to get into the building. They're dressed in thirties costumes, the women glittering in the evening light in their pretty dresses, their hair arranged into jaunty bobs.

"Oh my God, this is already the best date I've ever been on," he breathes, and I squeeze his hand.

"Me too," I say softly. But it's not because of the costumes or the air of excitement. It's to do with him and the thought that I'd be happy walking round Sainsbury's if I was with him. Nobody makes me laugh like him or challenges my brain so much.

I push the thought away and pull him over to the queue, which is moving quickly now that the doors have opened. Within five minutes, I've given the code to the bouncer dressed in a black suit with a white silk scarf thrown jauntily around his neck, and we're inside.

Jesse looks around avidly as we move past people giving their coats to hat-check girls dressed in tight, black silk dresses. The huge double doors are thrown open, and I hear his gasp.

The inside of the Art Deco ballroom is huge. A wide wooden dance floor is already half full of people dancing to the live jazz band that are playing, and the long bar is busy with people ordering cocktails. But what makes it most magical is the fact that there are no overhead lights on. Instead, it's softly lit by huge lanterns and the candles that are everywhere, sending shadows dancing up the walls as if the ghosts of old partygoers are still around.

"Oh my God, this is like a film on prohibition I watched the other day," Jesse shouts in my ear.

I smile and pull him close. "That's what they're emulating. They've taken over all sorts of venues, apparently. They set up and then pull it all down the next day and move on to another venue." I look around. "I must say this is a good place, though. Very atmospheric."

I pull him through the crowd to the bar, and after consulting him, I buy us each an Old Fashioned. We move off to a gilt table tucked in the corner with a view over the dance floor. A lively tune is playing, and for a few minutes we sip our drinks and watch people dancing. It reminds me of an old newsreel film, watching the almost courtly movements. Very different from a nightclub.

Jesse edges close to me, throwing his arm around my waist and resting his chin on my shoulder. "I love it," he says fervently. "This is amazing."

I shoot him a look. He's so beautiful this close up. "You really like it?"

He nods. "I've never done anything like this before. Thank you, sweetheart."

"I thought we vetoed the endearments," I say hoarsely, ignoring the thrill that went through me at hearing it.

He kisses me quickly and pulls back, leaving the faint taste of his cocktail on my lips. I lick over the taste.

"You vetoed it. I didn't," he says calmly and takes a sip of his drink. "Okay, why this for a date?"

"I wanted to do something different. I'd heard about this club where you pay membership, and they organise this, and thought you'd get a kick out of it."

"I do," he assures me, his eyes dark and shiny in the candlelight. "I really do."

"And I like this era," I say slowly. "It's fun to dress up like this and be a part of this."

"Why this era?"

I hum contemplatively. "It was a very glamorous time," I finally say. "It reminds me of my grandfather. He used to sing in the clubs. He was offered a recording contract at one point. They wanted to set him up to rival Frank Sinatra."

"Did he get it?"

I shake my mind. "No. They wanted him to go to America and he'd met and fallen in love with my grandmother by then."

"Did he regret it?"

"No, never. I asked him once and he said what could Hollywood offer him that he couldn't find with my grandmother. He said no woman could ever have been more beautiful than her. It must have been the right decision. They were married for sixty years." I shrug. "I think they were a bit nonplussed by my father's matrimonial habits."

He snorts. "Just a bit." He takes off my hat and brushes my hair back from my forehead, his fingers cool against my skin. "Were you close to them?"

"Oh God, yes. They were wonderful. They looked after me when ..." I hesitate. "When my dad forgot to. My grandfather was a bookie. Until the day he died, he would dress up in a full suit and his brown overcoat and his mates would come and pick him up and they'd go off to the pub. My grandmother always wore makeup and had the biggest laugh. She smelt of Charlie perfume," I remember suddenly, marvelling at the way the memories are being pulled out tonight. "And every night after dinner they'd put the stereo on and dance together to Frank Sinatra. They died a week apart from each other. Like there was no real point when their other half was gone." I swallow, and he kisses me quickly. "So, I like this era and the music. They seem close to me somehow," I say softly.

"My mum would tell you that the ones we love are never that far away."

"Do you believe that?"

He nods. "Oh yes. Definitely." The sureness in his voice soothes something inside me, and I kiss him.

"Well, we're going to have a nice night, Jesse. We're going to eat some food, drink lots of cocktails, and you're going to tell me some more embarrassing stories about yourself so I can flaunt my moral superiority."

He nudges me, but we quickly order more drinks, and that's what we do. We sit laughing close together, watching the dance floor and exchanging whispered observations about the people around us. We kiss and touch, unobtrusively at first, but he gets more daring as the evening wears to a close.

"I think I've changed my mind," he says into my shoulder where he's rested his head.

I kiss his hair. "What about? Brexit? The *Britain's Got Talent* final?"

He snorts. "No, about sex. I think we should definitely do some sex tonight."

I start to laugh. "*Do some sex*," I echo and he elbows me, his face alight with amusement and a true, pure sexuality.

"I think we should go home and fuck each other's brains out," he says cockily.

"What happened to getting to know each other?"

He smiles. It's knowing and very intense. "We already know each other, don't we, Zeb? We know each other better than anyone has ever known us." His words are a challenge, and I run my fingers down the sharp angle of his cheekbones.

"We could go on dates until the end of time and nothing will change that," I acknowledge, seeing his eyes flare.

"So, let's go now. I need you inside me."

A wave of heat runs through me but at this point the female singer steps up and begins to croon the opening words to "I've Got You Under My Skin."

I stand up. "Come on," I say, offering my hand. "Let's dance."

"What, now?" He gapes at me. "*Really?*"

I nod and smile. "Plenty of time for fucking. I want to dance with you first."

"And it's okay here?"

"It's fine. There's already a couple of men dancing together and two women over there. It's a friendly place. Anything goes." I wriggle my fingers at him. "I want to dance with you."

"Like your grandad," he whispers, and I snort suddenly, the deep moment severed the way he always manages to do.

"Well, I'm not quite that old."

"Oh shut up," he hisses, the twist in his lips showing his amusement as he stands up and follows me. "One dance and then we're fucking?" he says out of the corner of his mouth.

"You old sweet talker, you," I say, and he laughs loudly.

I step onto the dance floor, joining the other swaying couples, and draw him into my arms. He sighs immediately, betraying his pleasure, and I marvel at the fact that he fits like he's been made for my body, and it's as if every sinew recognises him. I pull him close, his head under my chin, and we sway together in the dim candlelight to the sweet song.

One Month Later
Jesse

I lie face down on the bed, sweat pouring off me. Zeb is a solid weight over me. I can feel the scratch of his chest hair on my back and the length of his cock inside me. I wriggle, and he chuckles and slaps my hip.

"Be completely still," he mutters.

"*I can't*," I groan, feeling sweat drip into my eyes. "I need to move. *Please.*"

"No," he whispers. "You'll lie there and take it, Jess."

"Oh, God," I moan as he moves in a slow glide in and out. He brushes over my prostate and it feels like it's swollen to twice its size. We've been doing this for what feels like hours. It's safe to say that if edging was an Olympic sport, Zeb would be standing on the podium with a bunch of flowers.

He thrusts in slowly, and I try to stay still, but I can't. Instead, I shove back on him, crying out in relief as his cock goes deep.

"*Shit*," he snaps, his fingers tightening on my shoulders, and I can literally feel the moment his control snaps and he starts to thrust hard and fast, his balls banging my arse.

"Oh, I can't–" I shout and he kisses my shoulder, the wet ends of his hair tickling my neck.

"You can come," he pants, and I dig my face into the pillow and scream as I come, feeling the heat of Zeb as he falls down over me, holding me down in a hard grasp as he fucks into me and groans his way to climax.

For a second there's just the sound of panting, and then I grunt as he pulls out of me and collapses at my side, his chest heaving.

"Shit," I breathe, and he snorts.

"You can say that again."

"Shit."

I wait for his laugh. It pleases me more and more to hear him do that. The amount he's done it over the last month has made me realise how little he laughed before.

I turn on my side and take the opportunity to ogle him while his eyes are closed. I have to seize these chances because he's a little self-conscious about his body around me. I'd love to know why because he's fucking gorgeous. I always knew he hid a good body under those swanky suits and I'm glad to report that I wasn't wrong.

The last month has been filled with so many quirky dates. We played board games on a rainy day at a little café in Waterloo and then ventured to climb the Whispering Gallery at St Paul's where I scandalized Zeb by whispering what I wanted to do to him. We played darts at a small club where we used the board to decide our next drinks. I'd even organised an escape-room date where I'd been vastly amused to watch Zeb organise everyone into the most well thought out and polite escape the place had ever had.

Stretching luxuriously, I smile at the twinge in my arse because it's well earned. Zeb and I have hardly set foot out of his bedroom for the last two days. We abandoned the dates and barricaded ourselves in, ordering in food occasionally to fuel us, but our attention has been totally on each other.

Each time the sex seems to just get better and better. The benefits of an older man in bed are legion, but chiefly because he has so much stamina, and that calm eye for organisation and details means that he can play my body like a fiddle. I've come harder and more often in the last month than I have in the last two years.

But it's not just all been sex. In the mornings we've escaped the flat when it's started to smell like an explosion in a salami factory. We've got coffee and wandered the streets of Covent Garden in the early morning sunshine as the shops started to open, wrapped in each other and talking intently.

For the first time I don't feel like he's looking at me as too young anymore. Instead he seems as fascinated by me as I am with him. We don't seem to run out of things to say, discussing politics and religion or saying the lines from our favourite songs.

Zeb seems to have softened in some way. He's still sarcastic. It's a trait he can't get rid of, and I'm glad of it. But he smiles more and laughs a lot, and I comfort myself that I can make him happy when Patrick couldn't.

The only blips have been the constant texts from Patrick which Zeb checks and then dismisses, but that's not going to work forever. Patrick is hovering on the surface like the dorsal fin in *Jaws*.

Pushing thoughts of the wanker away, I cough pointedly. Zeb's mouth quirks but he lifts his arm and I immediately snuggle closer, laying my head against that hairy chest and practically purring as he runs his hand through my hair in a lazy scalp massage.

We lie there for a few minutes as the sweat cools on our bodies. "I have a small confession to make," he says, stirring.

I tense and lift up, resting my chin on his chest. "What?" I ask slowly.

"Do you remember saying you hadn't done any pretend boyfriend jobs in ages?"

"Yes."

"Well, it wasn't by accident."

"What?" He fidgets under me and I reach out, trapping him with my arms. "Oh no. You have to tell me now, Zeb Evans."

I'm amused to see a faint flush on his cheekbones. "I stopped

Felix booking you for any with young men last year," he says so quickly that it takes me a few seconds to work out what he just said.

"I'm sorry, *what?*" I say.

He huffs a sigh. "I didn't want you to do them anymore," he mutters.

"Why?"

"Because I didn't want to book you for something and see you end up with the bloke."

For a long second I stare at him, a hot feeling of intense happiness and something stronger in my chest. I eye his awkward expression and opt to hide my jubilation.

"And do you feel better for that confession?" I ask. "Knowing that you could have deprived me of meeting my one true Prince Charming?"

"At someone's Christmas office party? You'd have just met vomit and damaging career decisions," he scoffs.

"You never know where you'll meet your prince," I say solemnly. "Zeb, I don't know what to say. This is such a new facet to your character."

"You're a massive pisstaker, aren't you?" he says in a resigned tone and I laugh.

"It's one of my many, *many* charming traits." I reach up and kiss him. "Thank you for telling me," I say softly.

"You're not bothered?" He sounds astonished.

"Nope. Why would I be?" He stares at me, so I elaborate. "You're telling me you didn't want me with anyone. Why would I be pissed off? It runs both ways."

"But I stopped you meeting someone."

"At *work.*" I grin. "Relax, Zeb. You didn't swallow the key to my chastity belt."

"That would have been like shutting the stable door after the horse had bolted years ago."

I start to laugh. "Anyway, you were right."

"I was?"

"I did meet someone on a pretend-boyfriend gig."

He looks worried. "Who?"

I shake my head. "You, of course, you idiot."

He looks pleased, so I kiss his nose and settle back in my place on his chest. He resumes stroking my hair and a peaceful silence falls as I hug my happiness to myself.

"So?" he finally says after a while.

I sigh. "I know what you're going to say, and the answer is no."

"So, you don't want to shag Jude Law?"

"Well, no. Hang on, you were not going to say that."

Zeb laughs, the merry sound ringing in the air, and I stare at his smiling face with his eyes creased in amusement. "No, I was going to say do you think we should get out of bed today?"

"I knew it." I lay my head back down and pat his hand to start the scalp massage again. "No. I want to stay here forever."

"When we die from malnutrition, the next people might object to sharing the bed."

"Will we die locked in each other's arms? That's *so* romantic."

"Oh my God, you probably liked *Romeo and Juliet*."

"The ultimate story of true love."

"Why? They died. It was the ultimate story of teenage strops."

"Oh my God, Zeb, you are the Grinch of love. What about *Ghost*?"

"It made me uneasy. Shouldn't dead people stay dead and not zip about making vases?"

I pop my head up. "This is so enlightening. I'm trying to think of more romantic films for you to destroy. Okay, what about *Notting Hill*?"

"That's not *romantic*, Jesse," he scoffs. "What's romantic about the fact that they're far too different and when they inevitably end up divorcing, she'll have to fork out half her money to pay for the mistake?"

I start to laugh. "Okay, what is romantic?"

He considers that, his arm flung over his head, showing the tuft of black hair that I always want to bury my face in.

"It's not about over-the-top gestures to me," he finally says almost shyly. "It's all the tiny moments that go to make a real love story. The funny things that go wrong like when one of you forgets your anniversary or does something silly. They all become part of your story. And you add to it with every argument or slammed door that you have. Every birthday or Christmas that you mould into a thing that only the two of you recognise. It's taking care of each other when you're throwing up or have a cold, it's huddling under the duvet together laughing so hard your ribs hurt. It's holding the other one when they're frightened, knowing you will do anything to make them feel better again. It's like being two pebbles on a beach. You start off individual shapes and then the weather and proximity means you rub the rough spots off so in the end you're smooth with a patina that only echoes one other person."

He falls silent, going red, and I stare at him with my mouth open. *I want that,* I realise fiercely. *I want that so much and I want it all with him.* I need to be with him over the years, watching the grey appearing in his hair, laughing together and living and fighting. I want to be near him. I can't say that though.

"Well, Zeb," I say slowly. "It isn't box office material, that's for sure."

He starts to laugh, pulling me down and hugging me, and I push my face into his neck, feeling the soft skin under my lips.

I send my hand over the sleek, tight skin of his hipbones. "Do you really want to get out of bed?" I say finally. "Because I have to say there are a couple of positions we haven't tried yet, and you've obviously ruled out the entirety of Hollywood's offerings."

"A couple of positions? There surely can't be any more. We could rewrite the *Kama Sutra*."

"One should always have goals," I say, mimicking the stuffy voice he's always used in my appraisals.

He laughs, but at that second his phone beeps again like fucking clockwork. I grumble as he detaches himself, but as soon as he's grabbed his phone I reattach myself to him like a limpet.

"Who is it?" I ask idly, following with my fingers the trail of black hair that leads from his belly button to his cock where it flares out.

There's a long silence before he says, "It's Patrick."

I come up on my elbow. "What does he want now?"

He scans the text. "He's reading me the riot act. The wedding is tomorrow. I've got to be at his hotel tomorrow morning at eight o'clock. His family and friends are going to have breakfast and then I've got to help him get ready. He's extremely disappointed in my absence this month and the fact that I apparently don't know how to be a good friend."

"And he does?" I say crossly. *God, I hate that cockwomble.* He's got an unerring instinct for where Zeb's weak spots are and he hits them every time. I look at Zeb's face and the reappearance of the wrinkle between his eyes. Yes, Patrick is still on his winning streak.

He looks at me, and I roll over onto my front, leaning on my elbows and cupping my face in my hands.

"You should really ignore that fucker," I advise, but his expression has already gone distant. I hate the way he looks when Patrick summons him. Like he's on the end of a very long lead. Patrick lets it out, but only so far, and he keeps a careful watch on where Zeb is at all times. I think I hate it most because sometimes I torture myself with the thought that Zeb is still in love with Patrick.

There's also the problem of his screwed-up feelings of responsibility. He seems to think he has to take on everyone's problems. If we'd been together for longer than a month I'd tackle that, but I can't because at the moment it would be overstepping so many boundaries I'd be up in court for trespassing.

"Well, I'm sure you'll have fun," I say lightly, rolling onto my back and staring at the ceiling.

"Wait. Are you not coming?" He scoots next to me. "Wasn't that part of the original arrangement we had?"

"Nope," I say, popping the p's. "My presence has not officially been requested by His Majesty, The Pampered Prince of Pillock, so I'm not going anywhere."

He rolls his eyes. "He's not so bad," he immediately protests. I stare at him and he cups my face, his fingers warm against my skin. "I want you to come," he says softly. "*Please.*"

I look at his imploring eyes. "Will you be wearing that morning suit of yours? The one you wore to Arissa's wedding to give her away?"

The smile creases the sides of his eyes. "I will."

I think of how handsome he looks in it and how Patrick will watch him, and against my will I nod. "Of course," I say, watching his look of relief. It warms me that he seems to want me around. But it doesn't take away the chill at the bottom of my spine that says that this is a very bad idea.

CHAPTER TWELVE

Jesse

That feeling hasn't gone away by the next morning as we orbit each other getting dressed. It gets deeper, and I feel a panicked twist in my stomach. I don't know what it is, but I have the feeling that this is going to go wrong. I'd discount it, but my mum is known for her form of second sight. She taught me to always pay attention to my feelings and they're currently screaming at me that today Patrick will try to fuck us up.

I'm dressed first, as I really don't care what I look like. I slide the morning suit on that Zeb hired for me and put in the boutonnière that arrived with Zeb's this morning, still wet with the dew.

I watch Zeb faff with the sleeves of his tailored, dark grey morning suit. No rental for him. The navy cravat suits him, enhancing those wonderful eyes. He rearranges the cravat and fiddles with the boutonnière and the feeling inside me bubbles up suddenly so strongly that I can't rein it in.

"Come to Devon with me," I say impulsively.

He stares at me. "*What?*"

"Come with me. I was going to visit my family. Come with me

and meet them. We could spend a few days away from here and tour round the countryside. I know loads of good spots."

I can hear the enthusiasm in my voice and for a moment a wild exhilaration shows in his face, but then even as I watch he smothers it.

"I can't," he says slowly, wincing at whatever he can see in my face. "I made a promise, Jesse. What would I be if I broke it?"

For a long second I stare at him. "A man," I say finally.

"What?" I watch as he looks at himself in the mirror and adjusts the handkerchief in his pocket. He looks back at me queryingly.

"Just a man. One who makes silly promises that he should never have been kept to."

Zeb shakes his head, and I feel my stomach clench. "I'm his best man, Jesse. Don't be silly. And what's all this about being kept to promises? I said yes, and I don't go back on my word."

"And he knows that and is using it," I burst out, feeling almost wild. For the first time this month I feel very young. "You shouldn't do this. He's going to marry Frances and still keep a fucking tight hold on you. He doesn't want anyone else to have you, but he isn't prepared to give up anything for you. It isn't right that he's played on your feeling of duty and got you to do this. It's bad for you." I pause. "*He's* bad for you. But you can't see it."

"Don't be utterly ridiculous. You're acting like we're in the plot of a Mills and Boon. I see everything," he says crossly, looking at me suddenly like I'm a disappointment to him. "I'm not blind. I know his faults, and I can quite categorically say that you're talking shit. Along with the fact that this really isn't about him but about you."

"What do you mean?" I say sharply and he looks almost apologetic.

"You think he wants me back, and I'm going to get back together with him."

"And are you?"

He stares at me for a long moment, annoyance and something else crossing his face. He opens his mouth to speak but his phone rings. Picking it up, he looks down at the display. "That's the taxi company's number. They'll be outside. We can't be late."

"You're still going to do this, then?" I say, hating the querulous tone in my voice. I sound like a nag.

Irritation crosses his face. "Of course I fucking am," he snaps. "I made a bloody promise and I'm not happy that you've had all month to say this and you're picking a fight right now before we leave."

"Patrick is not right for you because he doesn't see you properly," I say doggedly.

He exhales in exasperation and runs his hands through his hair. "*Jesse*," he says through gritted teeth. "Please stop."

"He doesn't see how clever you are and how fucking kind and how you live your life in tiny portions, trying so hard to be a good man that you've completely missed that you already are. The best man." I'm desperately trying to get everything out, and I know it's coming across very wrong. I sigh heavily. "Promises aren't as important as people. There's a middle ground between your father and you, Zeb. I wish for your sake you'd find it."

Silence falls for what feels like an hour. Then he picks up his keys, anger plain in his face. "Much as I hate to break up this session on the psychiatrist's couch, I'm going," he says tightly. "Coming or not? Last chance."

I stare at him and then sigh. "Coming," I mutter.

The journey there is tense. Zeb hardly says two words to me, and I'm not delighted that the theme continues when we get up to Patrick's suite. The rooms are full of his groomsmen and immediate family helping him to get ready, and as soon as we get into the suite, Zeb fucks off, drawn away by Patrick who directs one fulminating glare at me and then keeps him by his side as he reintroduces him to everyone. Zeb smiles and shakes hands and kisses cheeks, showing no sign of the argument that has twisted my guts.

I hover on the edge of the crowd, nimbly avoiding Nina and Victor. I make small talk and coincidentally feel myself getting smaller too. Smaller and more invisible.

Even when the members of the party sit down for the breakfast served on a long table in the lounge of the suite, I find myself relegated to the end of the table next to someone's grandfather who's extremely deaf. I answer his questions absentmindedly while watching Patrick and Zeb in the centre laughing over something together.

My temper kindles. It takes a lot to get me angry, but Zeb seems to be managing it ably. He hasn't spoken to me once. Just dumped me at the door like a child he's been babysitting and fucked off. There's been no thought as to whether I'm okay or comfortable, just complete radio silence as if I'm not even here. I don't think he's even looked for me once.

I watch him now from my position leaning against a wall, half hidden by a rather large pot plant. He's laughing at something a man is saying to him, his face alive with amusement and warmth. Anyone watching him would think he hasn't got a care in the world. Maybe he hasn't. Maybe it's just me who hates that we've argued, and he actually doesn't really give a shit at all. I look for his wanker of a sidekick but he isn't there. Then I catch a whiff of expensive aftershave and sigh.

"Hello, Patrick."

He comes to stand next to me. "Admiring the scenery?" he asks as we both watch Zeb.

I shrug. "Well, it is pretty."

He shoots me a sidelong look. "Oh, I'm aware of that. I looked at that view for years. It's the best I've ever seen."

"Can we dispense with the euphemism? You're starting to sound like an estate agent."

He takes a sip of his drink. "Okay. What would you like to talk about, Jesse? I can't help but be curious about the young man who's monopolised Zeb all month."

"Curious or threatened?" I say flippantly, a flash of temper appearing. But I know immediately that I've somehow made a mistake as his lips curl into a smile that lacks all humour.

"Oh, I'm not threatened," he says, staring at me. "Why would I be?"

"I really don't know," I say finally. "You're getting married, so I'm at a loss as to why you seem to be so concerned with Zeb's movements." I allow a smirk. "Talented as his movements are."

He shakes his head. "Don't get used to them. He won't stick around."

"Why?" I hate myself for asking him that, but I can't help it.

"Because you have nothing to offer him." He looks me up and down. "You're far too young. You're inane and probably stupid. He'll be bored within a couple of months." He laughs. "Hell, he's forgotten you already."

We both look at Zeb, who is in intent conversation with another man. At that point he looks up and smiles. It's intimate and devastating. Warm and almost loving. My lips tip up in reply but dip immediately as I remember the row and his behaviour and realise that he can't be smiling at me. I turn back to Patrick who's watching me intently, a pleased expression on his face.

"You see," he says. "It's not you he's looking at. It's me. It will always be me."

"So, if it's like that why are you not together and why are you getting married to a woman?"

He shrugs. "That doesn't mean anything. Frances knows that. She just wants to get married. And as soon as there's a baby on the way I'll pick up with Zeb again."

I shake my head. "That'll never happen," I say, confident for once. "He's the most honourable man I've ever met. He won't go for that."

"Really?" he purrs, looking vastly amused. "Well, obviously what you know about Zeb is not exactly much. Do you know when he agreed to be my best man?"

I stare at him, thinking back to the conversation I had with Zeb in the car. Somehow it seems like a long time ago. "You were getting on together again, I think," I say.

He throws his head back and laughs, and I briefly imagine karate-chopping him across the throat.

"That's one way to put it," he chuckles, rubbing his eyes.

"What do you mean?"

He shakes his head. "Jesse, we were in bed at the time." I stare at him, completely unable to say anything, and he smiles coldly with the light of triumph in his eyes. "He said he'd be my best man while my come was still running down his chest." He looks me up and down and smirks. "Well, I'll leave you with that. Enjoy the rest of your stay, Jesse."

I watch him walk away, assured and handsome, and I look intently at Zeb's face as Patrick comes near. The smile that plays on his face is warm, and I feel suddenly stupid. And very, very young.

I put my glass down and make my way into the bathroom. It's empty, so I lock the door and subside onto the chaise lounge in the corner of the room. I stare at my reflection and contemplate what Patrick said. I'm sure he wasn't lying. That was patently and painfully apparent. And I only have to remember Zeb's odd hesitation when he mentioned why he'd agreed to be Patrick's best man to know it's true. Fucking hell, he slept with Patrick knowing he was engaged to be married.

I shake my head. The Zeb I know would never do that. He has too many ethics, and he's too full of the desire to treat people well. Then I slump. "You obviously don't know him," I say out loud and the words are devastated, echoing the feeling in my eyes.

"Shit," I say, scrubbing my face. "Fuck." I make myself stand up. I can't sit here like a twat. I'll have to go back out there. I run cold water over my hot palms and brush my hair back. "Get a grip," I advise my reflection. "Go out there and behave like the adult that he doesn't think you are."

I still as a desperate thought suddenly occurs to me. *Maybe there's still a chance*. After all, he hasn't been with Patrick this month and his reaction to him has mainly seemed to be a kindness with a slight edge of impatience. I know he's enjoyed himself with me. The half-starved way he fell on me tells me that. Time and time again he's reached for me, entering me every time with a deep groan as if he's in heaven.

I know relationships have been built on less. But we've been together outside the bedroom too. Surely all the laughter and easy conversation have to count for something. *Not against five years though,* I think glumly. And Patrick is the finished product. Perfect exterior even if the interior is rancid.

Patrick could be lying, though. The thought comes out of the blue, and I seize it like it's a life raft. Somehow, despite what he said, I still cling deep down to my knowledge of who my Zeb is. A man who'd never entertain sleeping with someone who was with someone else. He'd rather cut his hand off than hurt anyone. He's kind and generous and thoughtful. How have I lost sight of that in the last ten minutes?

I straighten my jacket. "I'll go out and talk to him," I say out loud, seeing the resolution in my face. "I'll ask him what's happening. He won't lie to me."

My plan is foiled when I get back to the main room and I can't find him. The room is packed now with people talking loudly and happily. He isn't here. I come to a stop in the room. Where is he? Then I spot that the door to the patio is ajar, letting in a draught of cool air. I push my way towards it, but when I reach my destination I pause, hovering with my hand over the handle. I don't know why I'm so uneasy. He might not even be out there. He might have gone looking for me or be helping Patrick.

The nice thought gives me the encouragement to open the doors. They swing open, letting fresh air flow around me as I stand stock still, staring at the sight in front of my eyes. Zeb and Patrick are standing on the patio, their arms wrapped around each other and their mouths fused together in a hungry kiss.

For what seems like an eternity but is probably only a couple of seconds I can't move, standing looking at them. Then Patrick gives a low groan and it breaks my stasis and I step back, banging my elbow clumsily on the door. Then I'm gone back into the room, making my way towards the door and escape.

Zeb

For a too-long second I stand on the balcony held tightly against Patrick's chest, who seems to have developed hands like an octopus since we split up. Surprise keeps me there for a second but then reality surges back and I get my hands up and push him back forcibly. He stumbles back, his mouth swollen and his eyes at half-mast. Once, that would have done things to me. Now, I just feel a weary surge of disgust.

"What the fuck?" I say, wiping my mouth. "What are you *doing*? Have you gone mad?"

He rests back against the stone balustrade and shrugs, a half smile on his face. "I've always been mad. You know it."

"Yes, but not suicidal." I stare at him. "Pat, you're getting married in a few hours and you're trying to kiss your ex."

He shakes his head. "You're not my ex."

"I must have a powerful imagination, then," I say wryly. "Because I'm sure I remember a fair few screaming matches followed by you taking half my furniture and my pension."

"We'll never be over," he says stubbornly, coming back towards me, his arms outstretched. I sidestep them neatly, so he stumbles slightly.

"Why?"

He stares at me feverishly. "Because nothing and no one can get in our way. Not Frances, not your silly boy toy."

"Leave Jesse out of this," I say sharply. He laughs, and I narrow my eyes. "What have you done?" I say.

I feel the sense of unease again that started to gather this morning while I tried to catch Jesse's eye numerous times and failed. Every time I looked at him, he was resolutely staring away as if he couldn't bear to look at me. The one time I thought he was looking and I smiled, he turned away from me, and I felt nausea grip my stomach.

I regretted the row as soon as it happened. I just got cross when he wouldn't stop talking about going to Devon. Part of the anger was because I wanted to go more than anything. I wanted to apologise as soon as I saw his face fall at my rejection, but I couldn't find a way to get back to us, so I stayed silent.

It's given me a sour stomach but here was not the place for a serious discussion. I've therefore put on a good face for others all morning, but I've felt sick since we got here, and the only thing that's got me through is the thought that I can apologise to him when the wedding is done.

The uneasy feeling grows into a steady pressure on my chest. "Patrick?" I say loudly and he jumps.

"I told him."

"Told him what?" I can hear the panic in my voice and he smiles.

"Zeb, don't worry. He can't stand between us. I won't allow it."

"What did you tell him?" I say, enunciating each word slowly and clearly.

His smile widens. "I told him about the circumstances of you agreeing to be my best man."

My stomach knots so badly that I feel like throwing up. "Oh fuck," I groan, pacing away from him and staring unseeing over the balcony. "Why did you do that?"

"He had to know."

I whirl. "No, he didn't. He fucking didn't need to know about the one moment in my life I am most ashamed of."

"Why are you ashamed?"

I stare at him. "You just don't get it, do you?" I say incredulously. "Jesus, Patrick, you have less morals than a fucking polecat."

"What?" he says crossly. "It's just us."

"No, it isn't. It hasn't been just us for a very long time, and now there are two camps. There is you and Frances and there is me and Jesse and never the twain shall meet."

"But they did meet," he says smugly. "And fucked."

"We fucked because you never told me you'd asked her to marry you," I roar. "You gave me the impression you'd split up. You didn't tell me until after." I laugh incredulously. "And then asked me to be best man."

"So why did you agree to it, Zebadiah?" he shouts.

"Because I felt sorry for you," I say quietly, the soft words falling like rocks into a still pond.

"*What?*"

I nod. "Sleeping with you that last time made me realise that I'd never really loved you, Patrick. It was like the scales fell off my eyes all of a sudden and I looked at you and I realised that I pitied you."

He flinches. "Why?" I hesitate, even now unwilling to deal the blow, and he gestures sharply. "Get on with it."

"I pity you because you have never been true to yourself in your life. You tell lies to so many people, but the most important person you do it to is yourself. You're pretty, but there's nothing else to you, Patrick. You see yourself in other people's eyes and you exist to please them when you should be happy with yourself." I breathe in. "I've felt more for Jesse in this last month than I ever did with you."

"How can you say that? This isn't what was meant to happen."

"What was meant to happen?"

He stares mutinously at me. "You were supposed to wait for me, and we could have been together once the dust had settled."

"That dust is your marriage. Don't you care about Frances? She's a good girl. Aren't you bothered that we'd have hurt her?"

He shrugs, something cold showing in his eyes. "She knows the score."

"She's not a fucking umpire. She's a person with thoughts and feelings, and to be honest I really don't think you should marry her."

"Because you want me?"

"No, because she deserves more than you're capable of giving her." I pause, acid running through my stomach. "Oh my God, he was right," I say slowly.

"Who was right?"

"Jesse."

"Why? Did he get the answers for the homework you set him?" he says snidely.

"He said you were trying to get me back. We actually had a fucking row over it because I said you'd never do that." I stare at him. "He was right."

He stares at me for a long second, and I think we both see the years we had together fading away like sparks from a fire. Then he straightens up and buttons his jacket. "Whatever. I'm not terribly interested in that boy's opinions. Thankfully your stupid relationship isn't my business."

I nod slowly. "And Jesse isn't either. Please don't speak to him again unless it's just bland civilities. He's not your concern."

Spite crosses his face and I marvel that I ever thought I loved him. "I don't think he's yours anymore either, Zeb. Not after seeing his face a few minutes ago."

I go cold. "What do you mean?"

He smiles. "He saw us, Zeb. Stayed long enough to watch us kiss and then fucked off sharpish."

I feel vomit rise in my throat, and panic fills me. I dash towards the door just as he comes to life. "Wait, where are you going?" he shouts.

"To find Jesse."

"But I'm getting married."

"Not to me, thank goodness. You are now totally someone else's problem."

"What about my fucking best man?"

"Ask someone who still gives a shit about you. Good luck."

CHAPTER THIRTEEN

Zeb

I bang into the flat. "Jesse," I shout out. "*Jesse?*"

But the silence mocks me with the knowledge that he isn't here. I don't even need to look. He has a way of infusing a place with his presence and I always know where he is.

I see a scrap of paper on my desk and draw near, almost afraid to pick it up. It's a page that's obviously been torn from his exercise book and his messy scrawl fills up the page with impatient letters. I draw in a breath that hurts my chest and read it.

Dear Zeb,

I've left. To be honest it's looking like I never should have been here in the first place. I saw you and Patrick on the balcony earlier. I think that, along with your behaviour when I tried to stop you seeing him, tells me everything I need to know.

I lower the page and suck in a sharp breath, feeling moisture burn at the back of my eyes. Fuck. It just gets worse. I go back to the letter.

I realised when I saw the two of you that this whole month has really been about you and Patrick and never about me, which just goes to show my arrogance because I thought differently. I thought a lot of things which I'm glad I never said now.

Anyway, I wish you happiness. I'm not sure you'll get it to be honest because Patrick is a complete arsehole, but maybe that's what you need. And I realised today that I'd like you to have what you want because you spend far too much time catering to everyone else's needs and ignoring your own. So, if a spoilt man child is what you're after, then have at him.

Just please be happy. I don't think you are or have been for a very long time, but I don't think you pay any attention to that, which is sad. Be happy, Zeb, in whatever form it takes.

I won't be coming back to the agency so you can take this as my resignation. I'm presuming you won't hold me to anything. I just can't see you anymore. I don't want to. I'm going away for a bit so don't call round at the flat.

Jesse

My hands are shaking, and I push them behind my back as if to hide them. The idea that he thinks I've been using him to get back with Patrick is horrifying. My stomach clenches until I think I might throw up and I want to hold him so badly. He must feel dreadful. What did he feel when he saw me on the balcony? I imagine all that lovely vitality in his face dying away and I feel sick.

I want him suddenly and desperately. I want to say sorry for doubting him. I want to hug him and hold him close, listen to him laugh and inhale his scent of green tea. But the silence of the room seems to mock me with that wish, and I sink onto a chair, still holding his letter. *This can't be over. I won't let it.*

I think of this month. All the wonderful silly dates. Laughing together. That slow dance in the candlelight. I've never felt so alive or so seen. Jesse seems to notice things about me that no one else does. He seems to care more than anyone else has either. My childhood was so chaotic, and I clung to the notion that my father loved me. But he didn't really know me. No one does apart from Jesse. He is the only one who's ever cracked the shell I grew around me as a matter of survival when I was small. And even when he sees everything, I don't feel naked and exposed because he's seeing me with those warm brown eyes of his. Those kind eyes.

At times, this month has been scary because I have so many feelings for him. It's such a leap of faith to invest your heart with someone. It's something I've always resisted doing fully. I cared for Patrick, but it was nothing compared to what I already feel for Jesse. And it's only now I've lost him that I realise just how much he's come to mean to me. The thought of never seeing him again fills me with panic, and all my fears of him leaving me when bored fall away to nothing beside the pain of actually having lost him.

I stand up and pace over to the window, staring unseeingly out onto the yard. *Where would he go?* I think back to our conversation this morning and stiffen suddenly. He wanted to go to his mum and dad's house earlier on. "That's where he's gone," I say out loud. Then I frown. "But where the fuck do they live?"

A few minutes later I steam through the packed office downstairs, still dressed in my morning suit with my top hat under my arm and my gaze fixed straight ahead.

"Oh Zeb," Felix drawls. "When did the office uniform become so formal? Can't we talk about this?"

"Nope," I say.

One of my perennially dissatisfied customers, Miss Higgins, stands up, her face set in its usual querulous lines. "Mr Evans, can I just say–?"

"No," I say succinctly and bang into my office, slamming the door so her displeased whine is cut off.

I look around wildly. I'm sure the address I need is in the computer somewhere, but I'm also pretty certain it was on a piece of paper he gave me recently. But where is it? Deciding to leave the computer until last, I rummage wildly through the tidy paperwork on the desk, throwing it off when it proves useless. I scrape some of the files off and watch them cascade to the floor, so absorbed that I don't quite manage to catch the iMac that goes sailing past me too. It crashes to the floor, exploding in a bang and a flurry of sparks.

I hear the door open behind me, and Felix comes to stand next to me. "Redecorating?" he asks calmly.

I glare at him. "I can do without the customary backchat."

"That makes me sound quite a character." He pauses and winks at me. "I like it."

I run my hands agitatedly through my hair before bending to start going through the desk drawers. Felix stares at me, immobile until a stapler and a hole punch sail past his nose. Then he activates.

"What are you looking for? Also, much as I love this new devil-may-care side of you, do you think you should maybe have saved it until you're actually due in the office and not, say, when you're supposed to be at the church?"

The door opens and we both turn to watch Max edge into the room. "No," he says loudly. "No, you can't see him." He makes a gesture like a lion tamer, so I know he's talking to Miss Higgins, and then slams the door shut.

He looks up and grins at me. The smile manages to intensify for a brief second as he looks at Felix, like the last flare of a star, and then it dies as Felix glares at him.

I stare at Max. He's wearing a morning suit, but his hair is loose and longer than it's ever been and his beard is quite wild.

Felix sighs loudly. "Great. Who ordered the Jesus?"

"*Felix*," I sigh, rubbing my nose. "Can we concentrate on more important things?"

He shrugs. "He doesn't exist for me, so I'm a go with that plan."

"Oh, so I don't exist unless you're making unpleasant and quite anti-Jesus remarks about my appearance," Max drawls, sitting on the desk and folding his arms. "I'm actually offended."

"You're an atheist," I say baldly.

"It's the point of the matter," he says primly. He stares at me. "I have to query your pre-wedding game, Zeb. I must say I don't think I've come across many best men who've managed to fit in a spot of office reorganisation around their duties."

"I thought you were allergic to weddings, Max," Felix says coolly.

"Or was that commitment? What a silly twink I am." He smiles. "Ah, but now I remember. You've been a best man before. Now *that* memory is still evergreen for me."

Max winces, and I lose it.

"Shut up, both of you," I shout. The room stills and they both turn their heads at the same time and same angle. It's like talking to meerkats. "Good," I say. "Now, I need an address in Devon and that is *all* I need from you. No backchat. No smart remarks. Just the address."

"Any address or something in particular?" Felix asks, showing absolutely no sign of being cowed.

"I need Jesse's parents' address. I'm sure they live in some small village there."

"Well, that narrows the field," he says. Over-sarcastically, in my opinion. He pushes me out of the way. "And did you manage to find it before you became involved with chucking stationery and Apple products about?"

I scuff my foot. "No." It's more of a question than I'd like, but Felix is a scary person. The only person who isn't wary of him is Max, but then he did used to run towards gunfire, so he obviously has a death wish.

"It'll be on his employment records as his next of kin," he muses. He looks down at the sad sight of my computer. "Oh dear, maybe we could attach a string to it and shout the answers through the gaping holes in your keyboard."

"We'll use yours," I say decisively but he puts a hand up to stop me.

"Absolutely not until you calm down. You're *not* touching my computer in this current mood, and if you go out there you'll lose more customers if you don't watch it."

"I don't care," I say impatiently. They stare at me and I huff. "What? I don't."

"Why?" Max asks. He's staring at me as if I've gone mad. Maybe I have.

"Because I need to find Jesse, and I need to do it as soon as possible."

"What about the wedding?" Felix says slowly. "Aren't you supposed to be at the church soon?"

I shake my head. "I'm not going." They gape at me and I grimace. "What? I'm not going. I've got more important things to do."

"And to clarify, Jesse is that important thing?" Felix asks, folding his arms and leaning against the desk. I nod. "And what about your promises?"

"I'm an idiot," I say despairingly. "I don't care what promises I made to Patrick. Jesse is the important one."

He grimaces. "I'd give a rousing rendition of 'Hallelujah', if I thought the world was ready for the perfection of my voice, and if I wasn't also completely sure that there's more to this story than you're telling me."

He gestures to my seat and I slump into it. "I think he saw me and Patrick kissing."

"*What?*" The two of them shout it in unison and then very obviously avoid looking at each other. Well, Felix does. Max does what he does normally. He stares at Felix hungrily.

"He saw Patrick kiss me," I correct. "I shoved him off as soon as he landed on my lips, but I think it's given Jesse the wrong idea."

"Probably exacerbated by the fact that you're still keeping him at arm's length," Felix observes.

"I'm not," I say. Then I slump further. "Okay, maybe I am a bit. I can't help it. I think I'm still waiting for the other shoe to drop." I bury my head in my hands. "He asked me not to go, and I didn't listen. He said Patrick was up to something and asked me to go home with him instead."

"*What?*" Max says. "Why would you ignore his request?"

Felix stirs as if he's definitely wanting to say something, but he restrains himself and focuses his attention on me which always makes me a bit nervous.

I shrug. "Because if I'm not the man who keeps his word and his promises, then who am I?"

"A human being," Max says angrily. "And a bloody fine one too. Zeb, your dad broke every promise, and mostly everything he said turned out to be a lie. But that doesn't mean you have to keep every one of yours either. That makes you as stupid as he was."

I gape at him. "What?"

Felix shrugs. "Much as it burns with the force of twenty thousand suns to have to admit this, he's right."

"Hang on," Max says. "Let's just pause the conversation while I savour that."

"And you're back to being a dickhead." Felix turns back to me. "The trouble with you is that you're looking for structure with love."

"Is that my only problem? It sounds quite painful."

"If we don't focus on just the one, we'll be here all year." Max snorts and a smile tickles the corners of Felix's mouth. "You're looking for things that can't be there with real love. There aren't any rules in it."

"What about fidelity?"

"That's a *promise,* not a rule," he says. "And promises depend on both people in the equation."

There's a very strained silence, and Max is now doing the very opposite of looking at Felix.

"I feel like a whirlwind picked me up and shoved me through a steel fence headfirst and then rammed me into a cow pat next to a rose bush," I say sadly. Max and Felix blink. "It's too soon for me to have f-feelings," I finally say. "I don't think it's right to feel like this so soon."

"Like what?" Max asks.

"Like there aren't any rules." I pause. "And that I quite like it like that," I finish reluctantly. "Even though it makes me feel like I'm upside down on a very rickety and not properly policed fairground ride."

Felix laughs and shakes his head. "There aren't any rules for it.

That's the *point*. It has to be taken on trust because sometimes in your relationship that trust will be all you have to keep going." He shrugs. "There's no billeted list to check things off. It just happens. You have strong feelings for the person, you don't want to be away from them, you smile when you think of them. And away you go." He makes a flapping gesture with his hands.

"Surely that's infatuation?"

"Call it what you like, Zebadiah, but eventually you'll let it be love."

"Let it?"

He smiles affectionately at me. "I've always liked you, but God, you're an idiot."

"An idiot boss, I think you meant to say in a hyper-polite voice," I say faintly.

Felix carries on remorselessly. "An idiot who'd put the army to shame. You analysed and strategized and overthought everything and pottered along thinking that you had complete control. Then bam!" I jump, and he grins mischievously. "It hit you right between the bloody eyes. Jesse is perfect for you. Yes, he's younger than you, but you need that. He's funny and charming and impulsive, and he's stopping your slow roll into the grave through fear of feeling out of control. And you've let him in. You just haven't realized it yet." He rolls his eyes in quite a condemning manner.

"He's right," Max says somewhat piously. "You should listen to him."

"Ha!" Felix says.

I shake my head. "How is it that I'm sitting here letting you two lecture and advise me on love? It's like Henry the Eighth advising people on how to keep women happy." Felix opens his mouth, but I hold up my hand. "I just want the address," I say slightly pathetically. "That's all I want. I know I'm in love with him. I'm coming to terms with it slowly. I just need to get him back, explain things properly, and tell him to come home with me."

Felix and Max look at each other. "Good luck with that," Felix says slightly doubtfully.

"The address?" I say loudly.

"Oh, it's St Mary's Church in Dunsford."

"You knew it all along," I say indignantly.

He shrugs. "Of course. I knew at some point you'd fuck up on a grand scale and then need to complete a dramatic race to forgiveness."

I stare at him. "You're actually scarily clever."

"I know," he says over-loudly. "So clever that murdering someone and concealing their body would be very easy for me."

"I'm off," Max says quickly and within seconds he's gone.

I use the journey to Devon to overthink what I'm going to say. It's an abject failure. Normally, words come easily to me. They roll off my tongue, and I use them to soothe people. It's ironic that for the first time in my life I need them to serve a purpose and they're deserting me.

I try to marshal well-thought-out arguments, but all I can concentrate on is how Jesse must have felt seeing me with Patrick and how stupid I've been that I've somehow given him the impression that I want Patrick at all when the truth is very far from that.

I can see now that even though I've let him in this month, I've still done it with a hand holding him away slightly. So focused on how I'd feel when he eventually realised I was too old for him to see that I was actually making him go.

Eventually, I drive down a sleepy village street. It's typical of Devon, with old cottages set back from the road with vivid gardens full of flowers. I find the vicarage at the end of the high street marking the entrance to the old Norman church.

I park the car on the verge and look up at Jesse's home. It's rambling and very old and has obviously had a lot built onto it at some point. It's also very charming with wisteria smothering the brick and looking very purple in the sunlight.

Getting out of the car, I stretch after the long drive. I hope Jesse is here because otherwise I'm out of ideas. I unlatch the gate and walk up the path, inhaling the heady intense scent of roses from a bush near the front door. I look around curiously and it isn't hard to imagine a small Jesse here playing in the garden, mucky and happy. The smile is still on my face when the front door opens and I find myself staring at an older man.

He looks to be in his seventies, his hair thick and silvery. His glasses rest halfway down his nose and he's small in stature. He doesn't look anything like Jesse, but when he smiles at me there's something in the sweetness of the gesture that tells me instantly that this is his father.

He looks me up and down, and I fidget, suddenly aware that I'm still in full morning dress. I'd raced off without bothering to get changed and had therefore caused a few raised eyebrows in the service station surrounded by people in holiday clothes.

"Now at a guess I'd say that either fashion has become very formal in London nowadays or you've followed my son who appeared in the same style a couple of hours ago." His voice is warm and rich with an undercurrent of laughter.

"He's here?" I gasp, feeling relief pour through me and weaken my limbs.

He nods. "He got here this afternoon in a fearful temper. I set him to mowing the graveyard. That will make him cool down a bit and give us time for a little talk." He steps back, and, before I can blink, I find myself in a dimly lit hallway.

He ushers me into a study with lead windows open to the warm summer breeze. The walls are covered in floor-to-ceiling bookcases that are crammed with books and papers and all around them are piles of more books. I look at his desk covered with folders and more paperwork and my fingers itch to organise it.

He smiles at me and gestures me to a chair in front of the desk.

When I sit down, the leather is smooth and comfortable, obviously worn thin by the generations of penitent bums that have sat on it. He stares at me, and a silence falls, broken only by the sound of a mower in the distance. I wonder if that's Jesse and feel a powerful yearning to get to him.

"So, you're Zeb, then?"

I smile anxiously at him. "I am. It's very nice to meet you, sir."

He shakes his head. "Call me Michael." He looks at me assessingly. "Jesse told me about you last week. He seemed very happy. *Then.*"

I squirm. "It's my fault he isn't happy now," I hear a voice say and want to look around to see what idiot is talking, but it's me, and I carry on. "I pushed him away and hurt him."

"Why?" There's no condemnation in his voice. Just honest curiosity on that kind face.

"Because I still can't believe that someone like him would look at me."

"With his looks, you mean?" A shard of disappointment crosses his face, and I shake my head.

"No. Oh, he's pretty, but it's not that. He's such a good person," I say earnestly. "He's fun and clever and kind. And young." I spread my hands. "You must see how much older I am than him."

He sits back at his desk and gives me a wide smile that seems touched with whimsy. "There is a twenty-year age gap between myself and my wife. Jesse's mother. Did you know that?" I shake my head and he nods. "I felt very similar to you when I met Gianna. You say how pretty Jesse is. Well, she was the same. Vivid and stunning. Very funny." He folds his hands. "And I was smaller and older and far too serious."

"What did you do?" I finally say.

He smiles. "I fought it. I told her very pompously that she deserved better. Broke up with her and set her free."

"What happened?"

He winks. "I came up against the Bennici determination. Jesse has it too. A very passionate determination. Gianna declared that I was a fool, an idiot. She ranted at me in Italian for a very long time. Luckily, I didn't know the language." He smiles. "I still don't. When she shouts at me, I think it's probably best not to understand." I laugh and he waves a hand. "She declared her intention of not being bossed around by her husband. I refrained from telling her that I hadn't proposed yet, and instead gave in and got down on one knee. We married and all these years later we're still together." He looks intently at me. "There is still the age gap between us. That itself will never change."

"What did change, then?"

He smiles. "I realised that I would rather be with her than be alone. I would rather have her by my side than have years of regrets. I realised that I was being arrogant by forcing her to abide by my concerns, when the only person who had a say in whether she stayed with me was her."

I sit back in the chair. "I'm still worried," I say candidly. "I don't want him to regret being with me."

"And I like that," he says firmly. "It indicates a strength of character and a selfless concern for my son's happiness that I want to see in the person he settles down with." He pauses. "What I don't like is cruelty, Zeb. If you don't want him, set him free, but don't string him along. He has a good heart and doesn't deserve that."

I sit forward. "I won't. I promise." I shrug helplessly. "I hate hurting him. I'd rather cut my own arm off."

"Maybe keep your limbs and use your brain instead," he advises gently. "My son is impulsive and chaotic at times, Zeb, but he's the kindest and oldest soul you'll ever meet." He smiles at me, and I see an acceptance in his eyes that warms me. "I think you'll suit him very well. I think you'll actually suit each other. Relationships are all about finding that moment of balance and equilibrium so you don't fall over in life. You'll steady him out, and he'll set you free to move along without any brakes for a bit."

"I need to see him," I say, and I can hear the ache in my voice.

He stands up. "I've got to go up to the church because I left my sermon for tomorrow up there. I'll show you the way."

We walk out of the study, and I smile at the photos that line the wall. Jesse's mum is extraordinarily beautiful. She looks a little like Sophia Loren, with jet-black hair, prominent cheekbones and a slightly wild look. It's easy to see where Jesse's looks come from. I pause by one photograph. It's a black and white large photo of a young Jesse. He's standing in the garden staring at the camera with a huge gappy smile. The charm is evident in every inch of him even then.

His father shakes his head. "He was such a rambunctious boy. Always running and shouting. Never quiet."

"He's not changed much," I say honestly. "He's still extremely noisy."

He laughs. "He hated school. Couldn't abide to be caged up. It still amazes me that he's endured university, but I suppose that it was easier for him because it was for the job he wanted. He's the most astute and caring young man. He studies people because he likes to make them happy."

"He'll make an excellent social worker."

He nods and taps Jesse's face affectionately. "My mother always called him a merry soul. She wasn't wrong."

We walk out of the door and blink in the bright sunlight before he guides me to a path leading towards the stone bulk of the church.

"If you don't mind me saying, I'm a little surprised that we've had this conversation so easily," I say tentatively.

He looks at me and smiles. "Because he's gay and I'm a vicar?" I nod, and he laughs. It's Jesse's laugh. Warm and familiar. "I'm a man of God, Zebadiah, but my God is a loving one. I tell my congregation that when Jesus came to Earth to save mankind, he entered into a great compact with man. He went over everything that was wrong and needed to be fixed." He smiles at me. "He never mentioned homosexuality once. That's like Alan Sugar's lawyers forgetting to mention how much he's selling a business for. No, we are all created in God's image, Zeb. My son is as loved by him as anyone else. God doesn't make mistakes." He nudges me. "Besides, I wouldn't like to be him if he snubbed my son, and my wife got hold of him."

I laugh and follow him through the late evening sunshine. He comes to a stop by the huge curved wooden door. "Well, this is me," he says lightly. "You'll find my son round the back. Let him bring you down to the house for supper. Gianna is making her lasagna. It's not to be missed. Nor is your imminent interrogation by my wife." He winks. "I'm looking forward to both."

I laugh. "Thank you. I'd like that very much."

He vanishes into the church, and I follow the path around the building to a long graveyard. It's a peaceful spot. Ancient-looking trees hover over the gravestones, some of which lean to one side drunkenly. They're covered in lichen like a blanket for the dead. The smell of cut grass is heavy on the air.

I spot him immediately. He's sitting under an old, twisted chestnut tree. He's shirtless, dressed in faded blue shorts and wearing ratty-looking trainers that are covered in green smears. His T-shirt is a puddle of fabric at his side and sweat glistens on his soft chest hair.

I swallow hard. I've never in my life seen a more beautiful man than Jesse. Even though his mouth is drawn tight and a frown plays on that high-boned face, he's still stunning.

I walk softly across the grass. Someone in a house nearby is playing "Lucky Man" by The Verve and I hope it's an omen. The beautiful song drifts around us, mingling with the sound of birdsong.

"I like this one," I say nervously, and his head shoots up. Astonishment and gladness are there for a brief wonderful moment before he shutters them, and his face becomes a mask.

"Mrs Simpson likes them," he says coolly. "She went to all the festivals in the nineties and was in love with Richard Ashcroft. She always said that if he'd met her he'd have been writing happy love songs."

I stare at him. "Do you think that's true?"

He shrugs. "She's got seven children and five grandchildren. Richard must be quaking in his Clarks Wallabees."

I laugh and then shift awkwardly as his expression remains impassive. In my head this had gone a lot better. A lot easier. I don't know why I expected that. I certainly don't deserve it.

He looks me up and down. "You're a bit dressed up for a grave-yard, Zeb. How was your wedding?"

"*His* wedding and I have no idea. I left."

His stoical expression breaks. "What? Why?"

"I had to find you."

He shakes his head, his hair tumbling silkily around that thin face. "But what happened to your promise?"

He looks down as he pulls nervously at the grass by his leg, and I stare at his downcast head. "I realised that I was making promises to the wrong person," I say slowly.

He lifts his face and stares at me. His eyes are turbulent. "What do you mean?"

I shift my stance. "I mean that I shouldn't have kept old promises to someone who means nothing to me, when there was a far more important person in my life. I'll never stop being loyal and taking my word seriously and keeping my promises. It's just that this time I'll make them to the right person. You."

He shakes his head. "I don't understand you at all. You got what you wanted."

"Not yet, but maybe soon."

"I don't know what you're talking about. You're still sleeping with him. You were in bed when you agreed to be his best man. That's disgusting."

"*It is*," I say fiercely. "But I didn't know. He led me to believe that they'd split up, and I fell back into bed with him. It was more famil-iarity by then rather than passion." I pause and add honestly, "I didn't ask too many questions though, and that's on me. But in my defense, she was sleeping with him while he was with me. I didn't owe her any loyalty."

"I saw you on the balcony, Zeb. It looked pretty passionate to me. You were exactly where you've wanted to be. With him."

I break my stasis and crouch next to him. "It wasn't what you thought," I say fiercely. "He grabbed me and kissed me. If you'd stayed around a second longer you'd have seen me push him away."

"What happened?" His fingers have stopped their frenzied uprooting of the poor grass and I grab his hands and kiss the long, slender fingers. I can smell the scent of green tea from his pulse and taste a trace of salt on my tongue.

"I ran out of there. I got back too late to stop you leaving, so I followed you. Jesse."

"Why?"

"I'll always follow you."

"What are you saying, Zeb?"

I hate the caution on his face. He's meant for sunny smiles and that careless warm charm. "I'm saying I want you." I swallow hard. "I'm saying that I'm falling in love with you."

He swallows hard, something fierce and impassioned in his face that makes him suddenly look older. "Why? I'm too young and irresponsible and flippant and—"

"And perfect," I say quietly, cutting through the tumbling words. "You're just perfect for me."

For a long second we stare at each other, and I hope that's enough. I don't have any more words. I've said everything in my heart. Then he mutters something and throws himself onto my lap. Caught off guard, I flounder before falling backwards with him lying on top of me.

"*Oof!* Jesse," I get out before he kisses me fiercely. I taste a flash of blood and then hug him tight, lost in the kiss. I make a murmur of disgust when he pulls back, but he laughs jubilantly.

"You really love me?" I nod and he kisses me again. "I love you too," he says softly, and there is so much weight and passion to his words that I feel humbled.

"Really?" I ask almost shyly.

He nods, cupping my face in his palms. "I love everything. I love your sarcasm, your cleverness. I know you see age when you look at us, but all I see is the person I'm in love with. He's funny and clever and kind. He's protective, and he's vulnerable. I don't see how old you are or what you look like anymore, Zeb. I just see you and you–" He smiles. "You're fucking everything to me."

I kiss him then, feeling his weight and smell all around me. He feels safe. He feels right. He feels like my home. He's perfect.

EPILOGUE

Six Months Later

Jesse

I let myself into Zeb's flat with a quiet sigh of relief. It's eleven o'clock at night, and I'm bloody shattered. I've been at work since seven this morning and it's been a harrowing day with a case, but I can rest easy now because everything is settled and a mother and her child are now safe.

I look around the flat, inhaling the scent of vanilla and furniture polish on the air. He's left the lamps on for me, and they shed pools of light on the wooden floors and white walls. It's an oasis of calm and as far away from the feel of my workplace today as if I'd stepped into a house on the moon.

A clicking of claws sounds out on the floor and then a bundle of fur leaps at me from the shadows. "Clarence," I whisper. "Were you lying on the bed, you naughty little monster. You know Daddy doesn't like it." I laugh. "Just like he doesn't appreciate me calling him Daddy."

The dog pants and tries to lick my chin, his little face creased in what looks like a smile. When I encouraged Zeb to get a dog – okay, when I forced Zeb to get a dog – I thought he'd go for a pedigree dog. Something expensive and well groomed. Instead he marched off to the local dogs' home and came back with something small and unkempt that looked very much like a tiny sheep on spindly legs. God knows what breed Clarence is. There's some terrier in there and a few other breeds, but he's a bundle of love and slobber and he adores Zeb beyond reason. Wherever he is, you can be sure to find Clarence. The dog accepts me as an extension of Zeb, but we both know who his master is.

I take off my jacket, slinging it onto the back of the sofa, and wander into the kitchen, followed closely by Clarence who sussed out very early on that I'm a soft touch and will always slip him food. There's another lamp on in here and a plate on the island with a note propped against it. In Zeb's neat writing is written *I've left you some lasagne, love. I want you to eat it or you'll be ill.*

I smile at the prosaic note that still somehow manages to punch me in the heart. I've found that Zeb is very much like this in love. He doesn't overwhelm me with questions and demands. Instead he thinks hard and studies me and always looks after me. And because he's studied me over the months so intently and lovingly, he somehow gets it right every time.

I'd texted him when I knew I was going to be late without going into detail. But still he'd known that I needed him, and this is his way of showing me that he's with me always, regardless of physical presence, with my favourite meal that he learnt to cook from my mother.

I heat it up in the microwave, inhaling the delicious scent and feeling my mouth water and the knot in my stomach unravel. I love my job passionately. I think I'm good at it, and I know I'm helping people, but it still takes a toll, and it's good to be home. I still as the microwave dings. *Home. Is this my home?*

I look around the kitchen. It's still the same beautiful room as it was the first night he fed me dinner and asked me to pretend to be his boyfriend. However, I can see the new additions in the colourful blind that I picked out, in the photos on the fridge and windowsill, and the bright red teapot on the dresser.

I reach out and touch the corner of the photo I like best. It's a black-and-white shot of the two of us at a party. I'm laughing, and Zeb has his arm round me. A wide smile is splitting his gorgeous face, and his eyes are creased around the edges, but it's the way he's looking at me that I love best. As if I'm everything he can see. I smile. It's the way I look at him too, but he never realises that.

The microwave dings, and, using a tea towel, I grab my food and head into the lounge to eat on the sofa. Clarence jumps up next to me and gazes at me imploringly as if he hasn't eaten for a decade. I feed him a bit of lasagne and he licks my cheek affectionately afterwards.

Even here I can see my additions. Front and centre is the peony picture that Zeb bought me from the Cotswolds. I'd carried it here, blithely insisting that his place was a better backdrop for it. I'd worried that I was overstepping but he immediately hung it in pride of place over the fireplace, and he had a smile on his face the whole time.

Other bits of me are also here in the new bright cushions on the sofa, the painting I picked out when we were in Paris for the weekend, my trainers lying abandoned under a chair, and the pile of books on the coffee table. He'll grumble about them, but he won't be able to hide the smile. It's as if he loves these signs that I live here as much as I do.

I still with my fork halfway to my mouth. *I think I actually do live here now.* I calculate quickly how long it's been since I've stayed in my flat, and I can't remember. I think it was a few weeks ago.

I've been back to check on Charlie regularly. I'll always worry about him and his health, but he patently doesn't want fussing over and on my last visit he was talking about sharing a flat with Misha. My lip twitches. That should be interesting.

Then I frown. It's alright me thinking it's okay to stay here, but is it with Zeb? Is he just being polite and unable to hurt my feelings enough to demand that I fuck off back to my own house? I look down at my supper and smile and shake my head. He knew I was coming back here.

When I've finished my food and put the pots away, I wander into the bedroom. It's lit by the light of the moon and the streetlights outside, and the huge window is open, letting in the sounds of people moving through the yard outside.

I smile at the sight of Zeb. He's asleep, which is hardly surprising as he's been working all hours himself. He bought a house a few months ago with the aim of flipping it. I'd been surprised because as much as he loved his dad, he always seemed to shy away from any hint that he's anything like him. I'd also been amazed by the fact that he was doing most of the work himself.

But he's his father's son, and he knew a lot more about it than I'd realised, and he's thrived these last few months. He sends me off with a kiss to work before he zips off to the house, accompanied by Clarence with his head out of the truck window. Yes, Zeb now drives a dusty old truck and he dresses in disreputable old jeans and T-shirts as he goes to spend his day pulling up floors and demolishing walls. He comes home dirty and happy and it bloody suits him so much.

He promoted Felix to manager and hired someone to help him out when he bought the house, and the agency is thriving. Felix says he misses taking the piss out of him, but Zeb told me that Felix was always better at the job than him. I sometimes miss seeing Zeb in those sexy suits, but I like even more the lack of stress in his face and the way he glows these days.

Clarence huffs and jumps up onto the bed, curling into the corner of Zeb's legs and settling down happily. I smirk. When we first got him, Zeb had sternly laid down the law on where the dog could go, which didn't seem to be many places apart from his basket. However, Clarence is cunning and gradually circumvented Zeb's rules until there weren't many left.

I'd known that the dog had won when I came home and found him sitting by the side of the bath barking so that Zeb would throw water at him. The mess in the room clearly indicated a power shift that abides to this day.

Stripping off my clothes, I head for the shower and enjoy the cool water streaming down my body. Eventually clean, refreshed, and feeling as if I could sleep for a year, I pad back into the bedroom. Zeb has shifted position to accommodate The Dog Who Should Not Be There and is now lying on his side. His hair, which is longer than it's ever been, is a tousled mess and his full lips are slightly parted.

I stare at him in the soft light from the bathroom, feeling so much love push through me. I love him so much. Every day it gets deeper, rooted as it is now in the reality of Zeb rather than the glamorous view I'd previously had of him.

I love his grumpiness in the morning and his inability to ask anyone's advice to the extent that he won't ask for directions, which had led us on an hour-long tour of Falmouth once. I love the way his nose wrinkles when he's reading the paper and the way he looks at me with laughter and so much love in those bright blue eyes.

I know that this is it for me. *He* is it. My person. And that will never change. I'm a man who knows his mind and heart, and they're as full of Zebadiah Evans as they always will be.

The light catches on a piece of paper on his bedside table and I idly look at it, returning to look more closely when I see my name. I hold it up to the bathroom light and read it. Then I read it again. And again. And then I look at him and smile because it's so Zeb that I want to laugh out loud and smother him in kisses. It's a list in his neat writing and the subject is me moving in with him. It reads like a careful summary of all the reasons why he wants me to live with him, and I read them carefully again, feeling warmth spread through my stomach and chest.

Then I grab his pen and scrawl something on the list before climbing into bed and wrapping my arms around my Zeb and our dog as the sounds of London outside my window lull me to sleep.

. . .

Zeb

I wake up to sunshine streaming through the window, the smell of fresh bread on the air from the bakery next door, and Jesse's hair in my face. I edge back, pushing the silky strands out of my nose, and stare at him. He's curled around me like I tried to escape in the night, and I inhale the scent of green tea that clings to his skin. His face is gilded by the sunshine and his mouth half open as he snores gently. I smile and shake my head before pressing a kiss to his forehead that's gentle but no less passionate, as all my feelings seem to suffuse it.

I'm thankful that he sleeps on because he still looks tired with faint shadows showing under those ridiculously long eyelashes. He must have the morning off because his alarm never went off. I decide immediately to take the morning off too.

We haven't seen much of each other this week, apart from an odd few minutes snatched here and there, mainly because of a case he's been dealing with. I was right when I thought he'd be a good social worker. He's passionate and committed and farsighted. His dad called him an old soul, and it's true.

However, although he pays attention to other people's needs, he ignores himself, and I've noticed signs of him wearing thin this week. And that's what I consider to be my job. He's mine in a way that few things ever have been. I love him deeply and beyond anything I knew I was capable of, and, as such, all my caretaking impulses are out in full force with him. I'll therefore watch him a bit more closely this week, pamper him, and let him know he's loved. He, as normal, will in turn watch me with a wry look in his pretty eyes and love me back.

I still sometimes can't believe that he's with me. This vibrant, funny man could have anyone, and he chose me. However, I trust more and more every day, and we feel real to me. Inevitable and strong.

He influences everything that's good in my life now. He's life and light and warmth and laughter. Even the fact that I'm flipping houses is down to him in a way. Having him love who I really am gave me the courage to be myself again. I don't miss the agency and I'm going to make Felix a partner because I know that when I've finished this house, I'll move on to another. I find it so satisfying to do up an old house and watch it come alive again.

I find it equally satisfying that I now stop working at the weekends and nights so we can be together. And we've used the time properly. We travel a lot, visiting all the places that I wanted to, and one shelf on the bookcase is dedicated to travel guides. Their bright colours make me smile every time I catch sight of them.

We still have that map that he crumpled up in the bookstore, and Jesse insists that we'll visit one day and find the remains of the ancient barrow. I've agreed because I think I'll propose to him there. The thought doesn't even raise an inch of freaked out in me now. Just a desire to make us permanent and absolute.

Maybe that's because I'm finally happy and whole. I'm me. I'm Zeb Evans, not Eddie Evans's son, and I feel free to embrace the good characteristics I got from my dad without thinking I'm going to succumb to his worst ones. I know I can be funny like him and that I can command people's attention without having to then run off and marry seven people and rack up debts. Most of all, I know that by giving in and living my life fully, I'm not going to become him. I'm me, and I'm finally happy with that version because Jesse loves it.

I shrug and run my fingers through his silky hair. Then I ease quietly out of bed, shaking my head at Clarence who is perched on the end of the bed looking at me with bright eyes.

"Don't think I haven't noticed that you're somewhere you shouldn't be," I whisper as I step into my khaki shorts and pull on a navy T-shirt. I edge into the bathroom and clean my teeth quietly and then wander out to the lounge to grab his lead. I shake my head and tut as I kick my feet into Jesse's trainers that are, as normal, lying abandoned on the floor. He's like a very contained cyclone to live with.

"We'll go and get him some breakfast," I whisper to Clarence who dances about when he sees the lead. I clatter down the stairs and out into the early morning bustle of Neal's Yard. When he's had a wee outside, I put in our usual order at the bakery of some lemon curd doughnuts and the raisin loaf that Jesse loves, exchanging greetings with the lady behind the counter and answering questions about Jesse. I've lived here for ten years, and yet it's Jesse who knows all the shopkeepers. I've often thought rather fancifully that he's the bridge between the world and my insular tendencies. I can't retreat behind my walls when he's blown massive bloody holes in them.

I make my way through the office, laying Felix's breakfast on his desk as I go. He's standing unloading his bag onto the desk, and he grins widely. "It's like having a very buff houseboy."

"Thrilled as I am to have my whole existence reduced to my body and food-providing abilities, I'm going to have to pull myself away from your conversation."

"Your loss." He takes a sip of his coffee and sighs happily. "Except that it really isn't because I've just rolled out of an empty bed and yours is full of your young totty."

"Felix, someone someday is going to take a whack at that equilibrium of yours. I can't wait."

"That sounded slightly bloodthirsty and extremely implausible. I'm like Teflon emotionally." I stare at him because he wasn't always like this and it hurts my heart to know why. He waves a hand at me as if dismissing the look on my face. "So, asked him to move in yet?"

I shake my head. "I'm trying to find the right words."

"Actually, they're quite easy. 'Will you move in with me and be my boy toy until the end of days?'"

I roll my eyes as he laughs. "I made a list of arguments to persuade him."

"Well, of course you did. Not that you'll need it with him. He's nauseatingly in love with you. What's the matter?"

My face must show a horrified expression. "Oh shit, I left the list on the bedside table. Fuck. Maybe he's seen it."

He bites his lap. "Well, if he's read it, at least you've managed to cut out the terrible middleman bit of having to use words. Out loud."

"Fuck," I say again and dart up the stairs, Clarence trotting along behind.

"Good luck," he shouts after me.

I let myself into the flat and tiptoe towards the bedroom. "We'll creep in and get it," I whisper to Clarence at the door. "And he'll never know."

"Never know what?" comes a warm voice.

"Shit," I mutter to Clarence, who is patently unconcerned as he sits down to lick his balls. I come cautiously round the door to find Jesse sitting up, leaning against the headboard with the green sheets in a puddle around his lap. His hair is falling over his face, his eyes glowing with humour.

"Well, good morning to you," he purrs, lifting his arms up and stretching.

Unbidden, my eyes fall to his lap to see if I can get a glimpse of his dick, and then I remember my mission. I dart a quick look at the table and relax slightly when I see the paper still lying there.

"What are you staring at?" he murmurs.

"Nothing," I say shiftily. "Just checking I haven't lost my shopping list."

"Oh, your list," he says, biting his lip. "What's on it?"

"Why are you interested?"

"Humour me."

"Oh my *God*," I sigh. "You've read it." He bursts into laughter, giggling so hard that he falls into the sheets and writhes around. "You are such a twat," I say, shoving him gently as I walk past him. He laughs even harder. "When did you read it?"

"Your shopping list? Last night. I *really* hope you don't forget the bit about reminding me that you have a big wardrobe. Was that a euphemism?"

I shake my head but can't help laughing. "Why does nothing ever go as I planned with you, Jesse?"

He straightens onto his knees, the sheets falling away. He glows in the light but as ever, he's utterly unconcerned by his nakedness.

"Maybe that's a good thing," he says softly, his expression serious and all trace of laughter gone. "Maybe that's what you need."

"*You're* what I need," I say quietly, reaching out to cup his face in my palms. "You'll always be what I need." I trace the arch of one eyebrow with my finger. "I want you to live with me, Jess. I want to wake up every morning and go to sleep every night with you next to me. I want to laugh and talk late into the night the way we do. You're my best friend, and I don't know how that happened or what you see in me, but I want you to know that this is your home. Your safe place. Because *you're* my safe place."

He stares at me, his eyes looking liquid for a second. "When you go in, you're really in, love," he says faintly.

"So will you?"

"I wrote the answer on your list. I'm afraid I've messed up your bullet point system."

I snatch up the paper, and scrawled across it in his messy hand-writing is the word *yes*.

I swallow and look up at him as he nods his head furiously. "Of course I will. Zeb, I love you. I just want to be with you all the time. I can't think of anything nicer than to be with you for the rest of my life."

"And mine," I whisper. "I love you, Jesse Reed."

I hug him tight, loving the way he nestles into me so trustingly, loving the feel of him by my side in the way that I now have an inner certainty he always will be. I don't doubt him anymore. I don't think of the age gap or the future problems we'll probably face. Of course they'll come, but we'll be ready for them.

All the things that kept me from him for years now seem like nothing, because all I see is him. This maddening, impulsive man who is merry and warm and somehow just simply the best man I've ever known.

NEWSLETTER

If you'd like to be the first to know about my book releases and have access to extra content, you can sign up for my newsletter here

THANK YOU

My husband who's my best friend and can always make me laugh. This is for reading all of my stories, and then laughing a lot harder at T J Klune's books!

My boys. For being my pride and joy.

Hailey Turner. For all the laughs, encouragement, and wonderful friendship.

Edie Danford. For making me laugh every day and being such a wonderful friend. Also, for the Alexander Skarsgard pictures.

Leslie, Courtney, and everyone at LesCourt Author Services. I couldn't do it without you.

The members of my Facebook reader's group, Lily's Snark Squad. I love my time spent in there.

To all the bloggers who spend their valuable time reading, reviewing and promoting the books. Also, the readers who liven up my day with their messages and photos and book recommendations. I love being a part of this community, so thank you.

Lastly thanks to you, for taking a chance on this book. I hope you enjoyed reading it as much as I enjoyed writing it.

I never knew until I wrote my first book how important reviews are. So if you have time, please consider leaving a review on Amazon or Goodreads or any other review sites. I can promise you that I value all of them. When I've been struggling with writing, sometimes going back and reading the reviews makes it better.

CONTACT LILY

Website: www.lilymortonauthor.com
This has lots of information and fun features, including some extra
short stories.

If you fancy hearing the latest news and interacting with other
readers do head over and join my Facebook group. It's a fun group
and I share all the latest news about my books there as well as some
exclusive short stories.
www.facebook.com/groups/SnarkSquad/

I'd love to hear from you, so if you want to say hello or have any
questions, please contact me and I'll get back to you:
Email: lilymorton1@outlook.com

ALSO BY LILY MORTON

Mixed Messages Series

Rule Breaker

Deal Maker

Risk Taker

The Finding Home Series

Oz

Milo

Gideon

The Close Proximity Series

Best Man

Other Books

The Summer of Us

Short Stories

Best Love

3 Dates

Printed in Great Britain
by Amazon